a taste of her own medicine

medicine

a small town romance

tasha l. harrison

Copyright © 2019 by **Tasha L. Harrison**

Publisher's Note: This is a work of fiction. Names, characters, places, and incidents are a product of the author's imagination. Locales and public names are sometimes used for atmospheric purposes. Any resemblance to actual people, living or dead, or to businesses, companies, events, institutions, or locales is completely coincidental.

Book cover design: Tasha L. Harrison, Images: Unsplash.com

A Taste of Her Own Medicine/ Tasha L. Harrison. -- 1st ed.
ISBN 978-0-9909403-8-8

Other Titles by Tasha L. Harrison

THE LUST DIARIES
THE TRUTH DUET

Coming soon...
THE BAD IN EACH OTHER
a small town romance

Join my newsletter to get updates on
new releases and free short stories
about your favorite characters!

I'd love to hear from you!
Connect with me at:
Twitter | Instagram | Email

Visit my website:
TashaLHarrison.com

chapter one
Sonja

The strip of shops, eateries, and galleries in The Village of West Greenville were dark and quiet when I pulled my Subaru into the parking lot a few blocks away from *The CoWorking Spot*. In the last few years, this part of town had experienced some growth with the arrival of a few restaurants and specialty shops. But that was just a handful of businesses, most of which closed at or around six o'clock, leaving the streets quiet on a late summer evening. I took advantage of this moment of quiet. Closed my eyes and took a few deep breaths to settle the nervous butterflies in my stomach.

About a month ago, I allowed myself to be convinced to sign up for a six-week entrepreneurship course— something I'd regretted since the day the payment cleared.

What makes me think I could run my own business?

The only thing I'd managed in the last ten years was a household, and occasionally, the front desk at my ex-husband's real estate offices. Those skills didn't necessarily translate into the sort of hustle one needed to be an entrepreneur. But at the time, my sisters Birdie and Agostina, as well as my friend Estelle, made it seem like a great idea to start a business with the skincare products I made from the herbs and medicinal flowers in my garden. And I agreed. Or maybe the gallon of wine I drank that night agreed because now that I was sitting in my car with my brand new laptop, in my brand new laptop bag, I wondered if I'd temporarily lost my mind.

The *Bluetooth* in my car announced that I had an incoming call from Estelle Murphy.

"Hello?"

"Get out of the car, Sonja," she ordered.

"Why did I let you talk me into this?" I groaned and opened the car door, slightly annoyed that she knew me so well.

"Because you're more than ready for it. We've gone through this. Get out of the car, and I'll walk down there with you."

"Okay. I'm coming."

I'd arrived a good forty minutes early, mostly because I needed to stop by *Ink Blue Yoga* to get a pep talk from my Estelle.

Ink Blue, Estelle's yoga studio, was one of my favorite places. The front windows went floor to ceiling, which made the interior look and feel bright and warm. The smooth, shiny hardwood floors were warm in the winter months and cool in the summer. They welcomed bare feet, and I almost wanted to drop my bags, strip down, and get in a few vinyasas. Estelle was good at this business thing and was brilliant at getting her studio seen. If I checked our town's hashtag on Instagram on any given day, her yoga studio always showed up in the top nine.

"Hey, Soni," my friend said and gave me a knowing look as I came in. "Amelia?"

The woman sweeping at the far end of the studio looked up.

"I'm going to walk Soni down to *The Coworking Spot*. I'll be right back."

"No, problem. I'll get everything set up for the six-thirty class."

She grabbed two bottles of water out of the cold case near the cash wrap and handed me one. I opened it and followed her back out to the sidewalk.

"Okay," she said, falling into step beside me with natural grace. Estelle was just a few inches taller than I was but lithe, lean, and way less frumpy than me in her hundred dollar yoga pants. "Out with it. What are you feeling right now?"

I gnawed on my bottom lip. "I'm nervous."

"Be specific."

"I'm probably going to be the oldest person in the class —"

"And that matters because…?"

"It makes me feel self-conscious. It's been years since I've been in a classroom. I'm not sure if I can learn everything I need to know to make this thing work."

"Sonja, you're one of the smartest people I know. You'll be fine."

"How can you say I'll be fine? It took me six days to figure out how to use this fucking computer you made me buy."

Estelle laughed at me, and I joined her, realizing how pathetic I sounded. Doing something new was always scary. But it had been so long since I'd done anything new that this felt huge. She grabbed my hand as we walked the remaining two blocks to the building that hosted *The Entrepreneur Academy*.

"There's no need to be intimidated by anything you're presented with today. You're there to learn, and the instructor is there to teach you. Who's your instructor again?"

I laughed and rolled my eyes. "You sound like you're escorting your kid to their first day of elementary school."

4

"Aren't I?" she joked.

I pulled up the email they sent me after I registered for the class. "My instructor is someone named Atlas James. You know him?"

Estelle gasped, and her steps faltered a bit. "Yeah… yeah, I know him."

"What was that reaction about?"

"Uh, nothing. Atlas James is … he's an amazing teacher. I learned a lot from him."

"Yeah, but you gasped."

Estelle cleared her throat and smirked. "You'll see."

We arrived at the doors, and I turned to her with a smile. "So, I'll meet you next door when the class is over so we can have some drinks?"

"Oh, most definitely! Relax, and have fun. It's not nearly as hard as you think it will be. Especially not with Atlas teaching. I think you're really going to enjoy yourself."

I rolled my eyes. "Bye, Estelle."

Still laughing at my friend, I went inside the coworking space that doubled as the *Entrepreneur Academy* classroom on evenings and weekends. From what I read online, the two people who owned the business and ran the programs were dedicated to helping an underserved group of entrepreneurs get a foothold in the economy growing in Greenville. The businesses that students started after attending the Academy were conscientious and interested in blending into the existing community. That was precisely the kind of business I wanted to build--one that felt so familiar that my customers could easily imagine the hands that made the products and feel connected to the process.

I'd entered on the street level across from the *Village Journal* into a small lobby and seating area.

"Hi!" the young girl behind the desk said with a smile. "Welcome to *The CoWorking Spot*. I'm Chloe. Can I help you?"

"Uh, yes. Hi, Chloe. I'm here for the *Entrepreneur Academy Course*?"

"Ah, yes. Could you just sign in for me? They'll be meeting in the Community Classroom at the big table down there," she said, jerking her thumb over her shoulder. "But you're a little early, so feel free to grab a cup of coffee and look around or just hang out up here. Atlas is around here somewhere."

"Okay, thanks," I said as I signed in.

When I was done, I adjusted my bag on my shoulder and made my way down the steps to the *Community Classroom*. The big table was in an open area, with about ten or fifteen chairs around it. The group was far smaller than I anticipated it would be, and for some reason, that made me feel even more nervous. That and the fact that this Atlas person was somewhere in the building and if no one else arrived soon, I would be the first to meet him. All that tittering Estelle had done on the sidewalk made me wonder what the hell I was in for.

After choosing a seat on the far end of the table away from the big screen TV as the place to drop my laptop bag, I went back up to the lobby to grab a cup of that free coffee the girl at the desk had offered me. I was still considering the dark, strong-smelling brew when a young man bounded up the stairs.

One look at him and I swear my mouth went so dry that my tongue stuck to the roof of it.

"Hi!" he said cheerily, his lips splitting into a grin that lit up his face. And Jesus Christ was it a gorgeous face. He had smooth dark skin and the sort of distinctive features that were so unusual that it was hard to look at him without really staring. Full lips, a broad nose, and bedroom eyes with thick lashes that squinted when he smiled like he was doing now.

"Hello," I managed to croak, unable to tear my eyes away even though he was standing next to me now, and I had to look *up, up, up* to meet his gaze. This man was tall and built like he could plow my north field without a horse, with shoulders that he could probably throw a woman-sized stack of potatoes over. And by woman-sized, I meant me. I would like to be that woman-sized sack of potatoes.

That thought startled me. I couldn't remember the last time I looked at a man with little more interest than I gave a sturdy dining room table.

"Trying to get that last dose of caffeine in, huh?" he said casually as if his deep baritone wasn't designed to disintegrate my panties the moment he opened his mouth.

"Uh, yeah. I usually try not to drink coffee this late. It tends to mess with my sleep, but I'm not usually out after this hour, so—"

What the hell was I even saying? Why was I talking about my caffeine intake like some old lady who needed to be at home before nine to make sure she took her remedies?

"I hear that," the young man said as he tore open two sugar packets with the edge of his bright white teeth. His tongue swiped at a loose granule, and my pussy clenched like I knew how that tongue would feel between my thighs.

Look away, Sonja. Look a-damn-way.

He gestured at the still empty cup in my hand with the carafe of coffee in his hand, offering to fill it up.

"Yes, please." I held out the paper cup in my now trembling hand. "Thank you," I said once it was filled and finally turned toward the coffee station to add some sugar and cream.

"No, problem. I'll see you down there," he said, a smirk in the corner of his full lips.

"Oh! You're here for the *Entrepreneur Academy* thing?"

He pivoted around the corner to make his way back down the stairs. With his eyes on me, his smirk shifted into a smile. "I'm the instructor," he said just before he disappeared from view.

"Holy fuck … that's Atlas James?"

"Yes, ma'am, it is," the girl behind the desk said with a wistful sigh.

Leaving the cup of untouched coffee on the bar, I ducked into the nearest bathroom to call my so-called friend. Her self-satisfied giggle met my ears when she finally decided to pick up the phone.

"Really, Estelle?"

"What?

"You could have warned me that my instructor was a real-life action hero, so I didn't embarrass myself by drooling and blubbering like an idiot."

"You drooled and blubbered like an idiot? That's surprising. I didn't think he would get that much of a reaction out of you."

"And what the hell is that supposed to mean?"

"Sonja," she began gently. "I've known you for almost nine years, and I've never heard you so much as sigh at the sight of a pretty man. Even men that are universally handsome never seemed to move the meter for you."

I scoffed. "Yeah, well, Atlas James sure as hell did."

"Mmmhmm… six weeks of class with him was not an unpleasant experience."

"Estelle! You're happily married!"

"I'm married, not dead, Sonja."

"I get that, but…"

"Yes, I allowed myself to enjoy his personage, then I went home to my husband. And since you no longer have one of those, none of that should matter to you."

"I have no intentions on—"

"I gotta go. The six-thirty power hour is about to start. I'll meet you for drinks, and we can talk about how Atlas made you squirm in your seat for an hour and a half." Then she hung up before I could respond.

I glared at my phone's darkening screen for a moment and tried to figure out if there was a way that I could sneak downstairs, grab my new bag and twelve-hundred-dollar laptop, and duck out before the class started. Because I couldn't sit in the same room with that man.

Hell, maybe I didn't need to grab my stuff. Estelle could drive me home. My kids were there, so I didn't need to worry about how I would get in. I could pick up my bag in the morning or some other time when I was sure he wouldn't be here. Then I would quit the class because a woman my age should not be subjected to a man that young and that fine for six-long weeks without any sort of satisfaction.

Satisfaction?

I mean, seriously. What satisfaction did I want from this man? And more importantly, what satisfaction would he be willing to give? Did I want to know? Goddamn, he had successfully scrambled my brain. This was not right or okay.

I glanced in the mirror and smoothed my hand over my newly cropped hair.

Around the same time that I allowed myself to be convinced to sign up for this course, my sister Agostina thought it was a good idea to chop off all of my hair. "A woman who cuts her hair is about to make big changes in her life," or some foolishness she'd parroted from a mindfulness blog she read. Initially, I thought the cut looked cute. *Fun.* Now I just looked like a middle-aged woman who'd lobbed off her hair and dyed it to hide the grey.

I sighed and shook my head at myself, then turned on the water to wash my hands. I was making too big a deal out of this. He probably didn't even notice that I'd drooled over him. I wasn't unattractive, but I'd long ago realized that I'd become invisible to a specific type of man and definitely a certain age bracket. Atlas James fits that demographic. Yeah... I was worried about the wrong thing.

By the time I made my way out of the bathroom and toward the low murmur of conversation in the Community Classroom, I'd convinced myself that I was overreacting. I'd only assumed that he had noticed me noticing him. That didn't make it true.

And I believed that until I realized that my bag had been moved to a seat other than where I'd left it. It was now in front of a chair closer to the middle of the table…

Right across from where Atlas was setting up his laptop and unloading his backpack.

I glanced toward the place I'd left my things and saw that two girls were huddled there now. How wrong would it be if I put on my mom-voice and bullied them out of their seats?

"Decided against the coffee?" Atlas asked, pulling me out of my reverie.

"Uh… yeah. I had a couple of sips, but I'm jittery enough. It would have been a mistake."

"I probably should have done the same, but you know…Y.O.L.O."

I cringed inwardly. "Yeah...Y.O.L.O.," I echoed then pulled out the chair.

My son used that horrible slang phrase when he was in middle school. Was this Atlas in the same age bracket? Now I felt a little gross about lusting over someone who was probably only a few years older than my high school-age son.

Yuck.

I laughed at myself again. Unloaded my bag.

Stay on task, Sonja.

"Okay... It looks like everyone is here!" Atlas said. "Let's get started." He clapped his hands together and moved toward the front of the room. "Welcome to *The CoWorking Spot.* I'm Atlas James, and I'm going to be your instructor for this cohort of the *Entrepreneur Academy.* A little bit about me...Yes, my name is really Atlas, but I don't think my mother named me that in anticipation of me having shoulders big and strong enough to carry the world on them, but it helps that I grew into it."

We all laughed at that, and he seemed to relax a little bit.

"I'm a business coach for creative people who want to use their talents to make money. I've been at that for a little over six years, and before that, my best friend and I built a tiny home in a step-up panel truck, and I traveled to every state in the continental US because I was that anxious to get away from here. I have two degrees, business, and MBA in marketing, both of which used to build and run this business. Now..." He looked from one end of the table to the next, and then his eyes settled on me. "I'd like to get to know all of you."

My mouth suddenly went dry, and my nipples drew up into tight little buds against the thin silken fabric of my bra. I folded my arms, leaned forward on the table, and prayed that he didn't ask me to go first. Nothing but squawking high pitched sounds would come out of me if he did.

Atlas smiled at me then turned his attention to one of the young girls at the far end of the table.

Thank God.

"You there in the pink sweater. State your name, state your business."

Everyone at the table was at least ten or more years younger than me. They had internet jobs that I'd never heard of before — like social media manager and content strategist — that they'd joined the *Entrepreneur Academy* to grow. None of them had a business that sounded anything like mine.

"And what about you, Miss..." Atlas pushed up the sleeves of his shirt and pointed at me.

My brain short-circuited.

"Sonja..." I stammered. *Yes, that's my name.* "Sonja Watts and I want to open an online store to sell natural soaps, essential oils, hand, and body cremes, and maybe teas using recipes created by my Gullah grandmother."

The room fell silent.

"Excuse me...Sonja?" one of the girls at the end of the table began. She was sitting across from the girl in the pink sweater. I think her name was Ashley.

"Yes?"

"What is a Gullah exactly? You mean, like *Gullah, Gullah Island*? That show that used to come on Disney?" Ashley asked with a giggle that her friend in the pink sweater echoed.

Atlas turned his attentions to Ashley and regarded her for a long, critical moment. "Gullah people are Coastal Carolina African Americans who have maintained most of their West African culture, to include language and traditions," he explained finally. "They practice a lot of holistic medicine through cherished recipes passed down through generations."

He looked at me again, his eyes soft and...was that appreciation I saw there?

"I imagine your business will be no different than someone starting their own beauty brand."

"I imagine so..." I said, feeling for the first time in an hour that I was right where I was supposed to be.

chapter two

Sonja

Estelle had already grabbed us a couple of seats at the bar when I found her next door at *The Narrows*. I ignored the smug smile on her face and ordered a whiskey sour.

"Oh, come on," Estelle groaned. "You really can't be pissed off that I didn't tell you that your instructor was an intelligent, ridiculously gorgeous man. I feel like that was the best kind of surprise."

"To you!" I countered. "I don't like to be caught off guard by things like that. I like to be prepared for all situations so that I don't make a goddamn fool of myself drooling over a kid that's nearly the same age as my son."

"What? He's nowhere near as young as Winston. Atlas and I went to high school together. We're the same age."

So that made him thirty-one years old. That wasn't too young, was it?

Too young for what, though?

My brain stalled on that thought. I shook my head. Why was I even thinking about this? Atlas James had no interest in me. "I don't like to objectify young men this way," I said after taking a sip of my drink. "It makes me feel like a creepy old lady."

"Well, sometimes it takes just the right man to make a woman indulge in that singular pleasure," Estelle smirked. "So, what got you first?"

My mind slipped to that moment when he bounded up those stairs on those long legs. Those thighs... those goddamn thick-ass thighs. Or was it the mischievous light in his eyes or the knowing smirk in the corner of his mouth? Or those full lips that I could easily imagine on mine?

"The shoulders and definitely those thighs... but the shoulders first. I don't think I've seen shoulders like that outside of a fitness magazine," I said finally.

"Right? I mean, he was always tall and broad, but those shoulders—"

"He looks like he could plow my north field without a horse."

"Plow your north..." Estelle let out a screech of hysterical laughter.

We were still giggling and blubbering when the subject of our amusement mounted the steps, a soft cashmere scarf draping those shoulders I'd just mentioned. Just like earlier, my lungs refused to take in air. A slow smile spread across his face as he crossed the room to where we sat at the bar.

"Shitttt," I hissed under my breath and turned my back to the stairs. "He's here, and he's coming over here. Don't look!" I whispered, realizing just how immature that sounded as it came out of my mouth.

"What? Who's coming? Oh..." Estelle picked up her glass and waved. "Atlas! Hey! Come join us!"

"Fuck!" I cursed under my breath.

Estelle's eyes widened. "Sonja, language!" she scolded lightly.

"Hey, ladies," Atlas said, wearing a big smile as he shrugged off his jacket and draped it on the chair beside Estelle. " You mind if I join you?"

"Absolutely not. Pull up to the bar. It's been a while," Estelle said cheerily.

"It has! I hear that your yoga studio is tremendously successful."

"It is, thanks to you."

He nodded graciously. "And how you know, Sonja?"

"She's my best friend. We live across the street from each other. I'm the one who told her about the *Entrepreneur Academy*."

"More like she got me drunk and signed up for me. I wouldn't have done something like this without her encouragement," I volunteered.

"Awesome, thanks for that," Atlas said, giving Estelle a wink. "What do you think so far?"

"It's intimidating, but I'm excited to get started."

He nodded and signaled to the bartender. Apparently, they were well-acquainted because he immediately started making him a drink. "Don't be intimidated. I know it's a lot of information, but I have a pretty good track record for picking out which businesses will actually succeed in each cohort, and I think yours is going to be one of them."

I rolled my eyes. "Listen, I know I'm like the most ancient person in that class, and I will probably need a little more hand-holding than everyone else, but you don't have to patronize me."

Atlas's eyes widened. "No, I'm serious! I predicted that Estelle's yoga studio would be the most profitable in her cohort, and she was. And she knew just as much about running a business as you do."

"Hey!" she said, whacking him on the arm.

"What?" he said with a laugh. "It's true."

"Yeah, well, not all of us were math and computer science geeks in high school or had a GPA that had the ivy leagues courting us."

"Yes, I was an awkward, gangly teenager with bottle cap glasses who's love for numbers left him with plenty of time to learn how to code and master the stock market with the money he made cutting grass. Woohoo! Glad that paid off!" he deadpanned.

"I think it paid off in dividends," I said with a laugh, liking the thought of him as an awkward, sweet teenage boy who was more into his computers and math than girls.

"Was that a stock market joke?" he asked, then that sweet, awkward boy who'd grown into a strapping young man leveled me with a look that made my thighs snap together like that would protect me.

"It didn't land? Dividends are quarterly payments made on past investments, right?"

"Actually, it's on overall profits and revenue, but that was close enough."

"Do you want to sit beside her?" Estelle interrupted. "You're kinda leaning all the way into my space."

"Oh, shit. I'm sorry, Stelle," he said, looking slightly embarrassed.

"No worries," my friend said as she slid off of her stool and gestured for him to move into the space she'd just made for him. Atlas cringed a little bit but didn't hesitate to move onto the stool closest to me.

Christ, he smelled good. Like frankincense, and something sweet that I couldn't quite place, and maybe a little peppermint. "I'm sorry about my friend. She seems to think you might be interested in me and that you need help facilitating a... hook up? Is that what the kids call it?"

He smiled nervously. "I mean, I don't know what the kids are calling it these days, but you sound doubtful about me being interested in you?"

"I meant... romantically," I said for clarification.

"Uh... so did I?"

The way his sentences turned up on the end made me wonder if he was curious or unsure.

I angled myself toward him and looked him in the eye. "Did she put you up to this?"

"Who? Estelle? No... I didn't even know that she knew you. I...did I read this wrong? I sometimes have difficulty with social cues, but I thought we had a moment at the coffee bar before class..."

My body flushed with heat, nipples pinging into hard nubs again. "I...I'm sorry. I didn't mean to, like, ogle you. It's just that your shoulders are so broad and strong that I —" I shook my head, mortified that I'd almost told him that I imagined my knees over those broad shoulders.

He giggled. Atlas actually giggled, and his shoulders bounced as the giggle morphed into a laugh, and then I was sure he was having a go at me now. I'd made a fool of myself.

"I just made it really weird—"

"No, you didn't make it weird. I'm just astounded that a woman like you would doubt that I'm into you. Perspective really is a motherfucker."

"What?" I asked, now I was genuinely confused.

Atlas angled his body toward mine and leaned into the triangle of space the two of us made with our bodies. "You're stunning, Sonja. I couldn't keep my eyes off of you the entire class. I was afraid that I made you feel uncomfortable with all of my staring."

Uncomfortable in all the best ways.

"But I'm like nine years older than you."

"Ten if you round up, but what does that mean anyway? I'm a consenting adult. I'm of age," he said with a smile that bordered on lascivious.

A startled sound came out of me that was somewhere between disbelief and laughter. "You can't be serious. I'm forty years old."

"And you're beautiful and sexy as fuck," he said, his voice dropping into a lower octave that made me squeeze my thighs together again.

I shook my head and looked away from his intense, penetrating eyes. "I'm not. I'm a middle-aged woman with two kids, one of whom his on the way to college."

"Who the hell told you that?" he asked.

"I…"

Atlas chucked me under my chin, forcing me to look him in the eye. "Who the hell told you that you're not sexy or beautiful? Whoever told you that lied to you, Sonja."

Shit.

A lump was building in my throat. I was gonna cry. This was unacceptable. I blinked hard and bit down on my bottom lip to try and stave off the tears, but he teased my lip from between my teeth and swiped the pad of his thumb across it.

Goddamn, he might as well have reached down into my pants because I swear I was going to come on the spot.

"You probably think I do this all the time, huh? Like I'm some sort of charmer that has my choice of women."

"You don't?" I asked, arching my eyebrow.

He laughed. "Okay, maybe I do have my choice of women, but they are never usually the type of women I want."

"What type of woman is that?"

Atlas made a big show of dragging his gaze down my frame. "The woman right in front of me."

I shook my head, still in disbelief that this young man was giving me his attention. "I don't know how to respond to this."

"That's fair," he said, then leaned back a little. "Maybe just...think about it for a minute. Preferably when you're alone in bed tonight. Get comfortable with the idea that someone like me could want someone like you."

"Hey, Sonja," Estelle interrupted. "I'm gonna head out. It's bath time, and I need to get home to make sure Deacon doesn't let Christopher talk him out of getting his stinky ass in the shower."

"Okay, I'm gonna head out, too." I slipped off the stool, a motion that deposited me right into the triangle of Atlas's thick, muscular thighs. A soft, almost imperceptible moan slipped from him before he shifted back a bit more to give me space.

"I'll see you class?" Atlas asked.

"Yes, of course! I have a business to create!" I said as I grabbed my denim jacket, Before I could grab my bag, he picked it up and held it out so I could slip it on my shoulder. His fingers caressed the side of my neck, and I shivered.

"I'm looking forward to it," he said.

I cleared my throat. "Okay, well... thanks for the chat!" I squeaked then hightailed it out the door.

Estelle and I were parked in the same lot a few blocks up, so we walked together. I was in stunned silence until we reached the corner, but I could practically feel the smug satisfaction rolling off of her.

"Okay, maybe you're right," I said finally.

"Right about what?"

"Right about me being ...attractive to the opposite sex."

"I mean, I never doubted it."

"But that doesn't mean that someone like Atlas is even a possibility."

Estelle frowned. "Why not?"

"Look at him, Stelle! It's just not something that could or should happen. People will think—"

"Who cares what people will think?" she interrupted. She stopped walking and grabbed me by the shoulders. "No one is saying you have to marry him. You don't even have to date him. Clearly, he's awakened something in you, and it would be a shame to let that go to waste, don't you think?"

"What are you even talking about?"

"Fuck him, Sonja. If this opportunity is available to you, jump on it. And I mean that literally."

"I can't do that right now. I'm barely divorced."

"Do you really think that Eric isn't out there getting his dick wet?"

I clenched my teeth at her crude language, but the thought had crossed my mind. Eric hadn't said why he wanted a divorce a year ago, but part of me thought another woman had something to do with it.

"It doesn't have to be anything serious, Sonja. Just count this as part of your self-care regimen."

* * * *

Estelle's words weighed on me on the drive home, and by the time we both pulled into our garages, I was halfway convinced that Atlas wasn't someone or something beyond my reach. Those thoughts quickly dispelled when I walked into my house, though.

My daughter Nadia was sitting at the breakfast bar, eating a bowl of cereal when I came in. "Hey, baby. Is that what you're eating for dinner?"

"No," she said, shaking her head. "Winston took me to Burger King. This is just a snack. Where were you?"

"I told you that I was taking that business course down in the village. Why? Did something happen?"

She shrugged. "Dad called. He wanted to know if you had talked to us about the new schedule."

"Shit," I cursed. I dropped my bag and walked around the counter to embrace my daughter. "I'm sorry you had to hear it from him in that way."

"So it's true? The divorce is really final?"

I clenched my teeth against the anger that flared in my chest. We agreed that we would talk to the kids together. Break the news in a way that would answer their questions and leave them feeling secure in our love for them. Apparently, Eric had jumped the gun.

"Yes," I answered softly. "Daddy and I are divorced now, but that doesn't mean we don't love you and Winston any less—"

"I'm not a little kid, mom. You don't have to give me the 'we love you, but we're just not in love with each other' talk. Dad's been living somewhere else for more than a year, and when he was here with us, he was always distracted and distant. I'm just worried about you. You've always been so devoted to him. It's not fair that he gets to walk away and leave you alone after all this."

"Why do you assume that he's the one who asked for the divorce?"

"Isn't he?"

22

I looked at my fourteen-year-old daughter. She was bright and intuitive. I should have known that she would have been tuned in to what was happening between Eric and me.

"Listen, don't worry about me. I am okay."

"Are you? Do we have to move? What are we going to do for money? Are you going to have to get a job or something?"

"Baby girl," I said, taking her cheeks in both my hands. "I don't want you to be worried. Everything is going to be fine." I kissed her forehead and the tip of her nose. "It's late. You should get ready for bed."

My daughter went up to bed, and I did the rounds, checking the doors and the locks to make sure everything was secure before heading to bed myself. I hated that my daughter was nervous and afraid of what might happen now that Eric and I were divorced. That made getting everything I could out of the *Entrepreneur Academy* even more critical. I couldn't let her see me as a cast-off housewife unable to take care of herself. I had to prove to her and myself that I wasn't. My little beauty brand business had to be successful. And according to Atlas, it would be.

chapter three

Atlas

The bell hanging above the door jingled as I walked into the barbershop behind Kairo for our Friday appointment.

"Hey! If it isn't our two favorite customers!" Krissy, the cute bartender at the gleaming mirrored bar next to the door, chirped. She passed us our drinks — drinks that she had somehow memorized and had waiting for us when we came through the door.

Cutz 'n Cocktails was new in the Village with an old school vibe. Dark wood barber stations lined both walls with red leather barber chairs. Framed photos of local athletes hung above the comfortable waiting area in the back of the room, which was fitted with two overstuffed leather chairs and a couch.

The owners Jerricka and Sheba opened their shop a few months after we closed on the space that became *The Coworking Spot*.

It was completely unlike our old shop, which I counted as a good thing, but abandoning our old barber still felt a little like cheating. I'd thought about going back there, but I couldn't dismiss the fact that we were treated like valued clients when we walked in the door and never had to wait for hours to get in the chair. Besides, Jerricka was the best damn barber I'd had in ages. I couldn't have Kairo's fade looking tighter than mine. Even though that would probably be impossible because I swear she's in here on Tuesdays getting an edge up for... *reasons*. And that reason smiled at her as she emerged from the back office of the shop.

"Hey, you two!" Jerricka said with a grin. "What's going on? How you doin'?"

"I'm great," Kairo said, her smile flashing almost bright as Jerricka's. "My friend here needs some help, though. And I'm not just talking about his fade."

"You've been waiting all day to bring this up," I groaned.

"Oh! This sounds good! I'm just finishing up with Mr. Kemp, and I'll be with you two in a second."

"Don't be rushing through my cut just because that strapping young man came through the door. My money is just as green as his," Mr. Kemp groused, and I had to chuckle. If he'd been paying any attention, he would have realized that the smile and cheery disposition were for Kairo, the well-dressed stud seated next to me.

"Ain't no rush, Mr. Kemp. We're a little early anyway," Kairo said, giving Jerricka a wink.

And we were, which was also by design. How else was my best friend supposed to creep on the barber that she'd had a mighty crush on for over a year?

Kairo let out a soft groan and bit the corner of her lip as Jerricka moved around the barber chair, giving us a clear view of her fat ass.

I shook my head and laughed at my friend, then leaned in and whispered, "Explain why you're not asking her out again?"

She flared her nostrils and whacked me in the arm. "Shut the fuck up, Atlas. I already told you why," she gritted through clenched teeth.

I shrugged and leaned back in my chair. Kairo's explanation made sense—you don't fuck your barber because two relationships would end if it didn't work out. I understood where she was coming from, but damn...I haven't seen the kid crush this hard since seventh grade.

"Anyway, I would advise you to worry about yourself. Speaking of which..." Her face stretched into another grin, but this one was at my expense.

"Come on," I groaned, covering my face. "Can you please let this shit go?"

"Let what go? Share with the class," Jerricka said.

Kairo leaned forward and gleefully recanted my spectacular fail last night. And I couldn't really blame her. I'd relived that moment over and over in my head. It still sounded just as corny as it did when it came out of my mouth last night. Sonja Watts threw me off my game, and I had no explanation for any of it.

"Yolo, my dude? *Yolo?*" Sheba laughed, barely glancing up from the head she was cutting. "You have spent way too much time in Cali surfing with white dudes if you thought Y.O.L.O. was an acceptable phrase to use in a conversation with a Black woman in twenty-and-nineteen."

"Wow..." Jerricka said with a laugh. "What happened? I mean, I know it's been a minute. Are you just out of practice?"

"Nah... you didn't see her. This girl—"

"Woman," Kairo corrected.

"Lady," I conceded. "She's bad."

Kairo grunted in agreement.

"Hold on, now," Mr. Kemp said. "You can't leave a man hanging with that penny-ante description. Give an old man something to visualize."

26

"Mr. Kemp!" Jerricka gasped in faux-surprise. "Don't make me run across the street and tell Mrs. Kemp you're over here talking nasty."

"Sarah Kemp knows all about my nasty mouth. How do you think I landed her?"

"Whoa, Ernest Kemp!" Sheba, the barber in the next chair, protested. "Lemme find out that you're some kinda cat-daddy!"

"Some kinda... little girl," he twisted around in his seat. "You don't know nothin' 'bout me. I swear, y'all younguns think you invented sex. Now hush-up and let this man tell us about his woman."

A surprised laugh came out of me. I swear these old dudes at the barbershop are the best entertainment sometimes.

"Well, excuse me!" Sheba said with a surprised laugh. "I'm sorry I interrupted. Atlas, please continue to objectify women in a barbershop owned and operated by two women."

"Aww, come on," a couple of the other guys in the shop complained.

Mr. Kemp grunted and rolled his eyes.

"I got you, Mr. Kemp—" Kairo said eagerly as she scooted to the edge of her seat.

"Excuse me?" Jerricka snapped.

"I mean... I was just gonna say that she looks good," Kairo said with a sheepish grin and a one-shouldered shrug.

I was glad that I wouldn't have to hear a blow-by-blow of Sonja's looks from Kairo, but *good* was an understatement. *Good* was how you described a lackluster sandwich that filled the hole in your stomach when you were starving. *Good* was the girl your best friend paired you up with so they could take out the friend they've been trying to bag forever. *Good* was someone you shared a drink and passed the time with, but didn't bother to call because you just weren't that interested. Sonja Watts better than *good*. She was...

"You know how you hear someone's voice without seeing their face and reminds you of a song? But then you actually lay eyes on them, and the song feels like it's already part of a memory that you haven't even made yet?" I smiled, remembering how she smiled up at me, looking as nervous and shy as standing next to her made me feel. "Yeah, that's how she looks," I said confidently.

The room went quiet as a crept. I glanced around at the few faces I knew—the other Friday regulars— then back at Kairo. "What?"

The room exploded with raucous laughter. Loud, raucous laughter, punctuated with points and near tear-filled exclamations of, "did you hear this nigga?" And could I blame them? This whole thing was ridiculous. My reaction to Sonja — this illogical want she inspired in me — all of it was ridiculous.

"I thought it was beautiful," Jerricka said after the room quieted down.

"Beautiful? How can it be beautiful if it doesn't make sense?" Kairo asked.

"I understand what the young man was trying to say," Mr.Kemp piped up. "He met his wife last night and y'all in here cracking on him because he didn't describe her using some misogynistic metaphor."

Met my... "Whoa! Hold on, Mr. Kemp! I mean, she was beautiful and all, but I didn't mean—"

"Is that what made him act so stupid?" Kairo asked, interrupting me. "Because I swear I have never seen this man make a fool of himself the way he did last night. He turned into a pubescent boy the moment he saw her. I almost wanted to drag him out of the bar so he wouldn't embarrass himself further."

"You know… it's kinda insulting for y'all to keep talking about me like I'm not sitting right here—"

"Wait… it gets worse?" Sheba asked.

I cringed inwardly as Kairo nodded her head.

"We ran into them at the bar next door, right? This dude runs up on her like a big lab puppy and practically humps her leg."

"I did not—"

"He came on strong as fuck. Like… it made absolutely no sense. And then, even though this woman is *completely* into him, he precedes to make her cry and run her out of the bar."

"Hold on… I did not make her cry. I simply asked what asshole made her believe that she wasn't sexy and desirable, and she just started crying."

Jerricka dabbed a couple of cotton balls with alcohol and ran them along Mr. Kemp's hairline, making him draw in a sharp breath. "Sounds to me like she might be a little damaged," she said, unsnapping the cape.

"Or maybe she's a mother who just got wrapped up in raising her kids. That happens," Sheba volunteered.

"True. Does she have kids?" Jerricka asked, handing Mr. Kemp a mirror.

"Yeah, she said she has two."

Kairo groaned. "You didn't tell me that."

"What's that reaction? So the woman has kids. So what?" I shrugged.

Mr. Kemp settled up with Jerricka, thanked her, and kissed her on the cheek.

"Quit getting fresh, Mr. Kemp!" she exclaimed playfully.

"Oh, you ain't seen fresh," he said with a cackle. "Young man!" He pointed a finger at me. "Don't let these ashy motherfuckers in here talk you out of a good thing."

"Thank you, Mr. Kemp. I don't think she's interested, though."

"You made that woman's eyes well with emotion at your first meeting. She's interested," he said with a wink.

Gah. I wanted to believe him, but the "L" I took last night had a lot to say on the subject.

"Come on, Atlas," Jerricka said, waving me over. She let the chair down as low as it would go and laughed as I sat down, making the chair hiss and sink another inch lower. "I swear you're gonna break the hydraulics on this thing one day," she teased.

"Hahaha, very funny. Atlas is a big guy who breaks chairs by sitting in them," I said, my tone as dull and droll as I could muster.

"Oh, are we sensitive now?" she asked, shaking out the cape before snapping it around my neck.

"Not sensitive. It's just a tired ass joke. Figured someone as smart as you would've come up with something better by now."

"Aww...you are sensitive about your girthiness! Who knew?" Sheba teased.

Kairo scoffed. "Are you kidding me? Everyone knows the big fella has an ooey-gooey, marshmallow center."

I arched an eyebrow at my friend, and she went quiet. She knew better than to feed into that bullshit. I wasn't sensitive about my "girthiness" as Sheba called it. I was just sick of hearing it. At six-foot-four and two hundred and fifty pounds, it was fairly obvious that I didn't get this big overnight.

"Not that it mattered to Sonja. She's all into them broad shoulders," Kairo snickered. "And them thicc-ass thighs."

Kairo was the one who overheard Sonja telling Estelle that she would meet her at the bar after class. We went to high school with Estelle, and we've been known to have a few drinks from time to time— especially since she graduated from the Academy and opened her yoga studio a couple of blocks away. So it wasn't uncommon for her and Kairo to post up at the bar, and this time, Sonja had joined them. Before Kairo could introduce herself, Estelle and Sonja launched into some girl talk about me. Kairo's eavesdropping and covert texting resulted in some uncensored gems from Sonja. Sweet, little Sonja, who had presented as quiet and prim in my class, but apparently, was anything but. So by the time I'd locked up and joined them, I was sure she was interested. Damn, I really thought I had a chance.

"So you never answered my question," I said as Jerricka grabbed a pick and a spray bottle.

"About what?" Kairo asked for clarification.

"Dating a woman with kids. You've never done that?"

Kairo glanced at Jerricka. "I mean, I did when I was a lot younger, but I probably shouldn't have."

"Oh, really? Why do you say that?" Jerricka asked, her tone and body language suddenly combative as she sprayed my hair with detangler.

The corner of Kairo's mouth quirked into a smile, and I knew it was because this conversation was getting the desired reaction out of Jerricka.

"When I was like twenty-four, I dated a girl with a two-year-old son. It was pretty serious. We even moved in together, which I immediately realized was a mistake. I wasn't ready for the reality of parenthood. It was a lot more than baby Jordans

31

and cute videos of him dancing to the Migos. It was a lot of work, and when it boiled down to it, I wasn't ready to do that work. Nor did I want to."

"Hmph," Jerricka grunted then went back to picking out my hair…aggressively.

Goddamn, I wish Kairo would ask this girl out already. My scalp couldn't take this abuse every week when she decided to wind Jerricka up.

"But that was like ten years ago, and I'm a different person now. Back then, I was barely able to commit to a relationship, let alone help someone raise their kid. I'm far better equipped now. More stable and settled. But you, Atlas," she said, pointing at me. "Dating a woman with children is not for you."

"What? Come on. She's a forty-year-old woman who probably has pre-teens or teenagers. Not a twenty-something with a toddler—"

"Oh, wow! So she's a grown-ass woman? This Sonja most certainly doesn't have time for your childish games," Sheba volunteered.

"Damn, that woman is forty years old?" Kairo asked in disbelief.

"I know, right?" I said, echoing that same disbelief.

"But still, Sheba's right," Kairo said with a shake of her head. "This woman doesn't have time for your games."

"So, it's good enough for you, but not for me?"

"We're different people. You're not the settling down type."

If Kairo had made that same statement to me a week ago, I probably would have agreed with her. But today, three days after I'd met Sonja Watts, it felt less like the truth and more like an attack on my character. Unfortunately, I couldn't argue with her because my track record said otherwise. Past behavior

32

was the best predictor of future behavior, right? And my past behavior was... whorish.

I grunted noncommittally and decided to shut the fuck up, and thankfully, the conversation shifted away from me. Jerricka tightened up my fade, trimmed my beard, and I settled up with her.

"Am I picking you up, or are you going to Uber tonight?" Kairo asked as she settled into the barber chair.

"Where are we going again?" I asked with a frown.

Kairo gave me an incredulous look. "We just talked about this at lunch, Atlas."

I shrugged, still drawing a blank.

"First Friday? We agreed to visit some of the galleries and venues in the neighborhood so that we can connect with more business owners in the area and leave postcards? Spread the word about the courses we're offering? Is this ringing any bells?"

"Shit..." I grimaced. "My bad, fam. Pick me up around seven, I guess. That'll give me a chance to check in on my mama and grab something to eat before we head out."

"Yeah, definitely get something to eat. There's gonna be nothing but wine and finger food at most of these places. Nothing to feed the likes of you, and we can't have you getting hangry."

"Oh, no. We won't like him when he's hangry," Jerricka said, chuckling at her bland Hulk joke.

I huffed and shook my head. "You still got jokes," I said without the slightest hint of humor. "Text me when you're on your way, Kairo."

On my walk back to *The CoWorking Spot*, I attempted to shake off the conversation in the barbershop. But as I packed up my gear and jumped on my bike, it was still circling in my mind. Coming home to Greenville after being away for the better part of a decade sometimes felt like I'd gone back in time—and not just because it was a small town.

A lot of people had some long-held beliefs about me that I couldn't seem to shake. Like this idea that I was some sort of player... sure, I'd dated a lot of women in the last few years, but I'd only been involved with one since I came home. And yeah... maybe that was a bit messy, but was that really my fault? I was honest and upfront with Tatiana. If she wanted more than that one night, that had nothing to do with me.

Except maybe... *maybe*... I had no business fucking around with a twenty-two-year-old bartender in the first place, especially at a bar that I frequented.

Whatever. It was a mistake, and I course-corrected. I haven't even so much as flirted with anyone since then, and that was damn near a year ago. Unfortunately, that didn't matter because the drama that followed, fed everyone's preconceived notions about me.

Pedaling hard, I crested the hill that led to my old neighborhood, then coasted down the street to my mother's house. The cul-de-sac hadn't changed much since I left. The trees were taller, and a few neighbors had died or moved away, but my childhood home still looked the same. I propped my bike against the wall under the carport and walked in.

"Ma?" I called out, wiping my feet on the doormat.

"Hey, son!" she called back.

The brick ranch was tiny, with just three bedrooms and one full bath. Stepping through the back door, I found my mother at the stove, wearing a big smile that always made me feel like a kid again.

"Hey, mama," I kissed her on the cheek.

"I'm making oxtails, rice, and peas, and there's some cornbread in the oven.

"Yes!" I rubbed my hands together and hummed under my breath as I pulled out a chair at the small kitchen table.

"Excuse me, young man? I know you ain't 'bout to sit at my table without washing up first."

"My bad, ma." I made my way to the hall bathroom, ducking to get through the door. "So, how was your week?" I asked as I washed my hands.

"Oh, same ole, same ole. We started planning the menu for Thanksgiving dinner at the soup kitchen. Are you planning on volunteering again this year?"

"Yes, ma'am. Go ahead and put me down."

"Good! Meredith's granddaughter Prisma is gonna be there."

I rolled my eyes. Walked right into that one. "Last time I checked, Prisma was a sophomore at the University of South Carolina," I said, reemerging from the bathroom.

"She is! And she's pre-med. Smart and just as gorgeous as her mama. I know you had a crush on her mama growing up—"

"What? Mama, I was thirteen. And what does that have to do with —"

"I mean to say that Prisma is young and single, and I know she's your type," my mother said with a smile.

"Mama… she's a child."

She tsked and opened the cabinet next to the stove to take out two plates. "You're ridiculous. She is not a child. She's of legal age, and I think—"

"I think you should give that topic a rest," I interrupted. I didn't mean to be so short with my mother, but I couldn't stand another moment of the "get Atlas a wife" conversation. Especially after what went down at the barbershop.

In my peripheral view, I saw my mother falter for a moment before loading up my plate.

"I'm sorry, son," she said with a heavy sigh as she turned and set the plate in front of me. "You know I want you happy. Sometimes I push too much. I only do it because I love you."

"I know, ma." I looped my arm around her waist and kissed her cheek again. "But honestly, if we're gonna talk about anybody dating and settling down, we should be talking about you, Ms. Eileen James."

She swatted me with a dishtowel and chuckled. "Boy, quit talking foolishness."

"I mean, Mr. Bailey has been waiting for a chance."

As far as I knew, my mother hadn't dated anyone seriously since my father, and that was damn near twenty years ago. Considering how toxic their relationship was, I didn't blame her, but my mother, with her smooth brown complexion, glittering dark eyes, and sweet disposition, deserved to have a man in her life that wasn't her son. Unfortunately, I've never been able to convince her of that.

"That man already acts too familiar," she said dismissively.

Talking about my mother's love life was the best way to change the subject, though, so we moved on to other topics like the things she needed me to do around the house. So far, there was a possible leak in the roof, and the lawn guy needed to be fired because he'd trimmed her azalea bushes. Except I knew for a fact that he didn't trim those bushes because I expressly forbade him to touch the damn things. Not only that, the "lawn guy" was William Bailey, the same man who had hired me when I was a kid looking to make a few dollars. I trusted him implicitly for that reason alone. But even I knew this wasn't about Mr. Bailey. My mother just wanted me to work in the yard with her on Saturday mornings like I did when I was growing up.

"I'll talk to him, ma," I said as I wiped my mouth and pushed away from the table.

"Are you just gonna run off without letting your food digest?" she protested as I stood up.

"I'm meeting Kairo in a couple of hours. It's a work thing."

"A work thing." She grunted disapprovingly.

"Yes, mother. And trust me, I would skip out on this if I could." I scraped my plate clean, rinsed it, and put it in the dishwasher. "Anything you need me to do before I go?" I asked, turning toward her.

"Well, you can promise me that you'll try to meet a nice young lady tonight that will give me some grandbabies?"

I sighed and shook my head. "I'm not making any promises, but I'll try."

With another kiss, I left my mother's house and cycled home to get ready for a dull evening of networking. The conversation with my mother annoyed me, but I really wish I could give her want she wanted.

Cuz for real, for real? I wanted it, too.

Hell, I think I might've already found her in Sonja Watts. Sonja Watts with her pretty brown skin, bright, curious eyes, and that tiny beauty mark in the dip of her top lip. Sonja Watts, in ripped black jeans that covered an ass so juicy it took all of my willpower not to squeeze it. Sonja Watts in an old band t-shirt with a Stevie Nicks lyric emblazoned across palm-sized tits whose nipples peaked when I smiled at her. I had a visceral reaction to her last night and at the barbershop when Mr. Kemp said that I met my wife. I still didn't believe that, but damn... I wanted her. Unfortunately, Kairo wasn't wrong. She was a grown-ass woman, and I wasn't the settling down type. Even if her husky, blues singer voice reminded me of a song.

chapter four

Sonja

"There she is!" my baby sister Birdie pointed out the old school Econovan that belonged to our other sister Agostina in the parking lot. I pulled my Subaru alongside her van and tooted the horn. Agostina looked up, and a smile brightened her face.

"Get out and help me!" she shouted as I shut off the engine.

"Okay, okay!" Birdie chirped.

It was First Friday, and I was back in The Village to help my sister Agostina set up her weekend pop-up shop.

First Friday was a monthly gallery crawl that allowed the public to visit the private studios and gallery spaces in our now thriving arts district. During the holidays, they opened an event space and invited creators to sell their wares. My sister Aggie was a brilliant ceramist—though she more closely identified with being called an artist because she had so many interests. When she was feeling really badass, she introduced herself as a journeyman.

"What do you need help with?" I asked.

"I have eight more boxes of plates, mugs, and bowls. I already took the freeform stuff inside."

"Good. I've got these." I grabbed the other dolly out of the back of her van.

We stacked the boxes onto the dollies and wheeled them through the back door of *Artisan Depot,* a pop-up shop event space for makers, which just happened to be directly across the courtyard from *The Coworking Spot* and *The Narrows*—the scene of my recent humiliation.

Residual shame heated my face and made the back of my neck hot. Last night, a guy ten years younger than me told me that I was beautiful and sexy, and I cried like someone had never complimented me before. All night I'd thought about the way he'd caressed my bottom lip with his thumb and then looked at my mouth like he wanted to kiss it. God, I wish he had kissed me. I spent the whole night wishing he had kissed me or that I was brave enough to kiss him—

"Sis!" Birdie shouted. "Aggie's back here."

"What?" I turned to see that both of my sisters had stopped three stalls back. "Oh. My bad," I muttered. I wheeled the dolly around and doubled back to them. Agostina was staring at me, but I didn't dare meet her gaze. I didn't tell her anything about my first night of class or meeting Atlas, but if I looked at her, she would know.

"What's in that top box?"

"Uh…" I opened it and pulled out the plate on top. "The plates with the delicate sage leaves—oh! That reminds me!" I set the plate on the nearest shelf and pulled out the smudge stick I'd made for her. "It has all the good stuff for success and prosperity in there."

A smile spread across my Aggie's face, and she planted a kiss on my cheek. "Thank you, sis," she sniffed the bundle of herbs. "It smells like Christmas."

"That's the cloves. I had some sprigs leftover from the batch Mama gave me last weekend."

"Mmmm.." She hummed happily.

"Why didn't you tell me you were bringing her a gift? Now I look like an asshole because I didn't bring her anything," Birdie pouted.

"It's just a smudge stick, baby bird," I said and rolled my eyes.

Aggie gave the bundle of herbs another hard sniff. "This smells good enough to make a candle or essential oils out of it. You should put it in your shop. You got a lighter?"

I chuckled at her offhand suggestion and dug my lighter out of my bag. "Here, but let's get everything set up before we smudge. I also have a few live plants in the car to fill in the gaps."

"Yeah, you're right. That makes more sense." She set down the smudge stick and gathered her locs and tied them up on top of her head. "Let's get to work!"

My sisters and I worked for almost an hour, unpacking and styling her space to make it inviting for customers. When everything was just right, Agostina lit the smudge stick. She blew on it until the flame became glowing embers and sweet-smelling smoke.

"Prosperity within me and around me. Abundance within me and around me," she murmured, circling her head and crossing her shoulders until the smoke hung around her in a cloud.

I took it from her and paced around her space, waving the sweet-smelling smoke over the stacks of earthenware plates and bowls, being sure to speak her affirmations into them with intention. "So, what do you think of about my idea of us going into business together?" I asked.

"You guys are gonna go in on this together? Why am I always the last one to find out about these things?" Birdie whined.

41

"Can you give the bratty baby sister routine a rest for a moment? I just suggested it. Nothing is decided, but... what do you think, Aggie?"

Agostina made a familiar sound. It was her thinking sound. "It's a solid idea, Soni. But why are you really asking me to do this?"

That tone. I hated that tone because I knew it meant that she already had me figured out. Agostina was what our Great Grandmother would've called a medium or an empath, which meant that she felt a lot of feelings; hers and everyone else's. She often heard and understood the reason behind things before I was able to acknowledge it myself.

"Well," I began slowly. "For one thing, you wouldn't have to do these pop-up shops anymore if you didn't want to. We would have a dedicated space for you to sell out of—"

"I sell online and out of my studio. And my customers love my holiday season pop-ups. I create one of a kind pieces that they can't buy year around. Also? That's not the real reason why you asked me to do this with you," she said with a knowing raise of her pierced brow.

"So why did I ask you? Since you know so damn much."

"You're afraid of doing it alone," she stated in her plain-speaking way. "You're afraid of doing it alone because you're afraid of failing."

"And I oop!" Birdie said with a laugh.

I flared my nostrils and turned toward Aggie slowly, a retort on my tongue. But the moment our eyes met, the ire in me quelled. "You're so good at this."

"I know," she agreed with a smirk.

"And I need someone who has already done this to guide me through the process."

"Isn't that why you're taking the course that Estelle signed you up for?"

The mere mention of the course conjured images of Atlas in my mind. Not that he was ever far from my thoughts since that first night. And with those thoughts came the memory of how my body reacted to him, what he said to me in the bar that night, the way I wanted him—

"I mean, yes, but you're my sister. We're supposed to help each other with stuff like this."

Agostina narrowed her eyes at me. "Cut it out. That whiny bullshit doesn't even work for Birdie."

I sucked my teeth. "Come on, Aggie. It would be like opening mama's apothecary here in town—"

"If that's really what you wanna do, why aren't you asking mama to partner with you?"

"Because she's not gonna want to run the business the way I want. She would just want to make it *Eudora's Apothecary* in Greenville—"

"Or she will see your vision and support you," Birdie suggested.

"I don't know."

"Just ask her, Soni. You might be surprised by her reaction." Aggie cupped one of my cheeks in her hand and kissed the other. "Now sage that spot again. You got your icky, confused feelings all over it," she said, giving me a shove.

I rolled my eyes, grabbed the lighter off the table, and relit the smudge stick. "Prosperity…"

"Prosperity within me and around me," Agostina said.

"Abundance within me and around me," I said, picking up the affirmation where she'd left off and wafting the smudge stick over the dinnerware I'd already covered, cleansing the space I'd tainted with my confused thoughts.

43

Agostina and Birdie made it sound so easy. Like our mother, Eudora Malone wasn't some monument of a woman with a reputation as a healer around these parts that I couldn't begin to measure myself against. They were younger than me, so they never had to sit down with Mama and talk about the day when she would 'pass the mantle' to me. For a time, I was interested in it, but when I met Eric, I realized that I was no healer — no conjure woman. I just wanted to make soaps and lotions to sell to stay at home moms, for chrissakes.

The holiday pop-up shop opened it's doors at around four to welcome the people meandering up and down the sidewalk dressed in clothing that was more appropriate for late summer than fall. Agostina shooed me and Birdie away, deciding that our energy stirred up too much indecision around her booth, so we set out on the concrete to visit the galleries and shops open for *First Friday*.

The Village was transformed by this event, and it felt quaint and cute enough to feature in a Hallmark movie. We strolled, dipping in and out of storefronts and galleries when we were moved — gobbled up free wine and cheese while we considered airy watercolors, impasto oil paintings, and strange freeform sculptures. I didn't know much about art, but I knew what I liked.

We were heading back to see if Agostina needed anything or wanted a bite to eat when I caught sight of Atlas crossing the street.

"I think we should stop by the *Kinfolks Diner* and then go to *Oliver Green's* for ice cream," Birdie said. "I haven't had a good ole meatloaf dinner in a while."

Why did he look even better to me than he did three nights ago? He was wearing one of those shirts that were like a t-shirt but had three buttons at the throat, and noticing those three buttons drew my eyes to his broad shoulders.

Gawd, why did I cry and run out of the bar like a fucking weirdo?

"How's that sound, sis? I'm sure Mr. and Mrs. Kemp would be happy to see us."

"Yeah, yeah, sure…meatloaf," I muttered, then I tripped hard over a lip of risen concrete as I approached the crosswalk because I couldn't take my eyes off of him. "Oh, shit."

Of course, it made him look my way, and the moment his eyes landed on me, my whole body went hot and sensitive. My armpits pricked and itched with nervous sweat. My lips tingled. My nipples peaked, my skin erupted in a rash of gooseflesh, and my breath panted out like some gross representation of a woman in a Skinemax movie.

I waved then stood there, awkwardly.

"What the hell…" Birdie asked, looking from me to where Atlas stood with his friend on the opposite corner. "Who is that?"

"I… no one. Just the instructor of that entrepreneur course I'm taking."

"Well, damn. He's fucking fine. His friend is pretty damn cute too. I love her cut."

Atlas smiled and tipped his chin in my direction, acknowledging that he saw me. I was thankful for the street and traffic between us so that I could take a moment to get myself together. He tapped the woman with him. A gorgeous woman with a blonde, low-cut fade looked my way, smiled, and shook her head.

Great.

He'd probably told her how I cried and ran out of the bar, and now she knew my shame, too.

The two of them paused on the corner and had a conversation. I glanced up and down the street, begging to see a familiar face, or for a deluge of traffic to separate us, but only a few cars passed before the light turned red. The pedestrian sign flipped from stop to walk, and now I had no choice but to cross. Step by step, one foot in front of the other and watching the toes of my ratty Chuck Taylors, I made my way across the street. But I didn't dare look up until the toes of his boots were toe-to-toe with my ratty sneakers.

"Sonja Watts," he said in the deep voice, and I looked up, up, up until our eyes meet.

"Atlas James," I said softly.

"Sonja-goddamn-Watts," he repeated the corner of his mouth, hitching up into a smirk.

"Goddamn?"

He thrust his hands in his pockets. "You've been in my head all day like a song I can't forget—"

"Literally, all day," the woman next to him said with a smirk.

"Oh, nice. This is my sister Birdie," I volunteered, changing the subject because that thing he said about me being in his head all day was too much for me to process right now.

"Nice to meet you," Birdie said, then shook his hand and turned on all of her sparkle. My sister was damn cute.

"Nice to meet you, too, Birdie," Atlas said.

He barely glanced at her.

"My sister tells me that you're the instructor of the new class she's taking," Birdie said, smiling with all of her considerable sparkle.

"Yeah, I'm part owner of the Coworking Spot," he said, jerking his thumb over his shoulder.

"Hey, I'm Kairo McCullough. Best friend and business partner," the woman said, stepping forward.

I shook her hand then stared at her for a long moment. "Wait. You were at the bar the other night, weren't you?"

"Uh, yeah... I was," she stammered, let go of my hand, then shot a guilty look at Atlas that he didn't catch because he was still staring at me. "I'm gonna head up to the Center for Creative Arts—"

"I'll catch up," he said, thumping his friend on the back, then giving her a gentle shove to send her on her way.

Kairo sucked her teeth. "Nice meeting you," she said, then turned and walked up the block.

"Maybe I should go, too. Looks like..." Birdie glanced between the two of us. "Like you two have a lot to talk about," she finished a smile spreading across her face. "I'll be up at *Kinfolks Diner* if you're looking for me later...not that I think you will be."

I glared at Birdie, but she just waved and maneuvered around Atlas to walk up the sidewalk. Once she was behind him, she made some highly inappropriate sexual gestures at his back. "My God," I groaned. "My little sister is never gonna grow up, is she?"

"Wouldn't know. I don't have any. So what are you up to?" he asked.

"I was going to head over to *Ollie Green's* for some ice cream. What about you?"

"You know, that's such a coincidence because I was heading over to *Ollie Green's* for some ice cream, too."

I smiled. "Well, would you like to join me, Mr. James?"

"Indeed I would, Ms. Watts,"

Hm. That sounds odd. My married name paired with Miss. Maybe I should think of going back to my maiden name now.

47

Atlas offered his arm, and I notched my hand into the crook of his elbow. My hand curved over his bicep, and it bunched under my palm. I took a shaky breath and tried not to think about how that arm would look draped over my naked waist the morning after some hot sex.

"So... about the other night. I feel like I need to apologize," he said.

"For planting your friend at the bar so she could eavesdrop on my conversation with Estelle?"

"Uhhhh... she wasn't exactly a plant. She just happened to be there. And yeah, she did tell me that you and Estelle were talking about me... and that's why I came at you so hard. I took it too far. I'm sorry about that. I was too forward, and I made you cry—"

"You didn't make me cry." I interrupted, then looked up at him. "I wasn't crying because of what you said. I was crying because—"

Jesus. It was happening again. My throat closed up tight with tears. I dropped my gaze down to my feet. Atlas covered my hand with his.

"Sonja?" His step slowed, and he turned to me on the sidewalk.

With a finger under my chin, he tipped my head back so that he could see my face. I closed my eyes, and tears slid down my cheeks.

"I did it again? I made you cry again?" he asked, his voice soft and concerned as he wiped away my tears with his thumbs. "Say something, Sonja. You're making me feel like a monster here."

I laughed and opened my eyes. He was far too beautiful to ever think that of himself. "You're no monster, Atlas."

He smiled, and it was so bright it was like daybreak. "Okay, but why do you cry every time you're around me? Is it an allergy or something? Do I stink? Does my smell make your eyes tear up?"

I laughed at that. "No, it's not your smell. You smell delicious." I bit my lip, embarrassed that I'd said that out loud.

"Okay... that's good to know. So why the tears?"

I took and deep breath. "You see me. I've felt invisible for a while, and you see me. You see Soni, and that feels good."

"You are not invisible, Sonni. I see you. I see all of you." Atlas's gaze dropped to my lips, and his thumbs stroked my cheekbones. "Come on, let's get some ice cream for those tears."

chapter five

Sonja

The sun was setting, but it was still warm on my back as we walked half a block to *Ollie Green's*. The sweet smell of waffle cones assailed my senses the moment we stepped through the door. I got the Sunshine Sorbet, and Atlas got the PB & J, then we walked back down to the little courtyard between *The Coworking Spot* and the pop-up shop venue. The place was jumping, and from where I sat, I could see that Aggie was busy helping customers. She glanced my way, and her eyes widened with surprise. I shrugged and waved.

"Someone you know has a shop in there?"

"My other sister Agostina. She's a ceramist. Really talented."

"Cool. We should check her out when we finish eating our ice cream."

"Yeah, sure." Then I sighed and shook my head. "She's going to make a big deal out of this."

"Out of what? Us eating ice cream together?"

"Yeah... I don't date —"

"Is this a date?" he asked a big grin spread across his face.

"Wow. God. My brain turns to soup around you."

"I've noticed," he said, spooning more ice cream into his mouth and grinning even wider.

"You're so smug," I said, shaking my head.

He shrugged. "I'm sitting here eating ice cream with a woman who thinks I smell delicious and is so sweet and sensitive that she cries when I tell her that she's beautiful. And... her thigh is touching mine, and she's blushing, and that's really fucking cute. I think those are a few good reasons to be smug."

"Damn it, Atlas." I shook my head.

"Too much?"

I shook my head and blinked rapidly to dry my eyes. Atlas reached over and rubbed the middle of my back. It was a simple gesture. Sweetly comforting.

I cleared my throat and dug my spoon into what was left of my scoop of sunshine. "So, my sister Agostina... when you meet her, she might seem a little weird."

"Weird how?"

"She knows things sometimes,"

"What does that mean? That she's like... a psychic or something?"

"Or something."

He took my empty ice cream cup, and his then stood up to throw out our trash. "Well, let's see what she knows about me."

Agostina was ringing up a customer when Atlas and I walked up to her booth. I could tell by the empty spaces on her shelves that she had sold quite a few of her wares.

"Hey, sis!" I chirped a little too eagerly because I could feel Atlas at my side. And of course, she saw him because he was big. So big. At 5'9," I was pretty tall, and he made me feel positively tiny. His big hand was on the small of my back. I liked that. Too much. "Looks like you're selling very well."

"I am, but I always do," she said, but she wasn't looking at me. Her eyes were on Atlas. "Who's this?"

"Atlas James," he said, reaching out to shake Agostina's hand. "I own *The CoWorking Spot* across the way."

"Agostina, I'm the other sister. I have a feeling you met Birdie already. *The CoWorking Spot,* huh?" she asked, still holding onto his hand.

"Yes, me and my business partner Kairo run the place. Soni's taking my entrepreneur course—"

Aggie's mouth quirked at the corner eyes narrowed. "So you're the reason why my sister was so flustered when she helped me set up earlier today. Interesting."

"That is interesting," Atlas agreed, glancing at me.

"Atlas... what an unusual name," Agostina said then finally let go of his hand. "So, what do you think of my sister's business idea?"

"I think it's brilliant. It's original. I told her that she will probably be one of the few students who come out of this cohort with a successful business."

My sister gave me a self-satisfied look. "Told you that you didn't need me. You can do this all by yourself."

Atlas gave me a curious look.

"My sister sells her ceramics out of her studio and online, and I thought it might be cool if we went into business together," I explained.

"That's not what you said."

"That's exactly what I said."

"Okay, so maybe that's what you said, but you meant that you were scared to do it alone—"

"Maybe don't embarrass me in front of my instructor?" I pleaded. My face was hot, and I'd spent the better part of the afternoon blushing beside this man. *Show me some mercy.*

My sister winked at me. "Hold on, Atlas. I have something for you."

"For me?" He gave me a confused look.

"She carries rocks around in her bag," I began teasingly.

"Crystals!" Agostina corrected as she turned to dig around in her bag.

"Okay, magic rocks. And she gives them to people who need them."

Agostina turned toward us with something in her fist. "Don't be fooled. She believes in this shit too." She held the crystal in both hands, closed her eyes, and took a deep breath before she handed it to him.

"Star rose quartz?" I questioned.

Agostina smiled then gestured at Atlas. The palm stone looked pebble-sized in his hand. He grasped it between his thumb and forefinger and held it up to the waning sunlight.

"So what does it do?" he asked.

"What? You're not wondering why I gave such a big man a pretty pink rock?" Agostina asked.

"Well, apparently, it has something I need. I don't know much about this stuff, so I have to trust your judgment."

I made a small sound of surprise that drew his attention.

"What?"

"Nothing," I said, shaking my head. "You're just so open to this. It's a pleasant surprise."

Atlas shrugged. "I'm open to a lot of things."

And the suggestiveness of that one statement had my lips and nipples tingling again.

"So, what is it for?" Atlas asked again.

"Rose Quartz is the quintessential stone of love—love for oneself, one's life partner, children, family, friends, community, the Earth, the Universe, and the Divine. Hold it up to the light again." Agostina instructed. "You see that?"

His thick brows furrowed. "You mean that star?"

"Yeah. That's rutile, a mineral that's primarily made of titanium oxide. It accelerates and enhances the effect of rose quartz."

"And how is this supposed to affect me?"

"Do you meditate?"

"Not well... I have trouble sitting quietly with my own thoughts," he admitted ruefully.

Agostina laughed. "Sitting quietly with your own thoughts isn't the only way to meditate. Walking, running, and even dancing are excellent ways to quiet the mind."

"Dancing? Really?"

"Of course. What do you think tribal dances are about?"

A smile twitched the corners of his mouth. "You're right. I never thought about it that way."

She took his hand and covered the stone so that it was nestled between their palms. "So the next time you're meditating in whatever way works for you, hold this in your hand or next to your skin, focus on calming your mind, releasing worry, fear, anxiety, and ego-driven patterns. It will help you feel more open to receiving and sharing love." Aggie let go of his hand, stepped back, and gave herself a little shake. She always wore a necklace of black tourmaline and holly blue agate when she set up shop —crystals for clearing psyche energy — especially the holly blue agate. Her hand went to it now, sifting the beads through her fingers like a rosary.

"Ego-driven patterns, huh?" Atlas said thoughtfully.

I looked up at him. His features held no amusement or derision as he stared at the rosy pink stone in his hand.

"So, what do I owe you?"

"Nothing. It's a gift! I mean, unless you want to buy something else," my sister said, gesturing toward her wares with a smile.

"Let me take a look around."

He stepped away, and Agostina grabbed the front of my tee and pulled me closer.

"Hey! Don't stretch the Bob Marley! I've had this since high school."

"And it shows," she said with a disapproving grimace. "What's up with the man carrying the world on his shoulders?"

"Nothing. He's my instructor."

"And he makes you stutter and blush, and you're worried about impressing him—"

"He's just my instructor," I repeated so loudly that it could barely be considered a whisper. "And what's up with you giving him a piece of rutilated rose quartz?"

"That wasn't about you," she said with a dismissive wave.

I tipped my head and gave her a skeptical look. "Really?"

"Okay, it wasn't only about you, but damn, Soni. The chemistry is off the charts between you two."

I shook my head and looked at Atlas, who had his back to us, but was undoubtedly listening to our conversation. There was no denying that I was attracted to this man, and he was the first since I've had these feelings since my divorce. Still...that didn't mean that I was ready.

"Don't push."

"I'm not pushing!"

"Seriously, Aggie." I looked her in the eye. "Don't."

She stroked a finger down my cheek. "I won't. But I don't think you need a push. It's going to happen anyway."

There was no explanation for why or how, but the things Agostina knew always became the truth. If she said it would happen, it would, but I still felt the urge to resist that inertia. I'd let so much of my life happen to me— my marriage, becoming a stay-at-home mom instead of working once the

55

kids were born, my divorce. If Atlas was going to *happen* to me, I wanted to have a say in it; some sort of control over what happened in this next chapter of my life.

Atlas cleared his throat. "I don't mean to interrupt, but can I buy this whole set?"

I helped Aggie wrap and bag the set of four plates mugs and bowls Atlas bought. He selected a sacred geometric pattern called the Flower of Life. The shapes were etched into the natural colored earthenware and gilded with gold leaf. It was gorgeous but subtle.

Back in the courtyard, we turned to face each other. It was full dark now.

"Kairo is going to cuss me out. We were supposed to be networking tonight, and I spent the whole evening with you."

"I'm sorry."

"Don't be. I enjoyed myself. Didn't you?"

I looked up at him and smiled. "I did..."

"I hear a but coming," he said, those heavy expressive brows of his dipped into a frown.

"But... I think it's best if we didn't get...involved. I just don't think it's a good idea."

"Hm," he grunted. "And I suppose a gentleman would agree with you and back off."

"A gentleman would."

He groaned out his displeasure and looked up at the night sky. "A'right. I'll be a gentleman then."

"Thank you." And now I felt a little sad about that. Maybe I didn't expect him to be a gentleman about it. Or... maybe I didn't want him to be.

"I'll back off, but I can't promise I won't be a distraction," he said with a grin.

I rolled my eyes. "Goodnight, Atlas."

Me and Agostina closed up shop, I dropped Birdie off at her apartment, and then headed home to an empty house. I'd dropped Nadia off at a friend's house earlier in the day, and Winston was out with his girlfriend, which was why I was surprised to hear the TV on when I came in.

My first thought was that Winston had come home early. I didn't see his car out front, but maybe he'd parked further up block because the spot in front of our house was taken.

"Winston? Winston, is that you?" I called out as I rounded the corner into the kitchen.

Winston didn't answer, but someone was definitely in my house. The energy was off. Disturbed somehow.

Had I locked the door behind me when I left earlier? Was this an intruder? We had an alarm system, but the kids often forgot to set it when they went out.

I spun to my left and grabbed the biggest knife in the block. "Who's back there?" I called out as I crept around the entryway of the living room to the front hall, and down the hallway to my bedroom with my heart knocking against my ribcage. I kicked open the door to my bedroom and found Eric.

"Jesus Christ, it's me, Sonja," he said, throwing up his hands.

Relief washed through me and then anger. "What are you doing here?"

He shrugged and looked sheepish. "Winston said you were helping out Agostina, so I figured it would be a non-issue for me to come back and grab some things."

I glared at him, nostrils flaring. "You're supposed to call before you come over here."

He shrugged again. "I'm sorry. I didn't expect you to be here."

"That still doesn't mean that you can—you know what?" I held up my hands in surrender. "Get whatever you need."

I stalked back into the kitchen, and placed the knife back into the block before I took off my jacket and draped it in the chair at the kitchen table where I'd been working before I went to help Agostina. I was in the middle of the first assignment from class, discovering my strengths and weaknesses and identifying personal obstacles that might make keep me from being a successful entrepreneur. I guess I established today that one of my personal obstacles was fear of failure. But didn't everyone feel that?

Eric spent an hour or two in the bedroom and the office he kept at the end of the hall. I heard drawers opening and closing as he packed up his things, but I mostly ignored him until he came into the kitchen, wheeling two big suitcases behind him.

"Did you have a chance to talk to the kids about the schedule?" he asked.

Instead of answering him, I licked the tip of my finger and turned the page in the strengths finder book. Apparently, I was an activator. I would have never guessed that. After spending so many years taking care of other people, I can't imagine how that could be considered one of my strengths. Sure, I was good at helping other people turn their thoughts into actions, but I have never done that for myself, or even tried.

"Sonja, did you hear me?" Eric asked.

Slowly and deliberately, I set my book aside and looked up at him. "Yes, I have, but I assumed that is something you would set up with them."

"Okay, but how do you think they're feeling about it, and… what's all this?" he asked, looking down at the papers I had spread out on the island. He angled his head so that he could read the one right in front of him. *"The Entrepreneur Academy?* What's that?"

Eric was the last person I wanted to talk to about this. He had a way of diminishing anything I took an interest in until I felt like it was no longer worth the effort.

"Is this some sort of homework for Nadia or Winston?"

With a big sigh, I gathered up the papers, stacking them in sequential order. "Is there something else you needed from me?"

"What's with all this hostility?"

"This isn't hostility. I just have things to do, and I don't feel like chitchatting with you. You asked me if I talked to the kids and I told you that I have. There's really nothing more for me to say. I'm busy," I repeated more emphatically.

He laughed, but there was no warmth or humor in it. "You mean with this entrepreneur stuff? What are you trying to do? Start a business?"

"I'm not going to discuss this with you. Please, go," I begged.

At that moment, I realized that we'd had many arguments like this over the years. He would have called it a redirection to keep me from getting caught up in flights of fancy. I'd always compromised, acquiesced, even agreed that I didn't have the smarts or the wherewithal to handle myself outside of caring for him and the kids. But now I knew that wasn't true.

"I think you should go to nursing school," he suggested as if I'd asked. "You're good at taking care of other people."

I nodded. "I agree. Thanks for your suggestion."

Eric looked at me for a long moment. "I don't want this to be difficult for you, Sonja. I know that this divorce came as a surprise, but I'm not doing it to be vindictive. I don't want to hurt you."

"I'm glad you feel that way. The payout will go a long way toward helping me get established and to take care of the home I've made here in the meantime. You need not worry how I make that happen, though."

"Okay," he said, then put up his hands as if to rid himself of the responsibility. "I'll let you handle it." He grabbed the handle of his suitcase and began to make his way to the door. "Oh, and one other thing. I think we should go ahead and let our families know."

"Mine already does. I figure we could tell your family at Sunday dinner."

"Oh...I won't be there." He cringed. "But don't let that stop you. They should hear it from you."

I clenched my teeth. "Fine. I'll handle it."

Of course, he wasn't going to be there to let his dear old mother know that he made the decision to break up his family. Of course, that responsibility was going to fall to me.

"I'll be in touch with Nadia to schedule a day or weekend to spend some time with her."

"Hm," I grunted. Nadia probably had no interest in that, but I wouldn't stand between her and her father. "Eric?" I called out just as he reached the door.

"Yeah?"

"Please, knock or ring the doorbell the next time you come in. And arrange a time for someone to help you get the rest of your things. You don't live here anymore."

He turned to look at me from where he stood at the end of the hallway. Once again, he stared at me, but now it seemed as if he thought he was the one looking at a stranger. "That seems fair," he said finally.

"Thank you." I crossed my arms and watched him leave, then closed my eyes and took a deep breath. I didn't care how hard it was to start a business and make enough money to sustain the life myself, and my children had become accustomed to. I would do it, and I would do it without his help.

chapter six

Atlas

"Breh, if you ever want to be able to put your arms down again, I strongly advise you to move on from that arm and shoulder workout," Kairo suggested.

I looked at myself in the mirror and realized that I must've done way more bicep curls and shoulder presses than I initially intended. I now looked like I could lift a truck. *Fuck.* That was going to hurt later. Getting dressed would also be interesting now that I'd made it almost impossible to lift my arms.

"I'm so fucking distracted," I murmured as I repacked the dumbbells.

"Yeah, no shit," she snapped while mopping the sweat off of her face.

Three mornings a week, me and Kairo meet at the gym in my condo building. Ever since she read an article that said sitting was the new smoking, both of us made an effort to get at least thirty minutes of exercise a day. Not that either of us were a stranger to it. Working out has always been a sort of meditation for me. A way for me to block everything else out and just focus on moving my body and pushing the weight. It wiped all thoughts from my mind. Well, it usually did, but the moment I closed my eyes to catch my breath, I saw Sonja Watts licking Sunshine Sorbet from a plastic spoon with a smile on her lips and her dark lashes wet with happy tears. That mental image easily slipped into imagining if she would smile and cry happy tears when I had my mouth on her, or when I was inside of her…

Andddd now I was semi-hard again and thinking ungentlemanly thoughts.

Adjusting myself as discreetly as possible, I made my way over to the airbike to finish off my work out with a couple of high-intensity intervals.

"So I'm mostly done writing that welcome series we talked about this weekend. I think it will be a good funnel for the webinar idea you had."

"Yeah, yeah, sure. Did we settle on a topic? I forget."

Kairo dropped her barbell and turned to look at me. "Are you serious, Atlas? Yes, we decided on a topic! We spent most of Sunday brunch brainstorming it!"

I coasted to a stop, put my hands on my hips, and tried to catch my breath. This was beyond ridiculous. My brain refused to hold on to any thoughts besides thoughts of Sonja, and it was beginning to affect…everything. I'd joked about Kairo crushing on Jerricka, but she wasn't the one walking around with her brain between her legs like some preteen.

"My bad, fam. We did talk about it during brunch. I recorded the convo on my phone—"

"And thank fuck you did because it would have been lost forever. This level of distraction is not okay, my dude. You gotta get it together."

"I know…" I scrubbed my hands over my face. "I'mma get it together."

"Please, do. I get that you're into this chick, but you need to keep all the daydreaming to a minimum. We've got shit to do."

"Yes… I get it," I said, feeling slightly irritated by her scolding. "It's not like I'm doing this shit on purpose."

"Does that even matter? Look..." she tossed her towel over her shoulder and walked over to where I sat on the air bike. "That woman said she wasn't interested in pursuing a relationship with you. Respect her wishes and your self and move the fuck on."

"Is that what she said, though? I'm pretty positive that she said she didn't think it was a good idea. That doesn't mean she isn't interested."

"For fuck's sake—"

"I'm kidding!" I said with a laugh. "I hear what you're saying, friend. I'mma do better. I promise."

"You fucking better. I'll see you at the office," she said, then dapped me up and left me alone in the gym.

Once Kairo was gone, it occurred to me that I shouldn't have made that promise to her. This fixation on Sonja was completely involuntary. Despite my best efforts to redirect my thoughts, that perfect afternoon with her kept resurfacing. And damn, was it perfect. Too perfect. Just sitting on that bench with my thigh touching hers... I couldn't remember the last time I shared a moment so fucking simple with a woman that felt monumental. And I was supposed to just ignore this attraction— this magnetic energy— between us because she came to me learn how to start a business? And was that more important than kissing her?

Yes... it should be. It's definitely more important.

Stepping out of the elevator, I made my way to my apartment and let myself in.

Routine. That's what I needed. I should lean on my routine right now. It was important for me to focus on one goal at a time, and right now, that goal was the business Kairo, and I were building. This was not the time for big dreams and flights of fancy, even if that flight of fancy was laying down Sonja-goddamn-Watts.

I grabbed one of my premade frozen smoothie packs from the freezer and dumped it in the blender. While the almond milk, berries, and kale blended into something drinkable and nutritious, I woke up my computer. My to-do list populated on the right side of the screen, and I scrolled through it. Reviewing the audio from brunch with Kairo was on the list, so I could at least thank my past self for covering my ass.

Today was also the second day of class for the seventh cohort of the *Entrepreneur Academy*, and today's topic was Knowing Your Ideal Customer. It wasn't lecture heavy, which meant I could leave them to their own devices and focus on writing the scripts for the webinar—not Sonja Watts.

Goddamit.

This was getting frustrating. I'd made so many changes since I came home — a lot of self-improvement. But meeting Sonja had woken up that itch. It made the monotony I'd subjected myself to in an effort to reach my goals even more obvious. Routine served a purpose— yes. But I craved something new. Something… challenging.

But Sonja couldn't be that thing.

I drank my smoothie and sat down at my computer. I checked my emails because that's what I did at eight-thirty every day. After the emails were handled, I took a shower because that's what I did after I got my inbox under control. While the shower steamed up, I shaved. Once the neckbeard was managed, I climbed in the shower. Five minutes to lather and rinse. That's all I needed.

That was also where my routine ran off in a ditch.

Hot water beat down on my neck and shoulders, minimizing the damage I may have done overexerting myself.

I let my head sag on my shoulders, closed my eyes, and there she was. I'd spent the last hour or so scolding myself for thinking about her, but now... *sunshine sorbet*. How would that have tasted on her tongue?

I reached for the soap and lathered up.

No point in even pretending that I wasn't about to jerk off. To be honest, it was necessary to take the edge off at this point. I was going to see her later today, and I just needed...

Damn... that throaty laugh of hers. And the way she tipped her head back to let it out.

And her neck...

The long smooth column of her neck. I imagined my hand on her throat. Damn near felt the thrum of her pulse under my thumb. And her moan... would that be raspy and deep, too? Yes. Probably, yes.

And the way she said my name. Like she didn't want to, but couldn't help it.

"Oh, fuck..."

Dick throbbing in my hand, I braced myself against the wall and came.

But just like this morning, it wasn't enough.

Make it e-fucking-nough, Atlas.

* * * *

Later that morning, with my prepacked meals and my laptop in my backpack, I cycled to work at a leisurely pace. I took the Swamp Rabbit Trail and back roads, meandering through neighborhoods until I got to The Village. I waved at Estelle as I passed her studio, where she was conducting her cardio yoga class. I coasted by the bench where I sat thigh to thigh eating ice cream with Sonja and hopped off at the door of *The*

Coworking Spot. Chloe waved from her seat behind the front desk and smiled.

"Hey, Chloe!" I greeted her cheerily as I hoisted my bike on my shoulder and headed toward the stairs. "Kairo here yet?"

"Yeah, she's down there. You want a cup of coffee?"

"Yeah, that would be great."

"Or I could make you that turmeric latte I made you last time..." she offered hesitantly.

"Hmm... just a regular coffee will do. Thanks, Chloe."

I bounded down the stairs and tucked my bike in the alcove outside of the small office Kairo, and I shared in the back corner.

"The copy for that welcome series is in Google Docs," she said, by way of hello.

"Cool, I dropped an outline for the webinar in there this morning if you want to take a look at it."

"Nice..." Kairo said with a satisfied smile. She probably thought her little come-to-Jesus talk worked. "By the way, I'm sorry for laying into you earlier."

"No, don't apologize. I totally needed it." I sat down at my desk, pulled out my laptop, and got to work. "I've got my head on straight."

Well, I had it on straight for the next few hours, at least. But as time crept closer to when I would see Sonja, my knees started to bounce. I cracked my knuckles, cracked my neck. Shifted back and forth through tasks, and only made minimal progress on them.

"Oh, my god. Take a fucking walk!" Kairo snapped.

"You sure? I can keep working. I think I've almost—"

"You're shaking the whole table, and you damn near dislocated your neck just now. Go eat or something. Take a lap. We should have taken a break hours ago."

"Cool." I saved all of my work, grabbed my prepped meal, and went upstairs.

Chloe's eyes brightened when she saw me. "Hey, Atlas! I got all the new emails entered from the weekend and printed out these worksheets you needed for your class tonight," she said, tapping the stack of papers on the corner of her desk.

"Thanks, Chloe. You can take a break and go get something to eat if you want."

"Thanks." She sighed with relief and stood up. "Do you want me to grab you something?"

I held up my prepackaged, high protein meal. "Got it covered. I'll watch the desk and the phones until you get back."

"Thanks! I'll be quick."

'Take as much time as you need."

While my food heated in the microwave, I tried to visualize how I was going to handle seeing Sonja this evening. Visualizing a positive outcome was the best way to guarantee success, right?

So she would come in — bright and sunshine-y. I would greet her the same way I greeted everyone else. I wouldn't stare at her for too long. Wouldn't focus on her lips or say things to make her smile. I would keep my attention at eye level. I would...

Fail hard at all of this the moment I saw her.

She was early. Just like she was on the first day. And just like the first day, she wore ripped jeans and a concert tee. This one was from Outkast's last concert in 2014, and I wondered if she'd actually gone and what I would've done if I saw her there. Her hair was combed back from her face the first day, but today her short cut was big, with fluffy curls that fell over her brow and into her eyes. She was so damn pretty it made my chest ache.

"Are you always so punctual?" I asked as she dropped her bag.

Her eyes went wide. "Am I too early? Because I can go—"

"You're not too early, Sonja."

She smiled and let out a sigh of relief. "Good. So how was your weekend?"

"It was... uneventful. You?"

"Same. I went to my son's football game on Friday night and hung out with Estelle for a bit on Saturday."

I nodded. "Cool. Who does your kid play for?"

"Greenville High. He plays cornerback."

"Small world. I went to Greenville High, too, and played cornerback my junior and senior year."

Sonja frowned. "I thought you were a science and math nerd."

"I was, but I was also big and pretty fast, so football came naturally."

"I can see that," she said, the beginnings of a smile twitched at the corner of her mouth.

Fuck... I could kiss that smile, coax it out. Lift her onto the table and wedge myself between the thick thighs that peeked out of the rips in her jeans—

"So, I'm gonna go in the back and... think gentlemanly thoughts," I stammered, jerking my thumb toward my office.

"Okay!" she agreed, nodding her head.

"Don't look at my ass as I walk away." The throaty laugh that followed me back into my office made me almost positive that she did.

chapter seven

Atlas

The entire class was present and accounted for when I reemerged from my office. As much as I wanted to hang around and make small talk with Sonja, I didn't trust myself. The image of me bending her over the community table was way too real in my head. But once everyone was in the class, it was easier.

"Good evening, y'all!" I greeted everyone as politely as I could and got started on the lesson. "Let's get to it!"

Focus.

"So today we're going to talk about how to find your ideal client. Who are they? Where are they? How do we get their attention?" I qued up the slide deck for this lesson.

In my peripheral vision, Sonja shifted in her seat, leaned forward on the table, and pushed her glasses up onto her nose.

Focus…

"I know all of you have either a product or a service that you want to sell. But if you don't figure out who you want to work with, where to find them, and how to attract them, you're not going to make any money."

For the next thirty minutes, I presented the class with case studies that illustrated how they could go about finding their customer avatar. When the lecture was done, I turned toward the group and rubbed my hands together. "There's a worksheet in there. Work through those five questions, then we'll go over what you all have in about forty-five minutes."

They all nodded, put their heads down, and got to work.

Leaning on the far wall, I took a good look at the group and allowed myself to feel a bit of pride. I might be jumping the gun here, but this cohort was going a lot smoother than the three previous ones. It took me a minute to distill everything I'd learned in the six years since I officially became an entrepreneur. Despite the mistakes I made along the way, I managed to learn a few tricks to make this venture successful. At four hundred dollars a pop, we weren't making money hand over fist, but eventually, we'd both be able to do less consulting and more teaching, and honestly, I couldn't wait. Consulting paid good money, but I enjoyed helping women and other marginalized people build small businesses a lot more. This room full of women, ready and eager to launch their own businesses were exactly the people I wanted to serve.

"So who's ready to show their work?" I asked.

Heather and Ashley's hands went up first. I stifled an irritated sigh. There was always at least one know-it-all in the group, but I was lucky enough to land two this time.

"All right, Heather and Ashley. Which one of you wants to go first?"

The group shared their work, and I fought against my natural impulse to call on Sonja when she didn't raise her hand—hoping she put aside her shyness and speak up. I thought about how her sister had let it slip that she was afraid of going it alone and wondered if that played some part in it. Either way, she was the absolute last one to share.

"Okay, Sonja. I can see that you have the worksheet filled out with notes scribbled in the margins. Go ahead and share."

She bit her lip and blushed. Goddamn, she was cute.

"So first, I have to admit that I did most of the work before I arrived tonight,' she began.

"Okay, whatchu got?"

Sonja ran over her responses to the questions. Her answers were much more detailed than anyone else—partly because she'd worked on it all day and partly because she actually knew what she was doing.

"So what I want to give them is a hypoallergenic, all-natural product which would be an alternative to store brands that may have a long list of chemical ingredients — the effects of which you can't guarantee. My recipes are decades old and passed down to me from my mother and her mother and her mother's mother. You can't find them anywhere else... and..." She did a little wiggle and looked around the table. "I have samples."

Sonja pulled out a canvas bag and dumped the little round tins in the middle of the table. I bit my lip to hide a proud grin. My little overachiever.

"This is a recipe that I use for clarity and focus."

Each of the students reached for a tin.

"What's in it?" one of them asked as she opened it.

"Lemon oil, rosemary verbone, grapefruit peel, calendula flower extract, rosehip, ginger root, cardamom seed oil, and beeswax," she rattled off.

"And all of this is from your garden?" I asked, stepping forward to snag a tin of my own.

"Most of it. I get some of it from my mother. She has a few acres in Honea Path and runs an apothecary of her own."

I nodded as I opened the tin and sniffed it. "For clarity and focus, huh? And how do you use it?"

"Apply it generously to your pulse points— especially your wrists— so that you can smell it while you work."

"So... this is that Gullah, voodoo magic stuff, right? Is it real? Does it really work?" Ashley asked.

Sonja deflated a bit. The little fucking know-it-all was trying to steal her shine.

"Uh... the key ingredient that makes this work has long been used in smelling salts. The salts release ammonia, and that triggers your inhalation reflex by irritating the mucous membranes in the nose and lungs, which encourages you to take in more oxygen. More oxygen equals more blood flow to all parts of the body, including your brain. It can be invigorating."

"Isn't that dangerous?" Heather asked. "I swear my Gran-gran has always warned me about inhaling ammonia because it can cause, like... brain damage or something."

Sonja chuckled and shook her head in a way that said, *bless your heart* without saying it out loud. "No, Heather. You're thinking about gases emitted when you mix bleach and ammonia. This has the exact opposite effect. Also, mixing it with carrier oils like beeswax make it less harsh to inhale, but doesn't diminish the effect. Why don't you just try it?" she coaxed.

Officially cowed by Sonja's intelligent response, Heather and Ashley did just that, and I followed suit.

"Hmm..." I hummed, sniffing my wrist where I'd applied it. "It does smell good and sort of familiar, too." It smelled like her. Bright, sweet, herbaceous, and like sunshine. "What are you thinking about calling it?"

"I've been calling it clarity creme? But that sounds a little cheesy, doesn't it?"

"Oh, no. I think it's perfect," the woman sitting next to her, named Tina said. "I think the alliteration is fun for sales copy. Fun to say, easy to remember."

"Thanks," Sonja said with a satisfied smile.

"This was great, Sonja. Thanks for the sample. Now that we've got some clarity and focus, let's move on to the next part of today's lesson."

I went on for another hour or so, and everyone made good progress on their customer avatars. As I packed up, Ashley and Heather lingered... but so did Sonja.

"Come on...," Ashley whined. "Meet us next door. One drink. And it'll be my treat."

"I—"

"Don't say no. We saw you over there after the last class, so we know you drink," Heather added, cutting me off.

"Yeah, I do, but—"

"No, buts! Just say you'll meet us over there," Ashley said firmly.

I looked past them to see Sonja still packing up her stuff more slowly than was necessary. I dipped my head to hide my smile. "Okay," I agreed, lying through my teeth. "Let me wrap up some stuff over here, and then I'll meet you guys."

The delighted smiles on their faces almost made me feel bad, but I disregarded that when I remembered their side remarks to Sonja during class.

"Okay!" Ashley chirped. "Meet you over there, handsome!" she said with a wink. And finally, the two of them left, leaving me alone with Sonja.

"You've got quite the fan club there," she said, hugging the course binder to her chest.

"Who? Those two? Barely noticed."

She rolled her eyes in a way that said, *yeah, right.* "Do you mind if we talk a minute? I won't keep you long."

"Sonja. *Soni*... I have no intentions on meeting them for drinks. I just said that to get them out of here because I could see that you needed to talk to me." I walked over to where she stood and leaned on the table. "So, tell me what you need."

I hadn't meant to make it sound so... *suggestive*. But the moment the words were out of my mouth, I knew I would do whatever she asked. And the way she licked her lips... she felt those words the same way I did.

"I make you nervous, don't I?" I asked. But I should've cleared my throat first. Want had turned my voice to a sound like crunching gravel, and the sound of it made her face flush. She gripped the binder tighter. Were her nipples hard? Was the binder hiding them from me?

"Uh, yeah. It's ridiculous. I know it is. But you do," she admitted.

"It's not ridiculous. You do the same thing to me."

She laughed that sweet, husky laugh of hers. "You don't seem nervous."

"I'm just better at hiding it. Lots of practice with all the public speaking I do. I'm teaching myself to ignore the way my belly bottoms out when I see you. It's the only way I can govern my behavior into some semblance of cool. Did I pull it off?"

She shrugged and stepped a little closer. Still shy, but she'd clearly decided to be a bit bolder. "I think you pulled it off."

"Good," I said, smiling at her. "So, what did you need to talk about?"

Say you want me. Take back what you said the other night and say you want me and let me kiss you.

"Last week, when we were next door having drinks and then again on Friday, you said that you think my business was the most likely to succeed in this cohort?"

75

"I don't think it. I know it. Your idea is original. Tonight proves that you have the work ethic and the know-how. You and your business also have a story and..." I sniffed my wrist, and the sweet citrus scent opened my passageways. "It actually works."

She smiled. "My lotions and potions do work. I was never worried about that. It's good medicine tested over multiple generations of Malone women."

I frowned. "Malone? I thought your last name was Watts?"

"Uh... Watts was my married name. Which brings me to why I wanted to talk, " she said awkwardly, then set her binder on the table and backed away from me. "My husband and I just got divorced recently. Like...a month or so before this class type recent. I received a decent payout from him and the house, but I need to... I need to make enough money to keep it and maintain our standard of living."

What the fuck... that's why she pushed me away. It wasn't just that she *wanted* to start a successful business. She *needed* to.

I'm an ass. I thought this whole thing was about me. I'm a complete ass.

Sonja paced back and forth. Thoughts and emotions tumbling out of her. "I mean, my kids are older," she was saying, tears in her voice and her eyes — not happy ones. "My son is heading to college next year. My daughter just started high school and the house we live in? We've always lived there. My kids have never lived anywhere else. And my herb garden... I would have to start all over if we moved. I can't do that. I won't do that—"

The distance between her and me? I didn't even remember closing it. I didn't even remember standing up. But now she was in my arms. Tucked against my chest.

76

"Shhh," I quieted, my lips against the tiny shell of her ear. "What do you need from me?"

Her arms slid around my waist, and she fisted my shirt in her hands. "Besides this hug?" she asked with a watery laugh. She burrowed deeper and fuck... she fit against me just right. "It's been so long since someone held me like this without expecting me to give them something or do something."

"I can keep hugging you while you tell me what you need from me." I nuzzled into the curve of her neck. She smelled good there. Like the Clarity Creme. "But know that no matter what it is, the answer is yes."

Sonja sighed, and her hands spread wide on my back. "This course is good and in-depth, but I'm old—"

I pushed her away so I could look her in the eye. "Where do you get these ideas? You're not old," I corrected.

"Compared to everyone else in the room? Yes, I am. And the tech side of things is intimidating to me, but I want to learn it. I need to learn it."

"So what do you need? Extra lessons? One-on-one consulting?"

"Any and everything you can do for me."

"Anything I..." I noticed at that moment that my hands were on the curve of her hips. I gripped and squeezed her there, almost involuntarily. "Um... you better put some boundaries on that."

She laughed and stepped back until I was forced to let her go. "Any extra help you can provide to make my business successful," she clarified.

"I can do that," I said with a nod. "We can start right now if you want."

Her eyes widened with surprise. "But it's late, and you told those girls—"

I pulled out a chair. "Sit down. Let's go through this lesson, and you tell me what I can do to help you at this stage."

Sonja smiled and took a seat.

Bait was what she was struggling with. She knew her customer, but she didn't know what kind of bait she needed to bring her customers in. So we went over some options — a blog, a YouTube channel, mix-your-own-medicinal-salve classes that she could do online or in person. By the time Chloe packed up and left, we had some pretty solid ideas for places she could start.

"I'm free most Saturdays, and I can probably manage a couple of lunchtime sessions like this if you don't mind meeting on short notice."

"Okay." Her face flushed again. "I don't really have much going on besides this and family stuff. Maybe the occasional hike and yoga at Estelle's studio."

Sonja... doing yoga.

"Uh...yeah. Great." I shook my head to clear that sweaty, sexy visual from my mind. "Let me get your phone number," I said, taking out my phone.

She recited it for me, and I plugged it in then sent her a quick text so she would have mine.

"Cool..." She looked up at me. "I really appreciate this, Atlas. I know you're busy, and it's a lot to ask, so of course, I'm willing to pay you for your time."

"Sonya, I wouldn't dream of taking your money. I get it. I'm gonna help you in any way I can." I smiled at her. "Besides... it means I get to spend more time with you, so it's a win-win for both of us."

"That doesn't feel like a fair trade."

"Oh…" I allowed myself to take in her frame and how it had felt against mine when I hugged her. "It's more than fair."

She laughed and shook her head. "If you say so."

It was late, and Estelle had already gone home, so I locked up, grabbed my bike, and walked Sonja to her car. The street was quiet, with a bite of crispness in the air. A perfect night for a stroll. I wished we could go some place. Out to dinner or just to walk around downtown, drink hot cocoa, and window shop.

"I'm sorry to hear about your marriage."

"Yeah, me too," she said softly.

"How long were y'all together?" I asked as we made our way down the deserted sidewalk.

"Married thirteen years, but we've been together since high school."

"Wow. That's a long time."

"Yeah… it is," she said wistfully.

Why the fuck did I even ask that? Did I really care how long she'd been with her ex?

Well, actually...yes. I did want to know. Was she still hurting from that? Still in love with him?

Change the subject, Atlas.

"So… hoodoo magic. It's real to you, huh?"

She chuckled. "Does that make you uncomfortable?"

I shrugged. "I mean, my mother always warned me against women like you and your sisters."

"Women like and my sisters? What does that mean?"

"Women with… I don't know. Indian ways. She said women like you might put a root on me."

She laughed. "It's *work* a root, and the best way to avoid getting a root worked on you is to avoid doing anything to deserve it."

"I don't think it's that easy."

79

"Sure, it is. Every action has an equal and opposite reaction. If you're mindful of your actions and take care and consideration with others, you have nothing to worry about."

"I hope you're right about that."

"This is me," she said as she pressed the key to fob to unlock her car doors. "Thanks for giving me the extra help I need to launch this business so that I won't end up in a van down by the river."

My heart stuttered in my chest. "Is the situation that dire? Because I can go home right now and do some backend work—"

"Atlas, relax!" she said between giggles. "It's an SNL skit."

"An SNL... I've never heard of it." I searched her face trying to figure out if she was really kidding.

"Really? With Chris Farley, David Spade, and Alicia Silverstone? Chris is a motivational speaker?"

"The only familiar name in there was Chris Farley."

"Wow," she said with a stunned look on her face as she opened the driver's side door. She shook her head. "Google it. It's pretty funny."

"I will." I stepped in the way of the door before she could close it. "I'm glad you trusted me enough to come to me for help."

She laughed and looked up at me, and the moment our eyes met, her expression softened. "Thanks for the hug."

Her eyes said she wanted me to kiss her. I wanted to kiss her. "Thanks for hugging me back."

She smiled. "Goodnight, Atlas."

"See you soon, Sonja," I said softly, then closed the door for her.

She looked up at me. Smile on her lips. Want in her brown eyes, and as she pulled away, my first thought was I should have kissed her, but I knew if I had, she might not trust me again.

Be satisfied, Atlas. Be satisfied.

chapter eight

Sonja

The sun baked my shoulders as I plucked a few ripe zucchini and tomatoes in my garden. This should be my last harvest of the season, but the weather had been so warm that I'd probably get a bit more before the first frost. Either way, I had to get these veggies picked before they rotted on the vine. I'd already clipped some herbs, bound them, and hung them in my pantry to dry. My back said that weeding would have to wait for another day, though.

Wiping the sweat from my brow, I straightened and stretched.

"Hey, garden goddess!" my little sister Birdie called out as she came through the gate.

I looked up and smiled. "Hey! I was gonna call you. I've got some tomatoes and zucchini and a few peppers for you."

"And I will gladly take them," she said.

"Come inside, I'll get you a grocery bag."

My sister followed me into the kitchen, and I sighed when I felt the cool kiss of the central air. I loved the heat, but it's been sweltering lately. Uncharacteristically hot for this time of year, even for South Carolina. "Where's my niece?"

"She had a playdate with one of her friends from theater camp. I figured I'd hang out here until they're ready for me to come and get her," she joked.

"I guess it's just as well. Nadia is at cheerleading practice. She would have been bored if she wasn't here."

Birdie nodded. "And lord knows that none of us can deal with Amara when she's bored. I swear that little girl is running me ragged, " she said with a tired sigh.

"Well, it's no wonder! Taking care or a six-year-old all on your own is hard work. Especially when you're working chef's hours. Maybe you wouldn't have to work so hard if you reached out to her father," I said pointedly.

Birdie rolled her eyes. "God, when are y'all gonna leave that alone?"

Six years ago, Birdie was in culinary school out in Charleston. It was her dream to be a world-renowned chef, and her natural talent and tenacity made us all believe that it was possible. But somewhere in her third year, a big scandal that she refused to tell us about got her kicked out of school. Three months later, she announced that she was pregnant and refused to contact the father or even tell us who he was. Agostina had intuited that it was probably one of her superiors, which made sense. Revealing his identity might hurt the reputation she was trying to build in the kitchen. But it'd been six years. That's a long time to keep the identity of her baby's father from us -- not to mention keeping it from her daughter Amara.

"So you went to the second class for that entrepreneurship thing this week, right? How's that going? Are you and that instructor still eye-fucking each other?" Birdie asked, changing the subject.

"Jesus, Birdie," I complained.

I walked into the pantry and debated whether I should confess my fierce and instant attraction to Atlas as I pulled out a paper bag for her veggies. Was that really a conversation I was ready to have? Stalling for more time, I checked my

83

drying herbs to see which were ready for grinding or to be distilled in essential oils. Then something came to me.

"What a minute," I said, stepping out of the pantry. "Why aren't you at the restaurant? You have the night off from work?"

Birdie sighed. "So, I kinda wanted to talk to you about that."

"Did you get fired again, Birdie?"

Her mouth set into a thin line. "Yes, but it's not like you think. That work environment was toxic. You don't understand what it's like—"

"That's the third sou chef job you've been fired from since the beginning of this year."

"I know, but this guy was a fucking pig, Sonja."

"They're all fucking pigs, and you're never going to get to be head chef if you keep getting fired from sou chef jobs."

"Well, that's just bullshit. I'm better than half the chefs I've ever worked with—"

"Yeah, but you were working for them and not the other way around," I countered. Birdie's face crumbled, and she started to cry. "Damn it, Birdie."

I crossed the kitchen and pulled my sister into my arms. "I'm sorry. I don't mean to pile on you, but you've got Amara to worry about and those fucking student loans for a degree that you didn't even finish."

"Ugh, god. I know," she groaned, pushing me away. "I'll find another job, and I have a plan in the meantime."

"If you need help, let me know."

"I will," she said with a sniff.

"I mean, it Birdie. If you need money or a place to stay, don't be too proud to ask."

"I won't, and I think I might strongly consider moving in for a while. Eliminating that high ass rent would be a big help."

"Whenever you're ready," I said with a shrug.

"Thanks, sis," Birdie said with a smile. "But the class. How's that going?"

"It's going great!"

I filled her in, but I omitted the bits about Atlas. Surprise, surprise. I wasn't ready to talk about that yet. Hell, I wasn't even ready to feel it. "I'm learning a lot!" I said a little too eagerly, hiding my face because I was certain that something in my expression was going to give me away.

"Good! That's so good, Soni. You've been doing this for a while now, and it's beyond time for you to level up."

"You think so?"

"Yeah, I mean, I use your salve on my hands all the time. It's better than Mama's and smells twice as good, too."

"Okay, Birdie. You don't need to exaggerate for me to get it."

"Hey, I'm not exaggerating. Mama's formulas are great, and they're an awesome foundation, but you're doing something bigger here."

My stomach twisted with anxiety. "I haven't told her yet. Do you think she'll be pissed off?"

Birdie rolled her eyes. "Ain't no tellin' what Eudora is gonna say. She's wanted to go into business with you for years, though, so she might be a little salty about that part of it."

"I know," I said with a nod.

Eudora's Apothecary was practically a landmark in Honea Path, and my mother was revered and almost god-like to the people who frequently shopped there. And with good reason.

She's a talented healer. I just didn't see myself doing what she does.

"I guess I'll tell her this weekend."

"Hey…why don't I smell any food cooking? And why haven't you offered me a drink? Did getting divorced suddenly turn you into a shitty hostess?"

"Fuck you!" I said, throwing a dishtowel at her. "By the way, you're the chef. Cook me dinner for a change."

"Okay," she said then looked at the basket of vegetables I'd picked on the breakfast bar. "Do you have parmesan?"

"I think there's a brick in the fridge."

"Can I look in the garden and see if there's a yellow squash out there?"

"Of course. Go right ahead," I said.

Birdie slid off of the stool and headed out to the yard.

"While you're making dinner, I'd like to go over some of the recipes for the lotions & potions I want to put in my shop."

"Lotions & Potions?" she called over her shoulder.

"Yeah, that's what I've been calling them."

"You should call the shop Lotions & Potions!" she repeated.

"Lotions & Potions," I murmured to myself. It sounded a little silly, but I liked it. "I'll add it to the list."

While Birdie sliced the zucchini, yellow squash, and Roma tomatoes from the garden and arranged them artfully in a Pyrex dish, I dug out all of the old composition books I used when Mama taught me to identify herbs and medicinal flowers. Some of the pages were filled with the fat, looping childish script of my middle school self. In the later notebooks, my writing became tighter, neater, and more intentional.

"Do you still have Gigi's recipe book?" Birdie asked as she drizzled olive oil over the colorful ratatouille.

"Yeah, but the pages are so thin and fragile that I copied it into my own a long time ago," I muttered.

"Why are you the only one who knows all this stuff? Why didn't mama teach it to the rest of us?"

I shrugged and closed the notebook I'd labeled cold and fever remedies. "Well, I guess because I was the oldest. Passing down to the oldest daughter is a fairly common practice."

That held true for Mama and all of her sisters. She was the only one who knew how to work a root if needed. Not that my aunts were strangers to using good medicine. They just didn't make it their life's work.

"So, with a shop name like Lotions & Potions, I think I should stick to beauty and bath stuff, right?"

"No teas or essential oils? Everyone is really into that shit nowadays."

"Really? I didn't know."

Birdie rolled her eyes and put the ratatouille in the oven. "We gotta get you on social media."

"Oh! That's my homework for this week! You can help me. I mean, I'm on Facebook, but what's the point of Instagram and that Snapchat thing Nadia's always on?"

Birdie stared at me for a long moment then shook her head.

"What?"

"You're only forty. How are you this much of a fuddy-duddy?"

"Whatever. Are you gonna help me or not?"

"Of course, I am. Let me wash my hands."

While sipping whiskey and waiting for dinner to get done, Birdie got me set up on Instagram and helped me craft my first three posts. She was attempting to explain algorithms to me when Nadia called.

"Hey, sweet girl—"

"Is daddy coming? I'm waiting at the field, and everyone has left already,"

Did anger burn off alcohol? Because I swear, I got so angry that I felt stone-cold sober in seconds.

"What do you mean you're still at the field? Daddy was supposed to be there twenty minutes ago."

"Yeah, well, he's not. Are you coming?"

I shook my head. "No, I've been drinking. Did you call your brother?"

"Of course, I did. He didn't answer.

"Fine. I'll send you an Uber."

"Okay."

"And stand where there's plenty of light."

"Mom, it's not even dark."

"Just do as I ask without all the backtalk, please. I'm sending you an Uber. Text me when it arrives. Make sure you check the license plate—"

"I know, mom," Nadia snapped and hung up.

"Goddamnit, Eric," I cursed, pulling up the Uber app.

"What's wrong?" Birdie asked.

"Eric didn't pick up Nadia from cheerleading practice," I growled.

"Son of a bitch," Birdie said. "You're divorced a couple of months, and he thinks he can shirk his parental duties?"

"I don't know, but I'm about to find out," I mumbled.

The Uber was on it's way to Nadia, but I would be worried until my daughter came through that door. I pulled up Eric's number.

"Hey, Soni. Is something wrong?"

88

"Yeah, something's wrong. Did you forget to do something this afternoon?"

"What? Oh… shit. Nadia. Is she still at the field? I can go pick her up now—"

"It's handled. But am I going to need to make other arrangements?"

"No, it just slipped my mind. I got hung up at the office—"

"Whatever. Don't let it happen again," I interrupted then ended the call.

Dinner was made. Birdie made garlic bread to go along with it, but I wasn't hungry. I was too pissed to be hungry.

I paced in the front hallway until headlights pulled into my driveway. Moments later, Nadia came through the door.

"Don't, Mom. I'm fine. It's not like I haven't taken an Uber before."

"I know, but you've never taken one by yourself—"

"I'm okay, mom, really. Hey, Aunt Birdie!"

And just like that, my only daughter has shunned me to bask in the affection of my younger sister. Mine and Nadia's relationship had become strained since she hit her teens, but it's worsened since her father left. Part of me wondered if she blamed me.

Gah, now I sounded like my own mama.

I was just about to join them in the kitchen and pour myself another drink when the doorbell rang. Frowning, I peeked through the peephole and saw none other than my ex-husband.

"You gotta be kidding me," I groaned as I opened the door.

"Is she here? Is she safe?" he asked, his voice panic-stricken.

"Of course, she's fine—"

Eric pushed passed me and walked toward the kitchen. I followed, annoyed that he had shoved me aside to gain entrance to *my* house. I'd just asked him not to barge into my house anymore. To call before he came. To wait to be invited. But here he was, traipsing into the kitchen to interrupt Nadia and Birdie's conversation.

"Honey, I'm sorry. I got hung up at the office and lost track of time."

Nadia shrugged and stared down into the bowl of ratatouille my sister had made for her. "It's no big deal. Mommy called me an Uber, and I made it home fine."

Eric glared at me. "An Uber? You put her in an Uber alone?"

"I've been drinking. It was the responsible thing to do."

"You could have called me before you did that. I would've left—"

"You were supposed to pick her up in the first place. Why should I need to call you to do the thing you said you were going to do—"

"Guys!" Nadia interrupted loudly. "I'm fine. Don't argue."

Eric softened, then turned to her and gave her a kiss on the forehead. "I'm so sorry, bunny. It won't happen again."

"Okay," she said, but her tone said she didn't believe him.

"Do you want to go grab some dinner? I want to hear all about practice and the upcoming competition."

"That's okay. Aunt Bird made ratatouille, and I'm kinda tired and stinky."

Eric snorted. "You're definitely stinky." He kissed her on the forehead again. "We can do it tomorrow. Anywhere you want, okay?"

Nadia nodded. "See you tomorrow, Daddy," she said, dismissing him.

Eric looked around the room awkwardly, and that was when I noticed that Birdie had her arms crossed and was glaring at him with a look of complete disgust on her face.

"Okay, baby. I'll see you tomorrow," he said, then turned and made his way to the front door.

He'd barely cleared the threshold before Birdie growled, "That fucking arrogant asshole. I'm so glad you're done with him."

All at once, my daughter's face crumbled.

"Oh, shit, Naddy—"

"I'm fine!" She grabbed the bowl of ratatouille and dashed from the room.

I threw my hands up in exasperation. "Damn it, Bird."

"I'm so sorry, sis. It just came out. Do you want me to go up and talk to her?"

"No…" I covered my eyes with my hands and drew in a deep breath. "Go pick up, Amara. I'll take care of it. I'll handle it." And why not? I was expected to handle everything else.

chapter nine
Sonja

My parent's house out in Honea Path had been in the family for going on four generations. The land we grew up on was once part of a plantation owned by the Malones, some of whom graced a few branches of my family tree. Malones once owned land all around Greenville county and a few choice plots in the city. A few parcels had been sold off over the years -- sales that made my parents very wealthy, but my five still owned about ten acres, five of which they lived on and worked with the help of day workers.

Eudora was a hale woman of sixty-two, but she looked more than half her age, and that could be charged to her healthy, mostly plant-based diet, and the lotions and potions she treated herself, and all of us kids, with over the years. The apothecary she kept in a refurbished cabin at the beginning of her driveway was well-known in the surrounding area. It wasn't uncommon for people to come down from the North Carolina mountains to purchase her remedies. However, the sign on the door of the *Apothecary* said she was closed today. But that didn't mean that I wouldn't find my mother working, restocking her shelves, harvesting ripe vegetables, or hanging herbs to dry while dinner bubbled on the stove up at the house. She was the type of woman who couldn't sit still for too long.

I stepped inside, my childhood home and the old wood screen door banged closed behind me. "Hey, Daddy!" I called out to my father, who was installed in his recliner with ESPN blaring on the television. I swear he was half deaf. How my mother lived with the constant racket, I would never know.

"Who's that? Sugafoot and Sweetbread?"

I smiled. Daddy was the type to give you a nickname the moment he met you. It was usually nonsensical coupling of words that had no real meaning, like Sugafoot and my daughter Sweetbread, who earned that name three days after she was born.

Nadia barreled into the room and fell on my father, covering him with kisses.

"Whoa now, gal!" he exclaimed, a big grin on his face as he hugged her tight.

I leaned over them both and kissed my father on the forehead. "Where's Mama?"

"Out there somewhere," he said, gesturing toward the kitchen at the back of the house.

I went back into the kitchen and found the makings of dinner on the stovetop. Rice, black-eyed peas, and all the fix-ins for fried chicken thawing in the fridge, but no veggies. I opened the pot and stirred the beans. They were beginning to stick a little, so I turned the fire down.

"Keep an eye on these black-eyed peas, Naddy. I'm gonna go out and find GG," I said to girl-child before walking out the back door. On the porch, I found a big sun hat. I plopped it on my head, grabbed a basket, and made my way down the well-worn path to my mama's garden.

Truth be told, I'd arrived early for Sunday dinner, hoping that I would get a chance to talk to mama before the rest of my family arrived.

I found her in a row of snap peas. I could tell she came out here just to find vegetables for dinner because she was using her apron to gather the ripe peas instead of a basket.

"Did you check those beans?" she asked without turning toward me.

"Yes, ma'am. I stirred them a little bit, and Nadia is up there watching them now." She turned toward me and dumped the peas out of her apron into the basket I'd brought with me.

"Later on," she said, turning back to the row to pick more. "I'm gonna need you to come down to the apothecary and do a bit of inventory with me. Then later, I need Winston and your daddy to bring some crates in from the storage, but first, I need to know exactly what I need." She paused for a minute, took off her glasses, rubbed the bridge of her nose, and then turned to look at me. "What now, chile? You got a look on your face like you're here to bring me bad news."

"Not bad news… just news, I guess."

Mama took my hands in hers and looked me right in the eyes. My mother has always been somewhat of a medium. When we were younger, women came to her sure that she could find and match them with the man of their dreams. Maybe I was just too close to her, but I never saw that magic. Not in that way. But she did have one of the keenest intuitions I've ever witnessed. She always seemed to know exactly what was going on with us kids and how and what we needed to fix it. Mama Malone didn't give hugs and kisses. She gave poultices, balms, and words to say to yourself when you applied them. Some people called them spells. Either way, she knew how to fix what ailed you.

"Let's talk about this when we get inside."

Mama filled the basket to the top with beans, and we walked back to the house in silence. I hated it. I just wanted to

94

tell her what I'd decided to do and see how she felt about it, but Eudora Malone would not be rushed when it came to things like this.

In the kitchen, she dumped the beans into a colander, rinsed them thoroughly then grabbed two bowls from the cabinet. "Sit there and help me clean these sugar snaps."

I sat down at the kitchen table across from her, and we worked in silence, pulling the string from each pea pod and dropping it into the bowl between us. Repetitious work like this always put me in a sort of a trance. When we were kids, we joked that she did this so she could reach into our minds. Maybe there was something to that because she always knew exactly what I wanted to talk about before I even explained it to her.

"You've decided to become practitioner," she said finally.

"Yes," I said, slightly taken aback. "Well, kinda, but not the way you do it."

My mother tsked. "It's been a long time since you were an initiate."

"I know."

"This is not something to test or play with, Sonja."

"Of course it isn't, mama. I know that."

"And you want to do it out there?"

"Yes... but in my own way. I want to open my own apothecary. Online at first, but eventually, I want to have my own brick and mortar store like you have here." I gestured toward the Apothecary at the end of the drive. "That's how I want to take care of myself and the kids."

"And what's wrong with coming home to do that exact same thing?"

I shrugged. "Maybe I will eventually, but for right now...this is what I want to do."

My mother drew in a deep, expansive breath then stood up. She braced her hands on the table and looked down into the bowl of cleaned peas. "I have to tell you that I'm not sure how I feel about that."

"That's understandable. But I would love to have your support and help in this, mama. I need to be able to prove to myself that I can do this."

"I'll help you," she said with a tight nod as she dropped the peas in a big pot on the stove and turned on the eye under them. "I'll help you in any way you need."

"Thank you, mama." I went to her and kissed her on the cheek. She received it without returning the affection, but a smile lifted the apple of her cheek.

"Get me my mortar and pestle off the shelf in the pantry," she said.

"Okay." I went into the pantry and grabbed the mortar and pestle set that I'd coveted since I was old enough to know what it was used for. It was huge and made of olive wood that had the prettiest swirling grain pattern. Mama said it had been in the family for years.

"And I need the rose oil and a chunk of that John the Conqueror root."

I frowned and dropped the things she'd asked for in the mortar before bringing it out to her.

"Set it on the table," she said as she pulled out bags of unlabeled herbs from her cabinet.

Rosemary, patchouli, rose and hibiscus petals, Adam, and Eve root. She shuffled over to the table, added those things to the bowl, and then braced the mortar and pestle against her belly and began to grind them together.

"What are you making?"

"Come-to-me oil."

"Oh. Who's it for?"

"You, of course," she said, matter of factly, as if I'd asked for it.

"Mama," I said with a laugh. "I just ended my marriage I don't need—"

"Sonja," she snapped in irritation, still grinding the ingredients together. "You may not think that you need it, but you do."

Oh...Atlas. When she was nosing around in my feelings, she saw those budding feelings for him. "But I can't...I can't get involved with anyone right now. It's too complicated and--"

"There are no coincidences. People come into your life for a reason, Soni. Some for a reason and some for a season, and you'd do good to recognize it. You'd also do good to recognize that sex and love are good medicine, too. Sex is sometimes even better medicine," she said with a husky laugh.

"Mama!" I watched her for a moment, stunned into silence, but I knew she was right. Atlas was in my life for a reason. Whether it was sex or love didn't really matter. Mama Malone just told me so.

I cleared my throat.

"Can you show me how to make this? I've never really made one before, and I think it would be great in my store."

My mother smiled. "Get the sunflower oil, a measuring cup, a funnel, and one of those bottles from under the counter. Oh, and something to write with."

I gathered the things she asked for, then looked around and found an old pad of yellow paper and half a pencil.

She poured a generous amount of the sunflower oil into the measuring cup, scrapped the ground herbs shook it up. When she felt that it had, she just made into the bottle and sealed it

97

with a stopper before picking up the mortar and pestle again. As I wrote down the ingredients and got reacquainted with conjuring, my mother reminded me of what it took to be a good practitioner. I made a promise to come down at least once a week to reinvigorate the latent healing power within me.

* * * *

The time I spent with my mother that Sunday afternoon reminded me that making good medicine was more than just some sort of science experiment I conducted in my kitchen with a double boiler and dried flowers. It was a sacred practice, and I needed to make sure I treated it with the respect in deserved.

To that end, I renewed my focus for my business. I was going all-in with the modern apothecary idea intending to eventually open one of my own in town once the online shop took off. I spent a lot of time researching eco-friendly farms in our area, trying to find places that I could source things locally. My mother had a pretty extensive greenhouse and garden, but it wasn't large enough to support both my shop and hers. I would need to either build one of my own—which I was sure my home owner's association wouldn't approve—or I needed to find a local farmer who planted those flowering herbs year around. Sure, I could find them online, but I liked the process of walking through the rows and getting acquainted with the things I put on and in my body.

I was packing for such a trip when I got a call from Atlas. The sight of his name on my caller ID made my heart race inexplicably. I took a moment to settle my nerves before I answered.

"Atlas! Hey!" I said, completely failing at being cool.

"Hey, Sonja."

There was laughter in his voice. I was sure he was probably laughing at my eagerness. Why did this guy bring that out of me? I've never felt like this in my life.

"So, I have a free day, and I thought this would be a good time to meet up for that impromptu mastermind we talked about."

"Oh!" I looked at the lunch and thermos I'd packed for my little day trip. The farm was up in Brevard. I thought I might stop on the way back to hike a little and have a picnic.

"Is this not a good time or…"

"Well, I was about to make a trip up to Brevard for the day to meet a farmer who grows a lot of the medicinal herbs I would need."

"Oh…well…yeah. Maybe we can link up when you get back in town—"

"Or you could come with me?" I suggested.

"Up to Brevard?"

"Yeah. I, uh, packed a picnic. Just some turkey and swiss sandwiches, some grapes, and almonds. I was going to stop on the way back and hike up Ceasar's Head. Eat lunch up there."

"And you want me to go with you? You sure you want to be alone in a car with me for two hours?"

"Why? Do you get car sick or something?"

"No… it's just…" He made a strange sound, then cleared his throat. "Yes, of course, I'll ride up to a farm in Brevard, take a hike, and have a picnic lunch with you."

"Heh… when you say it all together like that, it sounds like a date."

"Is it?" he asked softly. "I mean, I wouldn't hate it if it were a date."

I smiled. "Okay, then. It's a date."

I made a couple more sandwiches and packed an extra stainless steel water bottle. He was a grown man and would probably bring his own water, but I wanted to be prepared just in case. As I was packing the lunch and water into my bag, one of the canisters clanged against something at the bottom of the bag. I dug around for a moment and pulled out a glass bottle with a cork stopper.

I knew without opening it that it was the Come-to-me oil my mother made for me a few days ago. But I didn't know how it got in the bottom of this backpack in the first place. I wasn't even carrying it that day.

"Hmph," I grunted to myself.

There's no such thing as coincidences, Sonja.

If this bottle appeared at this moment, there was a reason for it.

Sex and love are good medicine, too.

"Fuck it," I muttered aloud, then pulled out the cork stopper and applied a generous amount to all of my pulse points. I didn't say the words of power because…well, because I'm a coward, but there was probably enough intention behind it without them.

Thirty minutes later, I pulled up in front of a grey nondescript, condo building downtown near the Swamp Rabbit Trail, with the address that Atlas had sent to me via text. I parked my Subaru in a visitor's spot and walked into the building. The interior was cool and quiet. Empty, too. Like no one lived there. I mashed the button to call the elevator and went up to the seventh floor, which was apparently one level below the penthouse that needed a key to be accessed from the elevator.

When the doors opened, it was to a wall of windows that offered a gorgeous, expansive view of the Blue Ridge

Mountains that stole my breath. I didn't know what I expected, but this wasn't the home of some single guy scrapping by.

His door was one of four on the floor. I knocked tentatively and immediately felt a flush of nervous arousal at seeing him again. When he walked me to my car the other night, he had a look on his face like he wanted to kiss me. The scent of rose petals, jasmine, and coriander filled my nostrils — the oil had warmed in response to the heat my body released by my arousal --working its magic on me.

Shit... maybe it was a mistake to—

The thought blew away like so much dust when Atlas opened the door, a big smile on his face, and wearing a form-fitting white tee that made his dark skin look luminescent.

"Hey, Sonja." His eyes dragged up my frame, and at that moment, I remembered what I was wearing: super tight black compression pants, a tank top, slouchy tee combination, and hiking boots. I hadn't put much thought into the outfit. I wasn't sure if it even matched, but it must be working for him because he was frozen in place.

Was that the spell? He wasn't really close enough for it to work yet, was he?

"Hey," I said, snapping my fingers. "Are you gonna let me in?"

He blinked and shook his head. "Yeah! Yes, come in!" he said, stepping aside and opening the door for me to come inside. "I'll just be a minute. I need to grab my backpack and phone and all that."

"No worries. I'm not in any rush. I told the farmer I'd be there around elevenish. We have plenty of time."

"Okay, good. Feel free to look around," he said as he disappeared down a hallway behind the kitchen.

The same expansive view that I'd encountered when I stepped out of the elevator, stretched the expanse of his living room. The color palette of his room played off of that view. Greys, blues, muted greens, and the occasional pop of yellow. Most of the space was dominated by a big, deep sectional that looked like it would be perfect for cuddling and watching movies. On the built-in shelves were books and photos of what I assumed were his family, and Atlas in various locations. Always alone.

"You've traveled a lot," I said as I picked up a photo of him in what looked like Bulgaria. *Wow.*

"Yeah, I try to take a least a month off a year and spend it somewhere outside of the continental US."

"Hm," I grunted. I'd barely traveled the east coast of the continental US, much less anywhere outside of it.

"I'm thinking of going to South America next. Peru first and then maybe Rio. Everyone should experience Carnival at least once in their life, right?"

"I guess…" I murmured, setting the picture back on the bookshelf.

Suddenly, I felt foolish. I shouldn't have put on the come-to-me oil. This guy couldn't want anything from me, a middle-aged woman, with two kids fresh off of a divorce. He'd traveled the world. Experienced things that I'd never even considered.

"You always travel alone?" I asked, reaching for another photo, this one was of him kissing a dolphin in water that looked like clear, blue glass.

"Yeah, for now."

I gasped and realized that he was standing right behind me. His voice was suddenly low, and oh so close that I felt each word on my skin.

"Did I startle you?"

"A little bit."

"I'm sorry." But he didn't step back. In fact, it felt like he'd moved the tiniest bit closer. "I'm ready to go when you are."

But he said those words without conviction. Like he was totally okay with not going a damn place.

Oh, god. I had to get this damn oil off of me.

"Sure, but can I use your bathroom before we go?"

"It's down the hall on the left," he said, finally stepping back to give me room to move around him.

"I'll just be a sec."

Closing the door to his bathroom, I turned on the water while winding toilet paper around my hand. Putting that oil on was stupid. Was I some young girl desperate for the love of her teenage crush? Some neglected housewife longing for the attentions of the hot gardener?

I scrubbed at my neck and wrists until the skin looked a little red and irritated. Only then was I satisfied that all of the *come-to-me* spell was gone.

When I emerged from the bathroom, Atlas was leaning on the arm of the couch in that way I always scolded my son not to, but I didn't feel that urge with him. I just drank in his long, legs, those solid muscular thighs and the casual way his hand rested right at the crotch of his pants. He was looking at his phone, but while I watched, he grabbed the juncture of his thighs, gripping his length through the fabric of his sweats, and shifting it into a more comfortable position.

I tried to suppress the moan that wanted out of me, but a whimper still slipped through my lips and drew his attention.

He stood abruptly and dropped his phone. "Jesus," he cursed while bending to pick it up. "Now who's the one with kitten paws."

It's me. I have kitten paws and a kitten tongue that I want to use to lick every inch of your—

"Okay!" I said, probably a little too loudly. "Let's get moving shall we?"

We still had to spend an hour in the car with each other, and we wouldn't get anything done if I followed where those thoughts were going.

chapter ten
Sonja

It was a gorgeous morning for the drive up to Brevard. The sky was robin's egg blue, and once we got into the mountains, it was cool enough to let the windows down and open the moon roof of my old Subaru. Atlas was in the passenger seat with his hand out the window making waves in the wind.

"Tell me a little bit about what we're doing today," he said.

"Well, I've decided on the recipes I want to use for the shop, but after visiting my mother this weekend, I realized that I would need more medicinal herbs and flowers than either of our gardens can provide."

"Is this more in line with your idea to go bigger? To open a brick and mortar apothecary one day?"

"Yeah, what do you think about that?"

"Honestly?"

I glanced at him and then back at the road. "Of course, I want you to be honest."

"Okay, so last night I did a little bit of marketing research to see what sort of online shops were selling something similar to what you plan to offer," Atlas began.

"There really aren't any."

"You're right. Not any that make their own products anyway. Most of them have third party fulfillment. And you're going to be making and fulfilling all of your orders, right?"

"That's the plan. It doesn't work without my hand in it."

"Why is that?"

"Because it's not just about the product, Atlas." I sighed. "My mother ... she kind of renewed my dedication to making this more about good medicine and less about creating a product that can be mass-produced."

"Good medicine?"

"Yeah, good medicine is about supporting the whole person. Mind, body, spirit, all of it. And part of that lies in the intention the practitioner puts into making the medicine. That's why they're called recipes and not formulas. I'm not some guy in a lab coat mixing up chemicals."

He grunted, and the sound made me take my eyes off the road and look at him.

"What?

"I love that explanation," he said thoughtfully. "That is the clearest explanation of the why and what of your product that you've given me to date."

"Really? I mean, honestly, after talking to her, it's all coming together in a way that it wasn't before."

"That's so good, but I can't lie, Sonja. It's gonna make it difficult to grow the way you want in the time frame that you need. Hmmm... unless."

"Unless what?"

"Unless you presell."

"Presell?"

"Yes! You come up with the products you want to sell, make a few batches to send to influencers to drum up interest, presell, and then use that money to buy additional supplies and ship everything. It means you have to put in a little bit of money upfront, but after that, each drop should pay for itself."

"Is that legal? That sounds illegal."

Atlas chuckled at me. "Yes, it's legal, Sonja. New makers do this sort of thing all the time. We just need to figure out how much overhead you'll need so that we can price your products appropriately."

"Well, that's why we're here," I said, gesturing to the big sign that read *Welcome to the Randalson Farm.*

"Yeah, this is definitely a good place to start," he agreed.

Jerry Randalson was the one to give us the dime tour of his property and the big greenhouse I came to see. The greenhouse was impressive. At least an acre with rows and rows of flowering herbs that filled the moist, heated air with a lush floral scent.

"A lot of these plants can be found growing wild," Jerry said. "But folks don't really forage anymore, so that's why we expanded this greenhouse.

"Well, with the amount of herbs and flowers that she's going to need, foraging wouldn't cut it," Atlas said as he plucked a licorice leaf and brought it to his nose for an inquisitive sniff. I plucked a leaf from the same plant, put in my mouth, and chewed to let him know it was safe. Hesitantly, he mimicked the motion, and his face registered clear surprise when he realized what it was.

"What is that you said you were doing again, young lady?"

I smiled at that. "I'm opening an apothecary in Greenville."

"It'll be the first of its kind," Atlas bragged, making me smile.

Jerry nodded. "I used to know someone who ran an apothecary down in Honea Path by the name of Eudora."

"That's my mother. She's the one who told me about your farm and suggested that I come up here."

"Are you a practitioner, too?" Jerry asked.

I felt Atlas's gaze land on me the moment the question was out of Jerry's mouth. Well, no use in lying about it. "I am. But I won't be doing any old school conjuring like my mother does in Honea Path."

Jerry nodded, but the set of his mouth seemed to say that he didn't approve. "Well, that's a heavy mantle to take up. I hope one day you do decide to become a conjure woman. Her poultices and teas sure did help me when I had the cancer last year. Chemo is a poison that kills ya as it heals ya. Your mama's teas helped me maintain my appetite even when I could barely keep anything down."

"I'll make sure to tell her that." Pride flared in my chest. It had been a while since I heard about my mother's good works.

"Well..." Jerry thrust his hands into the pockets of his overalls. "Y'all two can wander around and see what you can see. If you have any questions, I'll be over yonder at the house."

"Thanks, Mr. Randalson."

"Thank you, sir," Atlas said with a tight respectful nod.

He waited until Jerry was out of the greenhouse before he turned to me with a look of shock on his face. "Your mother is a real, live conjure woman?"

"Yes. And her mother before her. And her mother before her. Who did you think I learned it from?"

"So, you're a conjure woman, too?"

"Don't make it weird, Atlas." I turned and walked up the aisle to check out some elderberries growing in the far back corner.

"I'm not...I just find it interesting that you didn't tell me. I didn't know there were conjure women outside of the Coastal Carolinas and Louisiana."

"My family is from the Coastal Carolinas. And my mother brought her traditions with her when she married my father and moved out here to be with him."

"I didn't know that any of those traditions made it this far inland."

"They typically don't. My mom was just the determined sort." I turned to him, took in his stunned and amazed expression.

Atlas moved in closer. "Seems like she isn't the only one. I thought you were just the keeper of the recipes. I didn't know that you were really into the magic of it all."

I looked up at him. "Is that a problem for you?"

"Absolutely not, but now I'm curious. Is that what it is?" he asked, gesturing between us.

"What are you talking about?"

"This attraction I feel for you…are you… spelling me or something?"

Guilt swamped me, and I felt compelled to tell him about the come-to-me oil, but then he reached out and slid his hand around the back of my neck, pulling me closer and angling my chin upward with his thumb at the same time.

"Hmmm, something tells me that you are, but I don't know if I care."

The first brush of his lips was hesitant. Like he was giving me a chance to pull away. Part of me wanted to. This thing between us already felt too intense. But before I could take a step backward, his mouth covered mine, and I swear my feet left the ground. His tongue tasted of licorice leaves as it invaded my mouth. His hands gripped me, holding me close to him so that I could feel the hard length that he had adjusted earlier this morning in his apartment. I angled my hips so that I could rub against it, drawing a moan from deep in his chest.

Oh, damn. Trying to resist this was pointless.

Was kissing always supposed to feel like this? So visceral that every cell in me responded in a way that made me wish I could just rub him on my skin and drink him in?

I wanted him closer. He hooked a hand under my knee and brought it up over his hip, lining the fabric-covered ridge of his dick against my pussy through my leggings. Sensation shot through me like lightning, and whatever resolve I had incinerated. I was practically climbing him. Somehow Atlas had the presence of mind to maneuver us against the sturdy planter box full of bright pink coneflower.

"God," he whispered. "You are so hot and wet that I can feel you through these pants." He slipped a hand down between us, caressing my swollen lips through the fabric.

"Oh, fuck," I whispered, rocking my hips forward, needing more pressure from his hand.

"You *are* spelling me. Aren't you, Sonja Watts?" he asked.

And I could practically taste the wicked smile on his lips as he found my clit with the pads of his index and middle finger.

The touch was too much and not enough, and he knew just how to bring me up to the edge, then back off, making that expletive fall from my lips again.

"Please," I whimpered.

"Is your little pussy aching?" he whispered, still torturing me. "Do you want to come, Soni?"

"Yes, please," I begged.

And then he slipped his hands down the front of my pants. Those same two fingers slipped inside of me with embarrassing ease. In an instant, he found my spot and circled my clit with his thumb. I bit his shoulder to keep from moaning loud enough to bring Jerry down from over yonder.

"Oh, Soni… sweet, Soni," he cooed, and I swear my stupid nickname never sounded so good to me before.

I rode his hand, too eager for the orgasm to worry about anyone walking in on us or how wanton I must look with my leggings halfway down my ass with his hand jammed in my pussy.

"Oh, there you go, sweetie. There you go…" he whispered as my pussy began to spasm around his fingers in tiny, fluttering pulses. "Go ahead and come, Soni. I've got you," he whispered in my ear while reaching around to cradle my backside with his other hand.

"Fuckfuckfuck!" I gasped as my pussy clenched down hard.

"Yes, sweetie…oh, god. You really needed that, didn't you? You should have just asked me, baby. I would've given it to you."

I held on, clutching him with my whole body until every spark of my orgasm dissipated. When I finally opened my eyes, bright spots danced across my vision before his smiling face swam into focus.

Oh, my god. What did I just do? Did I just let this guy finger me in public?

Shame washed over me, and I covered my face with my hands.

"Hey, no. Hey…" he whispered. He yanked up my pants and hugged me close as inexplicable tears poured out of me. "Come on. Let's get you to the car."

Sure that Jerry Randalson had heard, or worse, seen me have a screaming orgasm in his greenhouse, I sat in the Subaru while Atlas went up to the office to get a price list.

What the fuck just happened?

And why the fuck was I suddenly saying fuck so much?

Was I going through some sort of midlife crisis? Some late rebound triggered by finalizing the divorce?

I watched Atlas amble back to the car on those long legs. His eyes were obscured by sunglasses, but I was almost sure he was looking at me because he grabbed his dick and adjusted it. This time it wasn't some absentminded gesture. I knew it was about me.

He snatched the door open and climbed in. I stared at the emblem on the steering wheel, too afraid to look him in the eyes.

"It's lunchtime. Why don't we go somewhere and eat that picnic you packed so we can talk?"

With a tight nod, I started the car and pointed it toward Caesar's Head.

chapter eleven

Atlas

Motivated by shame or disgust, or I couldn't tell which, Sonja set a punishing pace on our hike up Caesar's Head. Well, punishing for her because she was determined to stay ahead of me — which was no small feat considering that she had to take two steps to match one of mine.

The place was strangely deserted. Normally it was crawling with tourists during the warmer months, but coming up on a random Thursday at the beginning of Fall guaranteed we had the place to ourselves.

Not that Sonja was even remotely interested in that. She barely talked in the car on the way here, no matter how much I tried to coax a smile out of her. What the fuck even happened back there? Had I misread the signals? It felt like she wanted that kiss. It felt like she wanted me to touch her. She didn't stop me or say no, but I was worried that had I barreled past a sign that she didn't want me to make her come.

God, but she was so fucking beautiful in that moment.

It took everything in me not to pull out my dick, bend her over that berry bush and sink into her.

But then she started crying. Her pussy was still clenching around my fingers when that look came over her face, and she cried. She cried like she wished I hadn't done it, and for the life of me, I couldn't figure out what I'd done wrong.

The foliage thinned at the end of the path, and the sound of rushing water reached my ears. Reaching the falls and hearing the water usually calmed me, but my thoughts were still racing.

Sonja wove through a few skinny trees to reach a grouping of flat rocks right at the top of the falls. She stretched and then put her hands on her hips. I hung back, unsure if I should move in closer or what.

Fuck. I really hope I didn't fuck this up.

Sonja squatted down to wash her hands in the river, and I tried not to look at her ass while I went to do the same. The moment I was shoulder to shoulder with her, she turned away and unzipped her pack.

"I've got turkey and swiss sandwiches, red grapes, and two bags of almonds," she said, then pulled out a blanket to spread over the flatter one of the rocks in the gathering, and sat.

I sat down across from her as she spread out our lunch. "There's three sandwiches here."

"Two are for you. I figured you'd be hungrier than me since you're a growing boy and all."

"Boy," said with a grunt. Was that what she really thought of me?

"Sorry... that was a poorly timed joke."

"No worries." I unwrapped my sandwich and took a big bite before I said something stupid. "This is good. Is that a spicy mayo?"

She nodded.

This was awkward. I made her come so hard that she saw stars, and instead of creating some intimacy, things were awkward, but in a way, I'd never experienced before. Was this about me? It couldn't be about me. This was something else.

"So…" she began in a soft voice. "Things got weird back there after I…" she stalled.

She couldn't even fucking say the words. *Wow*. Who did this to her?

"Yeah, but that's not what I think we need to talk about," I said.

"Huh?"

I looked at her. She was staring down her sandwich. I tapped her on the chin, and Sonja reluctantly looked me in the eye. "I don't think that's the conversation we need to have."

"Okay." She shrugged. "What conversation do we need to have?"

"Why don't you start by telling me what happened with your ex-husband?"

"My ex-husband? I don't see how that has anything to do with what happened at the farm."

"It's not just about what happened at the farm. But whatever happened between the two of you has everything to do with what's going on between us now."

I took another bite of my sandwich and chewed thoughtfully for a moment and watched the water. Hoping she would volunteer the information on her own, but when it became clear she wouldn't, I set the sandwich aside.

"At first, I thought it was about the age difference. It's slightly annoying that you think that I couldn't possibly find your desirable because I'm what… nine and a half years younger than you? As if that makes my desire less believable. As if you aren't desirable to everyone."

"I—"

I held up a finger to let her know I wasn't quite done. She had an opportunity to say her piece and chose not to. "But now I'm wondering… am I the first guy you've been interested in since you broke up with him? Did he cheat on you? Break your heart? Make you feel like you were undesirable? Tell me what I'm dealing with here."

Sonja's eyes were wide, wet, and unblinking before she dropped her gaze down to her sandwich and took another bite.

"Soni... Is that it? Is... did you respond that way because of him? Or was it something I did or said?" I asked softly. So softly that I was worried that she didn't hear it over the roar of the waterfall.

She kept chewing like she didn't hear me. This wasn't going anywhere. I shouldn't have asked her about her ex. I was fucking this up. Completely fucking this up.

"Sonja, look at me."

She sighed, her shoulders drooped, and she shook her head. "I don't want to talk about my ex-husband. I've spent a year sifting through the negativity around our divorce and... maybe I have some shit to unpack around my looks and how... how I feel like my best years are gone and..."

She lifted her head and looked at me. *God... Did she really feel that way?* "Your best years are not behind you, Soni."

"Atlas—"

"Why aren't you hearing me? I feel like we have something here, but you keep pulling away."

"You think we have something?" she shook her head and laughed. "What happened in the greenhouse only happened because I used my mother's come-to-me oil. I practically bathed myself in it."

I frowned. "Come-to-me oil?"

"A spell, Atlas. A love spell."

A love spell.

How much did I believe in this hoodoo? Most of it seemed too outrageous to be anything but fictional, but the thing was...

Sonja *did* believe in it. To her, it was as real as the good word my mother got from the pulpit every Sunday. And that belief had compelled her to use that magic — her good medicine — to make me fall in love with her.

"You used a love spell on me? Why would you do that?"

"It doesn't matter why I did it, really. But I guess I convinced myself that coincidences don't happen. That the bottle was in my bag for a reason. It was there because I was supposed to use it. So I did. And now it's doubled back on me and created this... mess."

Frustrated, she stood and paced back toward the water's edge.

"Stupid woman," she muttered to herself. "Stupid, desperate woman."

Stunned, I watched her go through a whole diatribe about her stupid uselessness, and I couldn't understand how or why she would be so down on herself. I stood up and went to her. Slipped my arms around her waist.

"First of all... you didn't need to use a love spell on me. I wanted you the moment I heard your voice." I pressed a kiss to the nape of her neck. "And you're beautiful, Sonja. I know you don't believe me—"

"It's not that I don't believe you. It's just—"

She drew in a breath and held it. I squeezed her gently, urging her to continue. The breath she drew in seeped out, and she relaxed in my embrace.

"My sisters..." she began hesitantly. "My sisters are beautiful, bold women, you know? They've always done exactly what they wanted and embraced all that life has to offer."

"Hm," I grunted, wondering where she was going with this. "I've met them, and they are pretty great. Agostina is definitely good people. Weird as fuck, but good. So are you."

"She is, but that's not what I mean."

"Okay, what do you mean?"

"I mean, that they're younger than me and they didn't have the same expectations hung on them, you know? They've done things, and they've had an opportunity to just… experience things. Eric was my first and only. So yeah, you're the first since the divorce and…"

"You've never been with anyone else," I finished for her.

"Yeah…" she said with a little nod. "When Eric asked for a divorce, he said that we'd outgrown each other. That he needed more fun from life and I understood, you know? Because I wasn't any fun. Not like my sisters or like other women, you know? And at the greenhouse… that was the first time I came like that with someone else, and I was—"

"Embarrassed?"

She shook her head. "Ashamed."

I sighed and pressed my lips to the back of her neck. *Ashamed.* That… I didn't know what to do with that. "Soni..."

"I mean, it's just pathetic, you know? I'm forty years old, and I never knew that I could feel that, and that makes me feel stupid."

"You're not stupid."

She scoffed and swiped at more tears. "I'm a forty-year-old woman discovering partner-assisted orgasms for the first time."

"And you're a really fast learner."

She laughed, and the sound warmed me.

"Can I finish telling you about how I felt when I met you?"

118

She swiped at her tears and nodded.

"Normally, I listen to music while I'm working, but my playlist had just ended, and I heard you come in. Your voice… it has a strange resonance to it. Has anyone ever told you that?"

She shook her head.

"It's kinda like a blues singer. You know how Nina's voice drops down low and deep, and it kinda makes you want to curl your body around it? That sound. Kinda like that. It hit me like that, and I felt it right here."

I slid my hand down low on her belly, fingertips grazing her pillow-soft mound, and I wanted to sink my fingers into her again.

"I don't know who I expected that voice to belong to, but when I reached the top of the stairs and saw you, I…"

She drew in another breath. Waiting and wanting to hear what I said next.

"I thought…I need to know this woman. How do I get to know this woman? I want to know what makes that husky laugh come out that gorgeous throat. And if she really loved Stevie Nicks or just the quote from that song? And then I ruined it all by being corny and awkward—"

Soni twisted in my embrace and cupped my cheeks with both her hands. "You didn't ruin it," she whispered then kissed me.

"I didn't?" I asked.

"You didn't."

That greediness that made me shove my hand down her pants, that needy, raw desire surged in me again, but I tried to hold it back. "And you really shouldn't feel ashamed about coming. You're beautiful when you come. So fucking beautiful, Soni."

119

Sonja moaned, deepening the kiss, tongue sliding against mine until we fell into a sort of hypnotic rhythm. Our breath synced, and I gathered her close. She undulated against me in a way that made me wish I didn't have any clothes on. That she didn't either. That both of us were naked on that blanket, under the warm midday sun, giving our bodies the completion we both clearly wanted. Her hand inched from my chest down to my crotch to cup and squeeze the part of me that so desperately needed to be inside of her. A sound came out of me that was at home in these woods.

"Soni, Soni, Soni," I chanted.

She tugged at the drawstring to my sweats, and that's when I heard it.

Laughter, heavy, careless steps and people talking excitedly about crossing the suspension bridge.

"Fuck," she cursed. Her head fell forward and hit the middle of my chest.

I chuckled. "I love that you're so turned on that you actually considered fucking me on a well-traveled hiking trail," I whispered.

I dragged my hands up her sides, over her breasts, and circled her neck. Her pulse fluttered under my thumb. I stroked it while tugging away the strap of her tank top then placed a soft, sucking kiss along the curve of her neck.

"As much as I would love to commune with you in the grass under these trees, I'd much rather make love to you for the first time without an audience."

"Make love?"

My brain tripped overhearing that phrase coming from her mouth. Had I actually said that?

While I was still considering why those words came out of my mouth, four young girls appeared on the trail. Sonja pulled away, creating more distance than I wanted or needed from her.

"Hi!" she chirped, giving the girls a little wave.

All three were dressed in gear straight from an Instagram ad. At least they were smart enough to wear hiking boots, but the sheer amount of visible skin almost guaranteed that one or all of them would leave the woods with a tick somewhere indiscreet if they weren't wearing bug repellant.

The girls returned Sonja's greeting and continued to the suspension bridge. A cloud of giggles erupted as they passed us, and Sonjas shoulders crept up around her ears.

"They're not laughing at us," I said knowingly once they were out of earshot.

She looked up at me. "What?"

"They're not laughing at us for the reason you think they are. They're laughing because you were practically humping my leg."

"You sure?" she asked, but it was wobbly at the edges. "They're not laughing because they saw a middle-aged woman molesting a man half her age in the woods?"

"No," I said with a shake of my head. "They're laughing because they damn near caught us rutting like rabbits."

"Atlas—"

I stilled her lips and quieted her protests by covering her mouth with mine. "I'm not going to let you talk shit about the woman I'm into anymore," I said softly. "You hear me, Sonja?"

She nodded. "I hear you."

"Good. Now let's finish lunch before the ants get away with our picnic." My stomach chose that moment to make a loud noise of agreement that made both of us laugh.

"You really are hungry," she said.

"Mmmhmm.." I sat down on the rock we'd abandoned and grabbed my sandwich. I dragged my eyes up her curvy frame until I met her gaze. "I can eat this now, but I guess I'll have to wait to eat you," I said and waggled my eyebrows.

chapter twelve

Sonja

The drive back into Greenville was quiet. I was still on pins and needles, but Atlas was relaxed and possessive in a way that I'd never experienced with Eric. He kept his hands on me the whole ride. I liked the way he gripped my thigh, squeezing intermittently, and then lightly caressing my plump folds through my leggings. By the time I parked in the visitor space outside of his condo building, I was wet and squirming in my seat, clenching my thighs on his big hand to try and get some relief.

"You probably have to go, huh?" he asked softly.

The clock on the dash read five-thirty. My kids were already home and probably wondering where the hell I was. "Unfortunately," I said with a nod.

"I figured," he said, then leaned across the console and gave me a soft, sweet kiss. "Thank you for inviting me to visit a farm, finger you in a greenhouse, hike to Rainbow Falls, and hug you after eating a turkey sandwich."

"I didn't invite you to finger me in a greenhouse," I corrected, a smile on my lips.

"Oh, yeah, you did. It was subtle and subliminal, but there was an invitation. Just like you're inviting me to finger you right now in the front seat of your Subaru," he said, then palmed my pussy through my leggings.

"Atlas…" I moaned.

"I know," he whispered, dragging his mouth across my cheek. "You have to go, but god, I wish you could stay."

Right away, I started thinking up ways I could stay with him. I could *Doordash* some food for the kids. Yeah…and if I got in after they'd gone to bed, I wouldn't have to explain. I wouldn't have to lie to them about where I'd been all day.

"Shhh… I'm not asking you to stay. I don't want to be that guy."

"What guy?"

He pulled away so that he could look me in the eye. "The guy that makes you abandon your responsibilities to make love all night."

"Jesus, Atlas. Is this some sort of reverse psychology? A Jedi mind trick to make me do exactly what you're suggesting?"

Atlas laughed. "I don't know? Is it working?"

The hand between my legs shifted to cup me more fully, the heel of his hand, creating a delicious pressure against my mound. I rolled my hips, and a bright spark of pleasure made my eyes roll back in my head.

"Poor baby…" he whispered. "Your tight little pussy is still aching, huh?"

This kind of talk, this dirty talk, I always thought it was silly. I wondered how it could be sexy, but I swear… when he asked me about my tight, aching pussy, all I could do was nod.

"I know it is. I'm aching for you, too." He shifted in his seat, and his right hand grabbed at his dick.

I watched him, mesmerized by the way he handled himself, wondering if he wanted me to handle him that roughly. I was never rough with Eric. He didn't like it that way. Could I be like that with Atlas?

"Hey…" he said softly, drawing my attention back to his face. "What were you going to do to me when you unbuttoned my fly by the falls?" he asked.

Now that the moment had passed, I suddenly felt shy about my thoughts and actions at that moment. "I didn't really think it through. I just wanted to feel you in my hands."

"Hm," he grunted. "You still want to?"

And just like that, with that simple suggestion, my palms tingled, wanting that intimate caress. "Yes," I said with a nod.

"I want you to… can you?" he begged.

"Right here?" I asked, glancing around. It was dusk, and the parking lot was full of cars, but no one was walking around.

"Right here… upstairs. I don't care where. I just need you to touch me. I don't think I can spend another night like this."

We kissed again, and I felt him tremble when my hand rested on his chest. He was practically vibrating.

"Right here," I said. "I can't go upstairs with you. If I go upstairs…"

He nodded, understanding the things I left unsaid. I wanted him. There's no denying that, but so much had happened today. I'd crossed so many boundaries, and I knew if I went upstairs with him, I was going to want more than just a touch. More than just a kiss. His hands wouldn't be enough.

"Okay," he agreed, then glanced around the still quiet parking lot. "Right here."

I gathered up his soft tee shirt and slipped my hand under it to touch his muscled chest and drifting lower to caress his belly, the ridged topography of his abdomen. When my fingers tangled in the trail of hair that led to the place between his legs, his whole body quaked.

"You okay?"

"Yes, I just…want your hands on me."

"Okay," I whispered and rugged at the drawstring of his sweats.

His desire was so acute it seemed like physical pain. I knew and understood how that felt. It's the same way I felt in the greenhouse, but I'd never known anyone to feel that way about me.

The dusk deepened around us, casting the world outside the car in shadow. Made the interior of the Subaru feel cocoon-like. Condensation formed on the windows, adding to that secretive intimacy as I reached into his pants.

He was big and hard in his pants and pulsed when my knuckles skimmed the silky fabric of his boxer briefs. I broke away from the kiss to look down at him. To watch myself reach into his boxers, take him in my hand. He was smooth and velvety soft against my palm.

Atlas hissed and lifted his hips to tug down his pants a little further. His dick, now free of its constraints, leaped into my hand. I closed my hand into a loose fist and drew it up his length.

"Oh, god. Sonja," he breathed. His head fell back against the headrest.

I looked at him. God… he was so damn beautiful. His eyes were closed, and his thick lashes made dark shadows on his sculpted cheekbones. He rolled his hips, urging me silently to draw my hand down his thick length and back up again. He swallowed, and I tracked the way his Adam's apple bobbed. I had no idea what I was doing. It had been more than a year since I'd even touched a man intimately, and I'd only ever been with my husband.

"Hey," I whispered.

Atlas opened his eyes and looked at me.

126

"Show me how you like it." I drew my hand up his length again. "Do you like it hard or soft? Do you want me to put my mouth on it?"

"Shit," he cursed, and his dick grew harder in my hand if that was even possible, and a bead of precum formed at the tip. I leaned over and lapped it up. "Jesus, Soni."

"Show me how to please you," I begged softly.

His big hand closed around mine, tightening my grip, then drew both of our hands up and over the fat, wet tip of his dick. On the downstroke, he thrust upward, forcing himself through my clenched fist. The sight of it was so erotic that my pussy clenched, releasing a gush of moisture that dampened the crotch of my leggings. Needing him inside of me in some way, I wrapped my lips around the tip of him again, and he whimpered.

"Like that?" I whispered. "Hard, but slow, like this?" I asked, squeezing him and drawing my hand up and over the tip.

"Yes," he nodded, thrusting into my hand again. "Just like that." He hooked his hand around the back of my neck and pulled me in. His kiss was deeper. Hungrier. More reckless. It took all of my willpower to keep my pants on. To keep my ass in my seat. To keep from sitting on the beautiful dick in my hands.

Atlas grasped at me, kissed me hard, then pulled away to watch, seemingly torn between wanting me closer and wanting me to make him come. I pulled away to take him in my mouth again. I've never felt so compelled to suck a man's dick before. To see this strong, devastatingly, handsome young man come apart because of me. I teased him, sucking hard on the tip, and each time his hips lifted the tiniest bit. Thrusting deeper into my mouth. I knew what he wanted, but I waited until he asked for it.

"Please, Sonny," he begged, his hips rolled upward again. "Please…"

I moaned and swallowed him down. Taking him in as deeply as I could, until his cockhead hit the back of my throat.

"Oh, fuck, Sonja…" he moaned loudly. "Oh, fuck."

I looked up at him. He was gone. Lost and on the edge of bliss from what I was doing to him with my mouth.

"Baby… baby, I'm about to come."

I hummed, closed my eyes, and took him in deeper.

"Oh, fuck. You're just gonna…baby, no." He made a sound that was somewhere between a chuckle and a moan, tensed, and came. Flooding my mouth and moaning my name. I swallowed him down, sucking and licking every drop from his dick until he started to twitch and jerk. He pulled me off of him, brought my lips to his.

"Why'd you do that?" he whispered, kissing me hard, that same hard, hungry kiss he'd given me at the start. Could he taste himself on my tongue? "Why'd you do that? You didn't have to do that," he said, his voice full of gratitude…and was that reverence?

"I know. I wanted to."

"You're amazing… Jesus, Sonja." He kept kissing me.

"It's been a long time since I've done anything like that or even wanted to." I pulled away a little, so I could look him in the eyes. "Thank god you came when you did. I was two seconds away from crawling over this console."

He shook his head. "This is a complete 180 from crying when I made you come in the greenhouse this morning."

I shrugged and slid my hand under his shirt. "Maybe it's the come-to-me oil, but there's no denying you bring it out of me."

Atlas sighed. "Same," he murmured. "So much same." He covered my hand with his.

"You laughed before you came," I said, remembering that moment. "Is that normal for you?"

"I...uh... I don't know. My attention is usually focused elsewhere."

"No one has ever mentioned it before?"

"No..." His brow furrowed. "Is that your way of asking how many girls I've been with?" he asked, smoothing his hand over my cheek.

"I... no. I just thought it was cute and unusual." But now I was wondering. How many women had he been with? Who was the last woman he was with? Was she my age or much younger with a firmer ass and a belly without stretch marks?

He stopped my self deprecating thoughts with another kiss. "Maybe we'll talk about that next time. When you actually come upstairs, and I actually get you in my bed."

I shook my head. "I can't—"

"I know. You can't tonight. I just wanted to let you know that this changes nothing. I still want you. So don't go home and lay awake all night recounting every minute that we've spent together today, looking for the one thing that you did that might have turned me off. Only one of us needs to do that."

I rolled my eyes. "You did nothing wrong."

"You mean, except come in your mouth after you sucked my dick for like three minutes?"

"Was it only three minutes?"

Atlas nodded and looked a little sheepish. "I glanced at the clock when you..." He rolled his eyes. "It was three minutes.

Maybe four. Andddd now I'm humiliated. Excuse me while I tuck my flaccid dick back in my pants."

"Atlas…" I reached for his hand and laced my fingers into through his. "It doesn't really matter how long you lasted. Especially since I can still feel you so big and hard in the back of my throat."

"Jesus, Sonja," he said for the third time this evening. He brought our joined hands to his mouth, where he grazed his lips across my knuckles. The look he gave me made me squirm in my seat again.

Maybe all of this dirty talk wasn't so silly.

"Can I see you sometime this week? Like… other than the class?"

"Are you kidding? Yes, absolutely yes," he said.

He grunted and leaned in to kiss me again. One of his hands curled around my neck, thumb stroking the place where my pulse thrummed and then slipped down to cup my breast. I arched my back, wanting more of his touch, and he granted it, stroking that same thumb over my taut nipple.

"We're never going to get out of this car, are we?"

Atlas pinched my nipple through the thin fabric of my shirt and smiled against my mouth. "Doesn't seem likely."

Oh, god, what am I doing? Making out in a car like a high school kid trying to get in as many kisses as possible before I broke curfew?

The hand on my breast drifted lower, tunneled under my shirt, skimmed along the band of my yoga pants. I sighed, curling my hips forward and opening my legs. He moaned, and his fingers slipped and slid through my drenched lips to find my clit.

"Did sucking my dick get you this wet?"

"Yes," I breathed. Now it was my turn to be slightly mortified by the wet, sticky sounds of my pussy in the quiet of the car as he thrummed his middle finger back and forth.

"You're gonna make me come again," I panted.

"Mmm, that's kind of the point."

"But you can't… we're even now. You gave me an orgasm in the greenhouse, and I gave you one just now."

"Are we keeping score?" he asked, amusement coloring his tone and sweetening his kisses.

"No…" My head swam, and I closed my eyes to quell the dizziness. "But it makes us even."

He chuckled. "Sweet, Sonja. Cute of you to think that one orgasm makes us even-Steven."

"What do you—" Before I could finish my question, he slipped two thick fingers inside of me, finding my spot like he's always known where it was, and circling my clit with the pad of his calloused thumb.

"I've made myself come while thinking of you almost every night since we met. By your calculations, I owe you at least a dozen. Probably more."

Something about that… the thought of him in that big bed that I glimpsed through the open door, flat on his back, dick in his hand, thinking of me while he stroked himself… The thought of that sent pleasure roaring through me.

Atlas didn't stop. Instead, he added a third finger, forcing his way through those intimate clenched muscles, lengthening the orgasm until it changed into something different. Something that rushed over the surface of my skin, sensitizing every inch of me until it arrowed back to my pussy, and I came again, harder, wetter. I grabbed his hand, and he stilled his fingers but kept them inside of me while my pussy clenched, and fluttered for what seemed like an eternity.

131

"Did you just..? Back-to-back?"

"Yes," I panted. My breath was soughing in and out of me like I'd run up ten flights of stairs.

"Wow, I thought that was a myth."

I laughed. "Me too. Hell, this is more orgasms than I've ever had in one day."

"Hmm, that's a sin." Slowly, carefully, he slid his fingers from me, dragging the moisture over my hypersensitive clit, making me twitch before removing them completely.

I sighed and opened my eyes only to catch him doing the most deeply erotic thing I've ever seen. His fingers were coated with the evidence of my orgasm, he slowly and deliberately, licked that evidence from each individual digit like it was the most normal thing to do. Eyes closed like the taste of me was like sweet icing or good barbecue sauce. I must have made some sort of sound because he opened his eyes and looked at me with eyes so dark with desire that I had to squeeze my wet thighs together again.

"You taste *sooo* much better than I imagined," he said. "I can't wait to have my face buried in your pussy. I think I'm going to spend a few hours just making you come with my mouth and fingers and nothing else."

I shook my head. "This is unreal. You are unreal."

"I feel the same about you, and this. I'm not like this with anyone. I've never been like this with anyone." He stopped short of labeling me as someone special and kissed me again instead. The taste of me on his tongue and lips had a strange and surprising effect on me. It sent my lust roaring to the surface again I groped for him, pulling him as close as I could.

"Fuckkkk, I gotta get out of this car," he moaned. "If I don't, we're going to end up in the back seat, and I don't want our first time together to go down like that."

"We could always do what you have planned the second time," I said, realizing that I was totally contradicting myself. But my line in the sand was just a reason to deny myself of the thing I really want, and hadn't I had enough of that?

I reached into his briefs, expecting to find him soft and needing a bit of encouragement, but gasped when I find him hard and ready.

"You're killing me," he whispered.

Then... my cellphone rang. *"Incoming call from Nadia,"* the handsfree feature of my car announced through the speakers.

Reflexively, I pressed the button to answer.

"Mom! Where are you? *The Voice* is about to start, and we were supposed to watch it together!"

"Oh, shit, Naddy. I lost track of time." I smacked my forehead. Me and Naddy watched *The Voice* together every Wednesday night.

"Mom! Are you serious? Watching this together was your idea!"

I grimaced, and Atlas pulled away, settling back into the passenger seat. "Nadia, I'll be home in a minute."

"Ten minutes? Thirty minutes? How many minutes, mom?"

God, my child, sounded like a spoiled, whiny brat. I didn't dare chance a look at Atlas. His dick had probably gone limp instantly from hearing her call me mom so many times.

"Nadia, I'll be home soon," I said more firmly. "Just record it so that we can watch it together from the beginning when I get there."

"Fine," she said with an exaggerated sigh. "Can you bring home some Krispy Kremes?" she asked. "But only if they're hot!" she added.

"Okay, I'll grab some Krispy Kreme. Bye, Nadia." I hung up before she could say anything else. "Sorry about that," I groaned.

"Don't apologize," he said, reaching across the console to grip my thigh. "You said you couldn't stay, and I kinda manipulated you into it anyway. If anyone should be apologizing, it should be me." With a deep sigh that wasn't unlike the one my daughter emitted a moment earlier, Atlas lifted his bottom and pulled his pants up. His t-shirt slipped up the tiniest bit, revealing that happy trail that I'd played with before I went down on him.

"Yeah, but that was probably a huge turn-off."

He laughed and shook his head. "I wish it was," he mumbled, then looked at me. "Text me to let me know you made it home, okay?"

I nodded.

Atlas leaned in and gave me one last soft kiss, then opened the passenger side door. Reluctantly and with a groan of complaint, he grabbed his bag and climbed out of the car. I watched him as he walked across the front end of the car, long-legged and confident, and he should be. He gave me two orgasms--three if I counted the second one that felt like it rolled into a third. At the entry, he turned and blew me a kiss, and hell...something happened in my chest. A great swooping giddiness came over me.

"Oh, fuck," I whispered to no one at all. "I'm falling for him."

chapter thirteen

Sonja

The sharp snap of Estelle's fingers brought me back to the present. "What?"

"Are you here to daydream or help set up?" she asked. Anyone else would have thought she was really irritated, but I saw the smirk in the corner of her mouth.

"This is your party, Stelle. I'm a guest. All I'm required to do is show up."

"Guest!" Estelle scoffed. "You ceased being a guest when you watched me push a baby out of my vagina in this very living room. Now grab the other end of this table and help me carry it outside."

Tonight was the first game of the college football season, and since most of us were University of South Carolina graduates, we often threw game day parties that everyone on the block attended. Estelle's were always the best. She went all out, and Deacon was a king on that barbecue grill. We hung out in her backyard, gathered at the various seating areas to watch the game on a big screen they had put in two summers ago. The kids ran around the yard or swam in the pool while we laughed and talked about stupid plays and whether or not our true freshman will ever be a good quarterback.

"So, are you going to tell me what has that dreamy look on your face, or are you just going to keep grinning to yourself like an idiot?" Estelle asked once we had the table in place.

"I'm not grinning like an idiot. Am I?" I asked, cupping my own cheeks. Now that I was paying attention, my cheek muscles did feel a little fatigued. Fuck, I was grinning like an idiot.

And still cursing.

Was this my new normal? Had my default state reset to someone who grinned like an idiot while thinking about a man seven years her junior who gave her three orgasms in one day?

Estelle smacked me hard on the ass.

"Yowch!" I screeched, rubbing the abused cheek. "Estelle! Why'd you do that?"

"What the hell is going on with you?" she demanded.

I chewed on my bottom lip and debated whether or not I should tell her. We weren't dating. We didn't even have sex…not really. Was this the type of thing you shared with your best girlfriend? I skipped this part of high school and college. Me and Eric were already together and had been since eighth grade. I never got a chance to be that giggly girl sharing secrets about her boyfriend.

"Do you need a drink to get this out?"

"I—"

"Stupid question. Yes, you need a drink. Come on." She ushered me back inside to the kitchen. From the cabinet, she pulled out two shot glasses and a bottle of tequila.

"Estelle, it's eleven o'clock in the morning."

She rolled her eyes and filled both shot glasses to the brim. "It's game day. We start drinking at breakfast. You know that. Bottoms up," she ordered, picking up her shot glass.

I shook my head and picked up the class, clinked it to hers, and swallowed down the fire hot liquid. "I spent the day with Atlas on Wednesday. He gave me three orgasms, and I sucked his dick," I blurted, then clapped my hands over my mouth.

Estelle immediately started choking. "What?" she strangled out. "You what and he what? Sonja!"

"I know! I invited him to take a trip up to the Randalson Farm and for a hike, but then he kissed me in the greenhouse, and fingered me up against the plant bed, and then again in the front seat of my car outside of his condo and who am I?"

"You're the bitch that's living her best fucking life, that's who!"

I covered my face, feeling ashamed, and ecstatic all at the same damn time. "I'm not some kid in high school, Estelle! I shouldn't be hooking up in cars like I'm Nadia's age."

"Uh, you told me about your sex life with Eric. You said that you didn't even know how an orgasm was supposed to feel until I bought you that vibrator for your birthday a few years ago."

"I know," I groaned.

"And Atlas, who is a fine ass young man, gave you three orgasms with just his hand—wait, was it just his hand? Was his tongue involved?"

"No, just his hands. His fucking magical hands."

Estelle suddenly went quiet and wide-eyed.

"What?"

"You look like a new person."

"Oh, shut up," I said, dismissing her comment with a wave of my hand.

"No, really," she said with a nod. "Those orgasms are great for your skin."

"I don't know about my skin, but they're definitely great for my vagina!"

"Sonja!" she squealed, then came around the corner and pulled me into a hug. "I'm so happy for you!"

137

"Really?" I squeezed her harder and buried my face in her neck. "Because I don't know what the fuck I'm feeling or doing. Seems like we're headed toward having sex, but I don't know anything about this guy. I'm supposed to let him see me naked?" All the emotions I'd tried to sort out on my own last night, and this morning came bubbling to the surface. "Let him inside my body?" I whispered.

"Sonja…" Estelle pulled away so she could look me in the eye. "Are worried about this because you've never been with anyone else, but Eric?"

I nodded. "And he's so much younger and good looking and has probably had a ton of sexual relationships. I just—"

"Okay, let's get everything set up so we can take this bottle of tequila out back, and I can tell you about Atlas James."

We put out all of the snacks, the cooler full of beer, and another full of sodas and juice for the kiddos before Estelle took me over to a bench swing in the far back corner of her yard. With our feet tucked under our bottoms and a more adult, and chilled version of our tequila shots in hand, she began to tell me about young Atlas.

"So this guy you see now, the confident one with the biceps, and the bedroom eyes, and a mouth made for sin? That's not the Atlas I knew in high school or even the guy I saw in passing when we were in college. That guy, the guy you see now? He was born during a period of amazing success that forced him to reinvent himself."

Estelle told me about Atlas's mother and how he was born from an illicit affair with the pastor of a local megachurch. The wife didn't discover his existence until he was like nine or ten.

"His mother was ridiculed, and he was too for a while. But instead of getting angry and confrontational, Atlas focused on reinventing himself and taking care of his mom."

She told me about the success of the stocks he'd bought when he was a kid and how, with the help of his friend Kairo, he built a tiny home in a panel truck and traveled around the country teaching people how to become laptop entrepreneurs, digital nomads who could make their money from anywhere in the world. There was a girl named Ruby in the story because, of course, there was a girl. They crisscrossed the country together for about three years, but ultimately, the relationship deteriorated, and they broke up. He sold the tiny home and booked a ticket to Europe, where he did the same thing overseas for a few years.

"Then he moved back here. That was three years ago. He hasn't dated anyone since he's been back."

I stared at her in disbelief. "No… seriously? Why?"

"I mean, there have been rumors, but nothing serious. Maybe a one night stand or two. But Atlas is… different. Ruby? The girl that traveled the country with him in that tiny home? She was a friend of a friend, and she said he was kinda dark and intense, but in like… all the best ways."

"But that doesn't explain why he hasn't had a serious relationship in three years."

"I guess he still feels like that awkward guy on the inside. Like he really can't believe that women find him attractive and desirable. I saw glimpses of that when he talked to you that first night at the bar."

"I gotta be honest, Stelle. That worries me a little. Dark and intense in all the best ways? What does that even mean?"

"I took it to mean that when he's with a girl, he's really with a girl and no one else."

"Hmm," I said, then took a deep swallow of my drink.

Was that dark intensity something I wanted or could even handle at this point in my life?

"What are you thinking about? I can see your brain working."

I sighed. "The ink is barely dry on my divorce, Estelle. I shouldn't be getting into anything serious."

"Okay, who makes these rules? And yeah, the ink just dried on your divorce papers, but you've been separated for a year and distant for much longer than that."

"Yeah, but I gotta be careful. I've got the kids to worry about, and I really want to focus on my business and make sure that gets off the ground—"

"Have you talked to him about this?"

"Um, no. I haven't even worked through all of this myself."

"Talk to him. He's a communicator. Shit...we gotta cut this short. The Bickersons are here." She stood up and tossed back the rest of her drink.

I looked across the yard and saw Owen and Robin Scott — The Bickering Bickersons. We've all lived on Earle Street for ten or eleven years, and never in all of that time have they ever a left a party or get together without getting in an argument.

And Owen had a weird crush on Estelle that Deacon thought was harmless, but I thought it bordered on creepy.

I downed the rest of my drink and followed Estelle back toward the house. "Woo! Go, Cocks!" I shouted, throwing a fist in the air.

Several hours, several beers, and chilled tequila shots later, I was debating whether or not the next play would be a draw or a slant with Deacon when Eric stepped onto the back patio.

My mood shifted almost immediately. Like someone had dumped cold water on me, startling me back into a reality where my husband no longer wanted me, and I was forced to navigate life as an ex-wife instead of a partner.

"What he really should do is call a pick— hey, what's up?"

Without a word, I stood up and went inside, maneuvering around the group Eric had gathered around him.

"Hey, Sonja? Are you leaving already?" Eric asked, as if he cared.

"Yeah, I've got some things to do. If you see the kids, send them home, okay?" As quickly as I could, I made my way through Estelle's house to the front door.

"Hey, Soni!" Estelle called out just as I grabbed the doorknob. I spun around to face her.

"Why's he here?"

"I don't know. Neither of us invited him. He must have heard about it from Owen or somebody."

"Cool," I said with a nod. "I'm gonna just go home—"

"Do you have to be so childish about this?" Behind Estelle, just inside the living room doorway, stood Eric.

My friend's nostrils flared, and without turning around, she said, "Eric, your assistance is not needed or desired here."

"Neither is your presence, to be honest," I grumbled under my breath.

My ex-husband scoffed. "Is that true? Am I no longer welcome in your home, Estelle?"

The look in his eye… Eric was itching for a fight. This was not something I wanted to inflict on my friend. "You know what, Stelle? I'm just gonna go. I'm tired—"

"Good, I'm gonna follow you," Eric said. "There's a few things we need to talk about anyway."

I opened the door and walked down the sidewalk and across the street to our— my house. It was dark inside. I flipped on the lights as I made my way to the kitchen, where I leaned against the counter and waited for Eric to enter the room and start a conversation that was guaranteed to piss me off.

He came into the room and looked around like he expected something about it to be different, then pulled out a stool and sat on across from me at the breakfast bar. I folded my arms over my chest as he regarded me quietly, and suppressed the urge to question him and just waited. The less I said, the quicker we could get this thing over with.

"So how have you been?" he asked finally.

"Great, actually. You?"

"Good. Well, things could be better. I've been trying to get Nadia to spend time with me, and she seems to be full of excuses. I was wondering if you could talk to her."

I frowned. "She's a teenager, Eric. I can't make her spend time with you. Either she wants to, or she doesn't."

"What do you mean you can't make her? You're her mother. Are you telling her to ignore my texts and phone calls?"

"Eric, I didn't even know you reached out to her."

"Well, she's been using you as an excuse."

"This is the first I've heard of it. I'll talk to her about the lying, but I'm not going to demand that she spend time with you, Eric. She's of age to decide how she wants to spend her time—"

"Goddamnit, Sonja!" Eric exclaimed, slamming his hand on the countertop and startling me. "Why do you have to make this so difficult?"

I took a deep breath and tried to settle my nerves. "I'm making it difficult?"

"Yes. You no longer wanted to be involved in the company and wanted me to buy you out. Fine. But I will not tolerate you creating distance between me and my children."

142

"Eric... I'm not making anything difficult. You asked for a divorce, and I gave you one. *Watts Realty* is your dream. Always has been. The support I provided was to help my husband because your success was my success. That's not the case anymore."

"That's still the case, Sonja. If the company is struggling to make profits this quarter, it's due to this divorce."

I shook my head. "I worked for free—"

"Yes, you did. And now I have to pay someone for your role as well as buy you out. It's creating a strain on our overhead."

"I'm sorry about that, but honestly, it's not my problem. I mean, what do you expect me to do, Eric? And as far as Nadia is concerned...you could be across the street bonding with her instead of sitting at the breakfast bar raging at me."

He scrubbed his hands over his face and sighed. "I'm not raging. I'm just voicing frustration with this situation—"

"The situation you created?" I snapped.

Eric dropped his hands and glared at me. "I thought we agreed that we would do this amicably."

"We didn't agree to shit. You told me you wanted a divorce, and I gave you one."

"This is how you talk now?" he asked, his left eyebrow arched. "Winston told me that you've been spending a lot of evenings away from the house, too. Are you going through some sort of rebellion?"

I shook my head and laughed. "Rebellion. Like I'm a child. You are so desperate to infantilize me--to make me think and feel that I need you. I don't need you, Eric. And I don't have to explain my comings and goings to you either. We're. Not. Married."

"But you're still the mother of my children and if you're negligent—"

"What? Get the fuck out."

Eric's eyes widened. "Who do you think you're talking to?"

"A fucking trespasser. Get the fuck out of my house! You dare accuse me of being a bad mother? When you're sitting here, begging me to repair your relationship with the daughter you neglected? Get the fuck out of my kitchen and out of my house, Eric!"

"Mom!" Winston appeared at the entryway of the kitchen, a stunned look on his face. "Why are you guys arguing? What's going on?"

"Nothing. Your father was just leaving."

"Sonja, I think you're overreacting—"

"Am I?" I asked, glaring at him.

"I only repeated what our son told us."

"Whoa, wait a minute. What are you talking about, Dad?" Winston said, holding up both hands in a palms out, vulnerable position.

"You told me that your mother has been spending a lot of evenings away from home."

"Yeah...working on her apothecary business," Winston clarified. "You asked me how she was doing. Like if she was sad and crying or whatever. I told you that she didn't seem sad, and she was keeping busy."

The smile that tugged at the corners of my mouth was one of deep satisfaction. "Oh, really? Thank you for clearing that up, Winston."

"Dad...it's not cool for you to ask me about mom as if you're concerned and then use what I tell you to like, antagonize her. And I don't appreciate you pulling me into the middle of this. I think Mom's right. Maybe you should go."

My heart about burst with pride. I've always encouraged my children to be communicative. To tell us how they feel when they feel it in a respectful way instead of holding it in. It did my heart proud to see my son, who wasn't a big conversationalist, use that tool in a moment where keeping quiet would have been easier. I crossed the kitchen to where Winston stood and placed a hand over his heart. Now that I was close to him, I could see that he was working to keep his emotions in check. *My poor baby.*

"Good job, son," I said quietly. "I think our boy is right, Eric. You should definitely go." And without even a backward glance, I grabbed a bottle of wine out of the fridge and went out back to sit in my herb garden.

chapter fourteen
Sonja

Dusk turned into dark. Cicadas sang in the trees, lightning bugs winked, and I drank my wine while breathing in the sweet scent of lemongrass, lavender, and rosemary. Usually sitting in my garden calmed me, but I just couldn't get my head right after that conversation with Eric.

I quickly abandoned the glass and drank my wine right out of the bottle because I might have been angry when Eric antagonized me, but now I felt…hollowed out. Sad to the point of emptiness. My marriage was done, and there was nothing I could do about it. This wasn't something I could fix for my kids, and that was torturing me. I wanted to cry about it, but the tears wouldn't come.

I didn't know how long I sat out there before my son came out to check on me. "Hey, honey," I said, sitting up straighter, hoping that I didn't look or sound too drunk. "What's up?"

"Nadia just came in. I wanted to let you know she was home."

"Okay," I said with a nod and a smile. Nadia had announced her arrival the moment she came home. I knew my son enough to know that this was just an excuse to come out and talk to me. "How are you after all of that? Are you okay—"

"I'm fine. I just…" He shoved his hands into the pockets of his sweatpants and looked around. Looked anywhere but at me. "I just wanted you to know that I would've never told Dad all of that stuff if I knew he was going to twist my words."

"I know that, honey."

He nodded. "Okay. I just wanted to make sure." He darted in and gave me a kiss on the cheek. "Good night, mom. I love you."

"I love you, too."

Nadia came out and said goodnight before she went up to bed, but still, I lingered on my lounge chair in the garden, trying to sort out my feelings. Why was I wallowing in this? Why couldn't I shake it off?

Then, as if the universe sensed the void in me, my phone rang. Before I even picked it up, I knew it was Atlas. I flipped the phone over and answered the call.

"Hey!" I said as cheerily as I could manage. "Did I send up a bat signal or something?"

His deep, dark chuckle vibrated through the phone's speakers, and my frayed nerves smoothed. "Is that your way of saying that you need me?" he asked.

"Maybe… maybe I just want to be rescued."

"Hmmm, rough day?"

"Kinda. It didn't start out that way, though."

"Okay, tell me the good bits."

I recounted my day of drinking and carousing with my neighbors and good friends. As I told him about Owen's bratwurst, Estelle's heavy pour mixed drinks, and the many rounds of corn hole, I realized how much I counted on my neighbors for built-in fun. Maybe that was why Eric showed up today. He honestly had no place else to go.

"Earle Street sounds like an awesome place to live."

"It is. It would really suck if we had to move."

"Hey... don't start thinking that way. Your business will be a success if I have anything to say about it."

"You can't make those kind of guarantees," I said quietly.

Atlas sighed. "You haven't talked like this in a while, sweetheart. What's going on? You can tell me."

But I didn't want to tell him. Eric had already taken up too much space in something that was supposed to be fun, carefree, and sexy, but goddamit...

"My ex showed up at the Game Day Party. Estelle says she didn't invite him, and I believe her, but the moment he came in the door, I knew that he was there to start an argument. I tried to leave, but he followed me and..."

"And what?"

"He accused me of sabotaging his relationship with the kids, when in reality, they never had much of one. We spent time together as a family, but he never really wanted to do anything with either of them individually."

"Okay, so you're not sabotaging the relationship between them. It's not even close to true. You know it, and he knows it. I can't even see you doing something like that."

"Yeah, but then he hit me with the two-piece and a biscuit." I laughed mirthlessly. "And honestly, I knew it was bait. I knew he was winding me up, but when he said it, I couldn't help but get defensive."

"What did he say, Sonja?" Atlas asked.

"He..." I paused and cleared my throat. "Apparently he's been talking to our son Winston on a pretty regular basis. He's been framing it as if he was concerned about me and how I'm dealing with the divorce, but Winston told him I was doing fine. That I was out most evenings and keeping busy with all of the business stuff. But when Eric mentioned it to me, he made it sound like my son was upset or worried about my absence."

"Oh, my god. This fucking guy—"

"And then he accused me of being a negligent mother."

"Shit, Sonja."

"But that's not the worst part!" I laughed again because suddenly this all seemed so tragically funny. "I got pissed off, right? Raised my voice for the first time ever and told him to get the fuck out of my house—"

"You said it just like that? Get the fuck out?"

"Yes."

"Good girl. You have every right to stand up for yourself. It's your house, and you don't have to take that kind of abuse under your own roof."

"I know, and I believe that. But then, Winston came downstairs. He overheard us fighting, and then he was forced to confront his dad about the lie. See… Winston only told him because he thought it was genuine concern for me. And at that moment, he saw his father for who he really is, and my heart broke for him."

Ugh. That was it. That's the feeling that I was trying to tease out all night. It was one thing for my fantasy of the perfect husband and perfect marriage to be crushed. It was another thing entirely to see Winston come to that same realization about his father.

"How did your son take that? Is he okay?" Atlas asked quietly.

"I can't really tell. Boys, you know?" I moped up my tears with the hem of my USC t-shirt. "My daughter will rage and cry and get it all out. But Winston…? Boys just don't share their feelings with their mothers. That's what fathers are for.

That's what they do. Now I'm afraid that neither of us will be able to really know how he feels."

"Hm," Atlas hummed thoughtfully. "I'm so sorry you're going through this, Sonja. I wish I were there with you."

"Me, too." But just him saying that felt like a hug. He was quiet while I cried, and that silence didn't feel uncomfortable. Slowly the sobs tapered off, and he cleared his throat.

"Listen, I know this might sound like I'm speaking out of turn. But you're not a negligent mother, Sonja. You love your kids. This is just a tough time, and you're trying to take care of everything, and that's a difficult adjustment. Give yourself some grace, sweetheart."

"Well, now I'm going to start crying again because that was ridiculously sweet. I'm a horrible mess, and you deserve to be something more than a dumping ground for all of my fucked up feelings."

He laughed. "It's okay. I've got broad shoulders for you to cry on. My name is Atlas, remember?"

I laughed snottily and wiped my nose again. "Thank you for letting me figuratively cry on your broad shoulders."

"They're available for you anytime. Literally or figuratively."

"You may regret that."

"Sonja, I don't anticipate regretting anything about being with you."

"With me?" I asked breathily because those two words felt more weighty than they should.

"With you," he repeated more firmly.

"Even if I can't be that for you because I have nothing left to give?"

"I already told you, spending more time with you is a win-win for me. Talking to you and knowing that you trust me with

150

your fucked up feelings is more than I expected to get from this conversation. I just wish I could hold you right now and figure out a way to make this easier for you."

I made a noncommittal sound of agreement because what does it even mean to know there was a man out there in the world that wanted to heal my hurts and fix things that he didn't break? "I'm feeling a lot better, so that'll do for now," I said finally.

"Good."

I sighed, then stood up and stretched. "I should probably go inside."

"You were sitting in your garden?"

"Yeah, it's where I always go when I need to be alone with my thoughts and feelings."

"It's good that you have that. I'd like to see a picture of it so that I can imagine you there next time."

"Hm. Okay."

"Yeah, you sound tired. I'll let you go."

"Okay, but hey, why did you call me?"

"No reason. I just wanted to hear your voice, is all. I was sitting at my computer working —or trying to because I couldn't stop thinking about you. So I decided to call because I wanted to talk to my little blues singer."

"Did you get your fill?"

He huffed. "Not really, but it will do for the night."

I laughed. "Good night, Atlas." The moment I hung up, a deep ache filled my chest. I wanted him here. I wanted to know what it was like to find comfort in his arms.

chapter fifteen
Atlas

A brisk wind rustled the dead autumn leaves as I peddled toward my mother's house. I was wearing a skull cap and a hoodie and my down vest, but I still felt the bite of it through my clothes. It was probably time for me to put the bike away and start driving again, but I wasn't quite ready for that.

I was meeting Mr. Bailey to discuss what needed to be done before terminating services until the next season. There wasn't much to do, but my mother had asked me to be around to supervise, and I had a few hours until tonight's class, so I didn't see any harm in it.

Bill and my mom knew each other from high school or church — I could never remember which. My mom had a thing about employing people from the church and the neighborhood, which I supported one hundred percent. Plus, I just liked Bill. He was an affable dude that was always super polite and gentlemanly with my mom. I heard her when she said she felt like he was too familiar, I'd never witnessed any disrespect from him. Nor did he strike me as the kind of man who would cross that boundary with mother.

As I coasted down the slight decline to my mother's house at the bottom of the cul-de-sac. I saw my mother and Bill standing at the edge of the yard with their backs to the street. My mother had her hands on her hips as Bill gestured toward the flower beds with one hand while he kept the one nearest her in his pocket. They looked like a couple. I would be lying if I said the sight wasn't endearing. And as a kid who grew up with a nearly non-existent father and never seeing my mother with another man, I wondered how my life would have been if the two had got together.

"Hey, mama!" I leaned in and kissed her cheek.

"Hey, baby! You rode your bicycle in this weather? Ain't you cold?"

I shook my head, smiling at her concern. "It ain't so cold once your blood gets pumping. What's up, Mr. Bailey?"

The man shook hands with me and then gave my mother a sidelong glance. "Your mother was just reading me the riot act. She seems to think I trimmed the azalea bushes —"

"I told her you didn't," I said, shaking my head.

"So explain why they're not flowering the way they should. This is the worst my azaleas have ever looked."

Mr. Bailey and I spent the next hour explaining what was going on with Mama's azaleas. It had been a very dry summer. Azaleas needed at least an inch of rain per week during their growing season, and since my mother never allowed me to put in the irrigation system, they didn't get the water they needed. Also, the tree in the front yard had grown so large that it was probably throwing too much shade for the usually hardy bushes.

Mama went inside, and me and Mr. Bailey aerated the lawn and laid down some fertilizer before she called us in for dinner. Chicken and gravy, rice, red beans, cornbread, and cabbage. Mine and Mr. Bailey's elbows were firmly planted on the kitchen table for twenty quiet minutes.

"Mmm," Mr. Bailey grunted. "That was delicious, Eileen James. My word. It's been a month of Sundays since I had a meal that good."

153

"Well," my mother said, a turned down smile on her lips. "Maybe if you kept the sabbath holy and showed up for a service every now and again, there wouldn't be so much time between those good home-cooked dinners."

I flinched at the barb, but Mr. Bailey just nodded and took it in stride.

"You might be right about that," he said in a quiet voice as he pushed away from the table. "But nevertheless, I deeply appreciate this home-cooked meal, Ms. Eileen James."

My mother was at the sink with her back to us. "Well, thank you for coming by."

Mr. Bailey gripped my shoulder as he passed. "Good to see you, son."

"Same to you, Mr. Bailey. I'll be in touch to schedule a time to trim back the bushes and discuss moving the azalea's next season."

"All right," he said with a grunt. "You have a wonderful evening."

"Mmmhmm."

I waited until I heard Mr. Bailey's old diesel engine pickup crank to life and backed out of the driveway before I said anything to my mother. 'Why do you feel the need to belittle Mr. Bailey so much?" I asked.

"Excuse me?" my mother said, glancing over her shoulder at me.

I sighed, already regretting the decision to start this conversation. "I just mean that he was thanking you for a home-cooked meal. Why did you feel the need to come at him about church?"

"I wasn't *coming at him*, as you say. I was simply pointing out that if he attended church more, he would be welcomed to this table more often."

I clenched my jaw, stood up, and pushed my chair in quietly. "Mama?"

"Yes, son?" she said, turning toward me.

"Mr. Bailey was the first and only man who took me under his wing and taught me how to hustle a dollar from nothing. How to take care of you and be the man of this house when the man you call my father never did—"

"I won't have you disrespecting your father in this house."

"How can disrespect a father I don't have?"

She didn't respond but stared at me for a long moment before she turned to the sink to finish washing the dishes.

Realizing that this battle was lost, I kissed her on the cheek and left.

* * * *

After a quick trip home to shower, I was back at *The Coworking Spot* setting up for class. Negative thoughts and emotions still plagued me from the conversation with my mother, but knowing that I would see Soni made me giddy with anticipation. We hadn't talked since that late-night convo, but that conversation felt like a breakthrough. I felt it. I hoped she felt it, too.

I cued up my PowerPoint presentation. Set out extra printouts of today's lesson, then went back into the office that Kairo and I shared to read and answer some emails until class started.

Students came in and settled at the community table, but I decided that I wasn't going to move until I heard Soni's voice.

I was deep into my work with Chloe appeared at the office door with a hesitant smile on her face. "Hey, Atlas. I hate to interrupt, but you're already about ten minutes late for the start of class."

"Really?" I glanced at the clock in the corner of my desktop. "My bad, Chloe. Let me save all of this, and I'll be right out."

My brain was still scattered, so I dipped into the bathroom to splash water on my face before I went out to greet my students.

Sonja wasn't among them.

What the fuck?

I checked my phone to see if I'd missed a call from her, but I hadn't missed any calls or text messages. I sent her a quick one to check in then shoved my phone in my back pocket.

"Hey, y'all. I got a bit distracted while responding to emails. Life of an entrepreneur," I said as I made my way over to my laptop to start up the slide deck for today's lesson. "So what have you all been up to since the last time we saw each other? Tina," I said, singling out a woman who often chatted with Sonja during class.

I got myself situated as she told me about her progress since last week but only halfway listening.

We hadn't spoken since that last vulnerable phone call, and I probably should have called her. I thought about it, but everything I wanted to say was 'me' focused, and she was already going through so much that I didn't want to be another thing she had to deal with. Was that the right decision?

"Thanks, Tina. It sounds like you made some good progress this week. That's great..." I glanced up at the empty stairwell. "All right, we should probably get started."

The front door alarm chirped, signaling that some had just come in. I resisted the urge to look toward the top of the stairwell again and instead started the PowerPoint presentation. But in my peripheral vision, I saw Sonni come down the steps, trying her best to be quiet. She grabbed the seat closet to the steps, and everyone's attention shifted toward her.

"Sorry, I'm late," she said, finally then dumped her course materials on the table. She seemed flushed and stressed.

"No worries! Glad you could join us." I caught her gaze and arched a questioning brow at her, wondering if she was all right. She nodded, and relief washed over me.

Good.

"Tonight we're going to cover branding," I said.

"Yasss!" Ashley cheered with a body roll. "Finally! My area of expertise!"

I rolled my eyes and folded my arms across my chest. "Yes, Ashely. Graphic design does have a lot to do with how your brand is perceived. However, branding is much more than cute logos and clever font choices," I said with a wink.

"Of course, I just—"

"A brand by definition is a name, term, design, symbol, or any other feature that identifies one seller's goods or services from another's," I interrupted. "Branding goes much deeper than that and precedes any font, color, or log discussions."

Ashely shrank into her chair and opened her corse binder.

It wasn't my intention to call her out, but she'd spent her time in this class checking me and everyone else down. Well, actually-ing every one of my lessons and the shit irritated the fuck out of me. I guess I'd just reached my threshold for her particular brand of fuckery today.

Not to mention the fact that she often went after Sonja. Demeaning her business idea and just making snide remarks. Putting her place was almost necessary at this point.

After I finished the lesson, I suggested they pair off to complete the branding worksheet. Tina and Soni paired off, which isn't who I would have wanted her to work with but whatever. Soni's habit of assuming she didn't know the information and needed to work with someone who did was slightly annoying. She was too smart and creative to second guess herself like that, but I had to let it ride.

Everyone was hard at work as I walked around the room to see if any of them needed any help. It was important to make sure that I gave each of them equal attention even if my eyes were drawn to Sonja more than once. Sonja was hunched over her laptop, with her tongue tucked into the corner of her mouth and reading glasses firmly in place. It was her adorable concentration face, and it made me want to kiss her.

"How are things going over here?" I asked, leaning into the space between her and Tina. The two were collaborating on the worksheet I'd assigned.

"Yeah," Tina volunteered. "Sonja is helping me with mine."

I plucked Soni'a worksheet from where she'd tucked it under her computer. I did a quick scan of her worksheet with one hand on the back of her chair. Her neck flushed, and I knew it was because I was standing so close to her. It took all of my willpower not to bend down and press my lips to the nape of her neck.

"This is good," I said though I'd barely glanced at it.

When I leaned in, I saw that the blush had spread over her cheeks and down her neck. Maybe this wasn't about me. "Are you okay?" I asked. "You look a little flushed." I placed a hand on the back of her neck, and her skin felt hot to the touch. A little shiver rippled through her, and her breath quickened.

158

"Yeah, I'm fine. I'm just suddenly very warm." She cut a look at me, irritated but clearly turned on. Seemed I was right the first time, and the thought of that made me want to pound my chest. It also made me think about our day trip to the mountains and making her come in a warm greenhouse.

"Do you need some water? I can get you a bottle of water," I volunteered.

"Hot flash?" Tina asked.

"Excuse me?" Soni blinked at the woman as if she were trying to make sense of what she said.

"My good friend Dana is perimenopausal, and she has hot flashes like that all the time. She uses natural herbs to combat it. Would you like me to send her a text and ask her what she uses?"

Soni's top lip curled with disgust. "I'm not perimenopausal, but if I were, I'm an herbalist...pretty sure I can figure out which herbs to use on my own."

Tina's cheeks flushed bright red. If I weren't standing next to her, I wouldn't have believed my sweet she was capable of that kind of venom. It was about time she stood up for herself.

"Oh...right," Tina said.

"Excuse me," Soni pushed away from the table and went to the bathroom.

When she disappeared down the hall, I went upstairs to grab her a bottle of water. In the quiet of the small break room kitchen, I took a moment to catch my breath.

"I am not an adolescent. This is not okay." I muttered to myself, then grabbed a bottle of water out of the fridge — downed it — then grabbled another for Sonni, who was just coming out of the bathroom when I made it back downstairs.

"Here you go. Drink up."

"Jesus... I'm fine," she said with an awkward smile.

159

"You didn't see yourself. You looked faint."

She looked up at me, a glint of knowing in her eyes. "What about you? Are you okay?" she asked in a voice so soft and intimate that all of the fine hairs rose on my body. She brought the bottle to her lips and took a few deep swallows, then wiped her mouth with the back of her hand.

Her mouth... those lips wrapped around my—

I clenched my teeth. "I'm fine."

"Thank you," she said as she screwed the cap back on. "That did help."

"Good. Can't have you passing out on me," I said with a wink.

Not unless it's from me giving you too many orgasms...

"Let's go around the room and share your answers to some of these branding questions, shall we?"

Ashley's hand shot up immediately, and I ground my teeth to bite back a nonverbal sound of annoyance. A huff or a tsk must've sneaked out because Sonja narrowed her eyes at me. I rolled my eyes in response and called on the ever eager Ashley.

After class, Heather and Ashely demonstrated their eagerness even further by trying to entice me into going next door for drinks. These two were fucking relentless.

"You ghosted us last time. What's up with that?" Ashley asked.

"I remembered that I had a prior engagement. You know how this," I said with a shrug.

"Yeah, right. Is that the excuse you're going to use tonight, too?" Heather asked with a raise of her brow.

"Nah, I just have somewhere else I gotta be," I said, giving her a surreptitious glance that neither Heather or Ashley noticed. But Sonja sure as hell did.

She rolled her eyes and disappeared into the bathroom again.

"Listen, ladies. It's just not gonna happen tonight."

Or any night. Just leave me the fuck alone.

"Fine..." Ashley said, but her tone said that it was absolutely not fine.

"See you on Monday," I said as they made their way up the stairs. They both waved, and I heard Chloe tell them goodbye and lock the door behind them.

Taking a deep breath, I made my way to the short hallway that led to the bathrooms. Sonja was still in there, so I leaned against the wall and waited for her.

Soni felt all that earlier. That electric want standing near her made me feel. Goddamn, I couldn't stop thinking of that day in the greenhouse, and the way she felt in my hands-- so soft and wet. She wanted it— wanted me.

Right?

I swear that I've never felt this unsure of a woman in my life.

The toilet flushed, the sink water ran, and Soni came out of the bathroom. The moment she set eyes on me, she started to giggle.

"What's so funny?" I asked, pushing away from the wall and blocking the short hallway.

"Nothing... you just look like some kind of 80s teen movie idol trying his best to look relaxed and sexy while leaning on that wall."

I laughed at that mental image. I may not have been trying out relaxed and sexy poses, but I was obsessing over whether or not she wanted me, so that tracked.

"Are you gonna go have drinks with your fan club?"

"Why would I do that when I plan to have drinks with you?"

She shook her head. "I can't go out for drinks tonight. You should just hang out with Ashley and Heather. They're obviously into you."

I frowned. "Did I miss something?"

It was dark back here, but I could still make out the subtle shift of her features. The wariness in her eyes.

"No..I just can't go out for drinks after every class. You shouldn't miss out on a good time because of me."

"What are you even...? A good time? I'm not interested in any sort of time with those girls, Soni. I want to spend time with you." I stepped closer. Close enough to smell the citrus of her Clarity Cremé.

"I've already been spending too much time away from home—"

"So I'll come to your place," I said with a shrug. "We can have drinks in your garden."

A laugh sputtered out of Sonja. "Are you crazy? My kids—"

"I'll come over after they've gone to bed."

She gave me a sardonic look. "They're teenagers, not toddlers, Atlas."

"I'm aware, Sonja. And even teenagers fall asleep by a certain time. So what time should I come over?"

She arched an eyebrow at me and was quiet for a long contemplative moment. "We can't do anything," she said finally.

I bit my lip, trying to hold in my smile. "I wasn't even thinking of doing anything but talking."

"Yeah, right. That filthy smile on your face is making a liar out of you."

"I wasn't. I assumed that sex was off the table when you said your kids were home."

"God," she whispered, covering her face with her hands. "You make me feel like such a pervert."

I laughed and leaned in closer, nuzzled her nose with mine. "Pervert, huh? I'd like to hear more of these perverted thoughts." I pressed a kiss to the corner of her smiling mouth. "What time should I come over, huh?"

"Twelve thirty? Is that too late?"

"It's right on time."

"Okay, then! Let me go home and get things ready."

She tried to pull away, but I slipped an arm around her waist and held her against me.

"Atlas…" she sighed.

"Last night? After we got off the phone? I wished so hard that you were in my bed." I dragged my nose down the line of her neck and nibbled at the place it met her shoulder. She purred and wiggled against me.

"Me, too," she said with a giggle.

Yeah, I'm a liar. I wanted this woman, and there was no way I was going to be able to keep my hands off of her.

"Oh!" a familiar voice squawked. "So, this is why you decided not to join us."

Both Sonja and I froze.

No, this isn't happening.

I closed my eyes and turned toward the doorway. When I opened them again, I saw Heather standing at the end of the table, glaring at us with wide eyes.

"Oh, god," Soni muttered.

"Can I help you with something?" I asked. One of my arms was still around her waist. I felt her wanting to pull away, but I held her close.

"I forgot my charger for my laptop," she snapped.

Heather seethed quietly as she unplugged the charge cord and wound it up. Without a second glance, she stuffed it in her bag and turned to leave. Each of her steps sounded as if she were trying to pound her heels thrown the concrete floors. We were both quiet until we heard the door slam, announcing her exit.

"Sorry, you guys!" Chloe called.

"Yikes!" Soni said, cringing.

"Yeah, it looks like the cat's out of the bag," I said with a chuckle.

She shouldered her bag. "Well…if you had any hopes of tapping that, she's no longer interested now that she's caught you with the old lady.

Again with this old lady business. I grabbed the waistband of her jeans and dragged her close to me again. "You are not old. And I'm glad she caught us. Now I can stop trying to find ways to let her down easy."

"Yeah, well, I'm glad, too. I was getting really fucking irritated by their syrupy invitations for drinks. Haven't they ever heard the word no? It's a complete sentence — what?"

My amusement must have shown on my face. "You were jealous, huh?"

"Jealous? Why would I be jealous of those two?"

"Not jealous of them. Jealous that they wanted my attention and that I might deign to give them what they wanted," I clarified with a grin.

"You should've been clear about your disinterest."

"Hm. Maybe you're right. I'll make sure I do that from now on."

"You better," she whispered as she slanted her mouth over mine.

I tried not to get too into it. I tried to let the kiss be sweet and sensual, but the moment her tongue slipped into my mouth. I pulled her right up against me. Deepened the kiss. Made it needier, and hungrier, until I had to pull away with more than a little force.

"So when you say we can't do anything… what does that mean, exactly?" I asked.

chapter sixteen

Sonja

In the tub, soaking in fragrant rose water, and furiously shaving my legs, I realized that I fully intended to do any and everything Atlas wanted. I'd already spent too many nights dreaming about how it would be. How he would hold me, how he would touch me and if he was as gifted with his tongue and his dick as he was with his fingers. I wanted to find out. And my body was going to be smooth and sweet-scented in preparation for it.

The alarm on my cell dinged to let me know that in exactly thirty minutes, Atlas would be at my door. Yanking the plug from the drain, I stood and grabbed a towel to pat my skin dry.

"Am I really doing this?"

The pink candles bathed in rose oil strategically placed in my side garden said yes. The body oil I applied to my still damp skin that was my own version of mama's come-to-me oil said hell yes.

The sweet floral scent of roses, jasmine, and honey filled my senses as I smoothed it on, paying special attention to the places where I wanted his hands.

Again the oil worked it's spell on me, smoothing away my nerves and making me feel more sensual and sexy than I had in months—maybe years. And that was more than enough reason to follow through with this clumsy seduction.

In my bedroom, I pulled on a dress that I loved but had deemed too indecent to wear beyond the back garden. It had a shelf bra, but the spaghetti straps had lost some of their elasticity and now revealed more cleavage than I was comfortable showing in public. However, it was perfect for lounging in my garden or snipping bundles of herbs before my neighbors woke up enough to be nosey. And I liked the way the soft, brushed cotton fabric felt against my skin. I liked it so much I didn't bother putting anything on underneath. I did pull on one of my favorite silk robes, though. The one that was covered in tropical flowers and made me feel like Blanche Devereaux.

Winston and Nadia were fast asleep with their televisions on when I checked on them earlier. It wasn't something I usually allowed, but with Atlas coming over, I figured a little added white noise might be a good thing. I didn't feel great about sneaking around, but it seemed smarter than introducing them to what might only amount to a fling.

Out in the garden, I lit the candles. The night was still holding on to a little of the day's warmth, perfect for sitting out here and chatting. The little deck in the midst of my flowering and fragrant herbs was bathed in a warm and inviting light when Atlas's text came through. My heart slammed against my chest, and I had to physically keep myself from tripping over my own feet to get to the door as fast as I could. As if making him wait, even one minute, would make him change his mind.

I made my way through the house, glancing at each individual room to make sure nothing was out of place. Excitement thrummed through me as I grabbed the doorknob and yanked open the door.

"Hey!" My voice sounded shaky and girlishly high, and I would have been embarrassed if Atlas didn't greet me with a

167

nervous-cited smile of his own. Like me, he'd gone home to change into something more comfortable and was now wearing grey sweats and tee with USC Upstate emblazoned across his chest.

"Hey," he said softly. His eyes dragged down my frame and back up again to settle on my breasts. I cleared my throat, and his eyes found mine again.

I stepped aside and opened the door a little wider. "Come in!"

"This is a nice neighborhood," he said.

"Thanks! We like it."

Atlas stepped across the threshold and into my foyer. Broad-shouldered and smelling scrubbed clean, his eyes darted around, taking everything in. "Wow! This is like... a real grown-up house."

I looked around and tried to see things the way he saw them. The gleaming hardwood floors and the haint blue walls and ceiling of the foyer that welcomed guests to move deeper into the cozy cocoon of my living room and the kitchen beyond it. "Yeah, I guess it is," I agreed.

"I brought a bottle of rum. I know you're supposed to bring wine when you visit someone. You know, so you don't come in empty-handed? The article recommended wine, but I've never seen you drink wine so. This rum is from the Virgin Islands. I hope it's okay?"

I laughed at his nervous rambling. "It's okay. This is weird, isn't it?"

Atlas turned toward me, eyes cast down, body bowing toward me with obvious restraint. "Yes," he said. "It's a little weird for me."

"I knew it would be." I held out my hand. "Come with me."

He took my hand, and I proceeded to lead him through the foyer, the kitchen, and out the back door. The flickering candlelight was just bright enough for me to see the wonder on his face as we navigated the pavers from the door to my side garden.

"Is this better?" I asked.

"Oh, wow. Yes," he breathed, squeezing my hand a little tighter. "So much better." His fingers slipped from mine, and he walked ahead of me, eyes wide and wondering, taking everything in. "So, this is your magical garden?"

"Yes, it is," I said proudly. "Please, have a seat. Get comfortable. I'll go grab some glasses. Do you want ice? Coke or juice to make a cocktail?"

"Nah, it's spiced rum. We can drink it neat."

"Okay, I'll be right back."

I dashed back inside to grab a couple of glasses. Before I went back out, I stopped at the stairs to listen for any sound from the kid's rooms. The faint murmur of their televisions told me that they were probably still sleeping, but I closed the side door behind me just to be sure.

Outside, I found Atlas sniffing the night jasmine and the bright orange marigolds that had really started showing off in the last few weeks.

He looked up as I approached and gave me a smile. "Your garden is beautiful, Sonja. Is all of this stuff medicinal?"

"Yes," I said, handing him his drink. "That one you were just sniffing is a natural anti-inflammatory. I use it often in teas and tinctures." I gestured toward the coach inviting him to sit.

"How do you remember all of this stuff?"

"Some of its just repetition. I've been helping my mother tend her garden and make remedies since I was a kid. I also have a notebook full of recipes handed down from my grandmothers and a few that I've created on my own."

"Like the come-to-me oil you wore on our first date?" he asked with a grin.

My cheeks heated with embarrassment. "That wasn't a date, and that was my mother's recipe. It was a bit heavy-handed. Tonight I'm wearing the one I made."

"So how does this work? I just take a deep sniff of you, and I will be overcome with the desire to ravish you?"

I laughed. "Yes... but only if that's what you want to do."

Slowly, cautiously, Atlas leaned in and buried his face in the curve of my neck. His breath tickled against my skin as he filled his lungs with the scent of me and kissed the round of my shoulder.

"And how does your mother's recipe work?" he asked.

"Most of the herbs she chose to use only inspired lust."

"And that's not what you want?" he asked, pulling away, but just enough to see my face and so I could see his.

"No...not *just* lust." My mouth went dry. I took a big gulp of rum. The spices made my lips tingle and burned the back of my throat. Atlas mirrored my actions then dropped his other arm along the back of the couch.

"So what is it that you want, Soni? How does your love charm work?"

I licked my lips, and his eyes tracked the path of my tongue. "Well, for starters, my charm works on the wearer just as much as it works on the object of her desire. It lowers her inhibitions and helps her tap into her sensuality. It's more about her embracing her sexuality than influencing someone else's feelings or emotions about her."

170

"Interesting. The intention is different, but the result is ultimately the same, right? The wearer makes the object of her charm fall in love with her?"

"Yes, but only if he's halfway there himself."

"Hm," he hummed as he took another sip of his rum, his dark eyes on me the entire time. "Seeing you here is really eye-opening."

"Oh? Even more than at the greenhouse?" I asked with a laugh.

"I mean, the greenhouse was eye-opening in lots of ways, but this is like a secret peek at the real you in your natural habitat. Like some barely tamed little thing caught in candlelight."

I laughed at that, envisioning myself as some sort of wood nymph or fairy that felt more at home in my garden than I did inside. It wasn't far from the truth.

Atlas trailed his fingers along the nape of my neck and around the edge of my cleavage. My skin lit with goosebumps, and he leaned in to kiss the hollow of my throat. The wet tip of his tongue lapped at the place where I'd generously applied my love charm.

"I think about you in the greenhouse all the time," he murmured. "But now, my fantasies are probably going to feature you in this garden."

"I'm in your fantasies?"

"Aren't I in yours?"

"Of course, you are. Look at you," I say with a laugh, gesturing at his gorgeous personage.

"I'll take the compliment," he said with a grin. "But it really pains me that you don't see yourself the way I see you."

"How do you see me?"

Instead of answering, he pressed soft lips to mine. The hand on the back of the couch cupped my neck and pulled me closer. He nipped and lapped at my lips until I had no choice but to open for him. His mouth tasted sweet and hot, flavored by the spiced rum. I savored the taste. Sucked it from his tongue and lips.

Atlas pulled away for a moment to take our glasses and set them on the table before pulling me into his lap. Facing him, straddling his strong thighs, I cupped his bearded jaw in both of my hands and brought his mouth to mine. His hands settled on my hips, thumbs stroking at my splayed hipbones through the soft cotton. Just that simple touch made me crave him even more.

God...I've never wanted a man like this.

Never wanted someone so much that I felt like I was coming out of my skin. Atlas pushed my dress up my thighs. I gasped as the night air found the moisture between my legs. I watched his face as his hands slid higher to find me wet and bare under my dress.

"Shit, Soni," he whispered. "Do I deserve this?"

I pulled away so I could look him in the eye. Desire painted his features darker and sharper. Hungrier. That hunger was for me, and it made me feel like a wanton passionate thing. A thing meant to be worshipped in the way I saw in his eyes.

"Yes," I whispered back. "You deserve it, and I do, too."

He leaned back, resting his head on the back of the couch so that he could look at me. With a touch so soft that it made me quiver with anticipation, he hooked a single finger into the strap my dress and tugged it down until one breast was exposed. A tiny crinkle formed between his brows as he cupped it then dragged his thumb over my peaked nipple. I

172

arched into his touch, and my hips tipped, positioning the hard length I felt in his sweats against my pussy. Atlas watched me quietly, like he was learning me, cataloging all the ways I reacted to his touch.

"You're a fucking goddess, Soni." The hand on my breast slid upward to grasp my neck, and he pulled me in for another kiss. The hand resting on my hip slid around to palm and grip my ass, kneading the flesh greedily. His tongue, hot and thick, thrust into my mouth. Both of his hands were on my ass now, and the way he lifted and parted my cheeks made me roll my hips and grind my pussy against the thick length in his pants.

"Atlas, please," I begged. The desperate sound of my voice surprised me.

"Shhhh," he quieted, then circled my waist with one arm. "I'm gonna take care of you. I promise."

With careful precision, he stood, carrying me with him, and then turned to place me on the nearby chaise on my back. I scooted backward until I was bolstered on the pillows. Atlas stood over me and looked at me with lust hooded eyes.

"How nosy are your neighbors?" he asked.

"They're an elderly couple who are usually in bed fast asleep by seven every night. And there are no windows on this side of the house so they won't hear us if we make any noise."

Atlas's lip parted in a wolfish grin. "Oh, we're definitely gonna make some noise," he said as he pulled his shirt up and over his head.

Another gasp slipped from me at the sight of him. He was all hard lean muscle that rippled as he tugged at the drawstring of his sweats—loosening them but not pulling them down. Making just enough room for him to reach a hand inside.

"Pull up your dress and open your legs for me, Soni."

173

Pushing aside any shyness or apprehension that attempted to surface at his request, I lifted my hips, pulled the length of my dress up around them, and let my thighs fall apart.

Atlas licked his lips and gripped his dick hard enough to make the muscles in his forearm flex. "Wider, baby. Show me everything."

I took a deep breath, and on the exhale, I opened my hips and felt my pussy open with them. A deep moan rumbled out of Atlas's chest, and he dropped to his knees at the foot of the chaise and licked my pussy with a broad, flat tongue.

"Oh, god," I moaned in disbelief. Had this always felt this good? Just that one lick had me on the brink of orgasm.

Atlas wedged himself between my legs, spreading them wider with his broad shoulders and cradled my ass in his hands. He parted my pussy with his thumbs and looked up at me. "I want you to let me know what feels good," he said. His warm breath played over my exposed clit, and a ripple of pleasure made me clench deep inside. "Okay?"

"Okay," I panted.

"Mm…you're so wet, Soni," he whispered, eyes sinking closed as he lapped at my opening, the tip of his tongue slipped inside just the tiniest bit. "And you taste so good."

His lips closed over my clit, and he sealed his mouth to my pussy. He licked and sucked me, and I swear, my eyes rolled back in my head. This felt more than good. It felt decadent. The stroke of his tongue across my clit was so perfect and precise that it felt like this wasn't the first time he'd ever kissed my pussy. Like he'd always known exactly how much pressure to apply with his tongue, how to suck on that little bundle of nerves just right. So right that my hips rolled under his mouth and when he raked the edge of his teeth across that nub, a bright, quick, delicious climax rushed through me, surprising me and him.

"Jesus," I moaned and tried to catch my breath.

Atlas chuckled. "So you like it when I use my teeth. We have that in common. Noted."

"Yes…your teeth, your tongue…everything you did down there was amazing.

"Good…" he shifted his weight on to his forearms and covered my inner thighs with soft, wet kisses. I cupped the crown of his head in my hand, and he looked up at me. "Come here."

Atlas shook his head. "Not yet."

"Not yet?"

He shook his head and smiled. "I think I can make you come one more time."

Stunned, I watched Atlas reposition himself between my thighs. He blew on my heated flesh. I flinched, and he hooked my knee over his shoulder. I wanted to tell him that it wasn't going to happen. That there was no way I would come again, I was too sensitive, but I didn't need to say a damn thing because he slid two thick fingers deep inside of me and covered my clit with his mouth again. It felt so good that I let out a quick surprised shout. I swear I felt the corners of his mouth twitch into a smile against my pussy as he dipped his fingers deeper. Forcing those still tense muscles to soften and relax.

"Oh…shit…how?" I whispered as he sucked harder, using his teeth and tongue, instinctively knowing that I needed more pressure on those overstimulated nerve endings. The pads of his index and middle fingers worked my spot, and my pussy gripped them, the pleasure a faint promise of the second orgasm he was going to pull from my body. I rode his hand, trying to tip myself over the edge, but it wasn't enough, so I begged.

"Please, please, please…" I moaned until he gave me something I didn't even know to ask for. Slick and dripping with my need, his two remaining fingers slid into my ass, and my back arched off the chaise.

"Yes, Soni," he urged, as his fingers worked between my thighs.

An unladylike groan slipped from my lips, and I came so hard that my lungs refused to take in another breath for what felt like an eternity.

Atlas peppered my clit with soft kisses and licks until all of the tension left my body, and I melted into a puddle on the chaise. Only then did he come up for air. Still kneeling between my knees, he wore a self-satisfied smile as he wiped the evidence of my orgasm from his chin.

"I promised I would take care of you. You believe me now?"

"Yes," I whimpered.

"You thought you couldn't come again."

"No… but how did you…? Why did you…" The words for the deliciously dirty thing he'd just done to me wouldn't leave my tongue.

"Why did I put two fingers in your ass? And how did I know to do it?"

Mortified, I covered my face with my hands. Atlas grabbed my wrists and pulled them away before he leaned in to kiss me with smiling lips.

"You're cute when you get all shy."

"You enjoy embarrassing me."

He shrugged a shoulder and nodded. "I do. But to answer your question, I did it because I knew you needed another sensation. A little bite of pain to make you come."

"Like when you used your teeth?"

"Yes."

I observed him quietly as another thought came to my mind. "Do we have that in common, too?"

A nervous smile twitched at the corners of his lips. "Are you asking me if I would like it if you slipped your fingers in my ass?"

The visual that created in my mind made my sex clench so hard that I drew a startled breath. "Yes…that's what I'm asking."

Atlas nuzzled his nose against mine and brushed his lips against mine. "Yes, we have that in common."

"Noted."

I breathed in and savored the laughter in his kiss. He wrapped his arms around me, holding me close and bracing himself over me at the same time. I wrapped my legs around his waist, loving the feel of him on top of me. Atlas moaned and ground his hips into the mattress of the chaise as I ran my hands over the expanse of his back.

"Sonja?"

"Yes?"

He pulled away and looked me in the eye. "Take me to your bed," he whispered.

"You sure?" I asked, remembering how nervous he had been just standing in my front hallway.

Atlas nodded. "I want to make love to you. Take me to your bed."

I blew out the candles while he grabbed his shirt and the bottle of rum, then we went inside.

chapter seventeen
Atlas

The house was dark when we went back inside. Sonja said something about the lights being on an automatic timer, but really... I was so hard that she could have just grabbed me by my dick and led me to her bed. Flickering candlelight glowed in a hallway near the front door, and she led me toward it. That scent that was all over every inch of her skin was stronger here. It overwhelmed me a little, made my head swim in a way that made me wonder if her spell was really working or if I was just light-headed because all the blood in my body had rushed to places further south.

Sonja dropped my hand as she crossed the threshold, let her robe slip off of her shoulders, and turned toward me.

"Goddamn..." I murmured, then leaned on the door jamb to just fucking look at her. She looked like one of those women in an old, Harlem renaissance photo who draped themselves over chaise lounges, smoked cigarettes, and broke hearts.

No hearts were broken on Soni's chaise, though. Stolen maybe, but not broken.

"Are you just gonna stand there looking at me all night?" she asked, a tremble in her voice as she pushed up her chin defiantly.

"Maybe," I murmured, letting my eyes take in every inch of her; from her wavy curls, to her pretty tits with those nipples that I couldn't wait to get my mouth on, to her pink painted toenails. I reached for my dick, squeezed, and didn't bother trying to hold in the moan.

The corner of Soni's mouth quirked, and she began to gather her dress in her hands. Slowly…it inched up her long legs, over those shapely thighs, revealing the sweet pussy I'd just had my mouth on and hips I would definitely grip when I —

She yanked it the rest of the way off and dropped it to the floor.

My knees wanted to bend.

They literally weakened, and I barely had enough blood in my lower extremities to kick the door shut and close the distance between us.

Soni backed away until her knees hit the bed, and then she turned and crawled onto it— ass in the air like a cat begging for attention.

I was making sounds. To my own ears, it sounded like grunting and growling, which was so fucking cliche for a man my size, but I'd forgotten how to make words as I fished a roll of condoms out of my pocket, yanked off my sweats, and climbed in after her. Soni cast a look over her shoulder that was probably meant to be coy until I gripped her hips and yanked her toward me. She drew in a sharp breath, and I felt a little tremble rush through her. Instead of sliding inside of her the way I so desperately wanted to, I crushed her to me, wedging my dick in the crease of her ass. Sonni wiggled a little and rolled her hips. I laughed and kissed her shoulder.

"You're playful. That's a pleasant surprise." I slipped my hand down her belly and found her hard clit. "I have condoms—"

"You don't need them," she said in a rush.

179

My hips twitched involuntarily at the thought of being inside of her, skin-to-skin. I didn't usually ask. Condoms were an unspoken rule. I always used them. *Always*. But something about being with Soni made the thought of any sort of barrier between us almost unbearable.

"You sure? I have no problem wearing one." I slid one hand down between her thighs.

Soni licked her lips. "I know we should…" A soft gasp slipped from her lips as I slid my fingers inside of her.

Fuck. So wet. So tight. "We should," I agreed. "But…"

"I don't want to," she whispered, clenching around my fingers.

"Shit…" I felt a small twinge of guilt. This conversation should have definitely happened before I had my dick out.

Soni curled one hand around my neck and twisted in my arms so that she could reach my mouth. She kissed me, and I pressed my fingers deeper, held them firm against that bundle of nerves until she made little whimpering sounds as her pussy grew wetter around my fingers. Fuck… I wanted to be inside of her.

"Oh, my god," she whispered. "I just need you, Atlas."

"You sure?" I asked again.

"Yes…" She opened her eyes and looked deep into mine. "I'm sure, Atlas."

"Okay," I said with a smile. "Is this how you want me? From the back?"

"Yes, please," she said breathlessly. Her polite response made me smile.

I rocked my hips backward—just enough for my dick to fall from the crease of her ass so that I could slide it through her drenched pussy lips. "With your pretty, heart-shaped ass in the air? Or like this? With me holding you?"

I rolled my hips against her, and the tip of my dick skimmed her entrance. It took everything in me not to ram inside, but something told me she needed to go slow.

At least the first time.

"Yes, Just like this."

"Okay, baby."

I shifted so that my thighs were splayed, and she was nestled between them. She titled her ass just so, and I angled my hips and slid the tip of my dick inside of her. Soni reached down between her legs, fingers slipping through her wetness to where we were so tenuously joined. She grabbed my shaft, and I swear I saw stars. With her hand holding me steady, I slowly slid inside of her.

"Ohh…" she sighed, a note of surprise in her voice.

"You okay?" I asked.

"Yes!" She laughed, a throaty, sexy sound then rolled her hips, taking me deeper.

Her pussy fluttered and rippled around me, stretching to let me sink deeper. "Oh, fuck, Soni." I clutched her tighter.

She drew in a sharp breath. "You feel so good," she whispered breathlessly.

I thrust deeper and let out a breathless moan of my own. "Damn… you feel good to me, too. So good…" Like a dream. I reached down to play with her clit again, and the moment I touched it, her pussy clenched hard on my dick, and it felt so good that we moaned in unison. I took that moment to thrust deeper still until my hips were flush against hers.

"Oh, god," she whimpered, and then she was coming.

I fucked her right through that orgasm and on the other side of it? I met the real Soni. Bold and wanton, she braced her hands on either of my thighs and circled her hips, stirring my dick inside of her, so deep that for a moment, all I could do was grip the sheets and try my hardest not to come. Just like in the greenhouse, I was struck by how much she needed this. Needed something and someone to help her let go, and I had no qualms about being that someone. Fuck... I kinda always wanted to be that someone.

"Yes...Soni. Use my dick to make yourself come," I encouraged.

And then she did. Hard and wet, and I was beginning to think that sweet little Soni might be more into the dirty talk than even she realized.

Spent from her back to back orgasms, Sonny sagged in my arms. "Hmmm... is it my turn yet?" I asked.

A smile spread across her lips. "I don't think I can—"

"I seem to remember you saying that outside in the garden, and here you are, three orgasms later, coming all over my dick," I whispered in her ear. Deep inside, I felt her body respond to my words, and I laughed, rocking my lips left to right just slightly, loving how it felt to have her hold me inside of her just like this.

"Atlas..." she moaned.

"Shhh..." I said. "I've got you, baby."

I lowered her to the mattress on her belly. From this point of view, I could see where my dick split her, and the sight of it almost made me come on the spot. I gripped her hips, thumbs notching into the dimples at the small of her back. And fuck... she rocked back into me, and it felt so perfect.

"Yes... just like that," I growled between clenched teeth.

Sonni whimpered and did it again, and this time I met her halfway. *Oh, fuck... so deep.*

When I pulled out, her pussy gripped my dick like she didn't want to let me go. I didn't want her to let me go either, so I thrust in again, pulling her hips back to meet mine. Soni's hand clenched into a fist, and she moaned loud and long into the pillow. I've heard that sound before. The memory of how fucking beautiful she looked when I made her come in the greenhouse filled my mind. I didn't get a chance to in the garden because I was so focused on making her feel good. That was all for her. But now…

"Turn over," I whispered. I slipped out of her, and she made a sound that was close to weeping. "I know, baby," I whispered then kissed a trail up her spine. "Turn over for me. I wanna look in your eyes when I come. I want you to see what you do to me," I whispered.

I braced myself over her on hands and knees, giving her room to roll over onto her back. Her pretty face was flushed. Her lips pinked and plumped from kissing, her lashes wet and spiked with the tears she'd cried into the pillow.

"Hi," she said with a shy smile.

"Hi…" I answered. *Goddamn, she's sweet.*

Soni reached for me, her hands smoothed over my chest and up around my neck. "Kiss me," she demanded.

And of course, I obliged. The moment our lips met, my sweet Soni attempted to devour me with her mouth. Her hips rolled under me until the very tip of my dick notched between her slick pussy lips. She rubbed my claves with her feet then notched her ankles together at the small of my back. With every stroke of her tongue, her hips opened wider and made tiny undulations until I couldn't wait for another second to be inside of her again, so I didn't.

"Oh, God, Atlas," she cried out.

And she was right. It felt different in this position. I could see her face, and *oh, fuck*, the way she met my thrusts…

I felt every bit of her from the tip of my dick to the base.

Somehow her knee found it's way over my shoulder and fuck if I wasn't deeper inside.

Was this real? Did it really feel this good? I slid my hand under her shoulders and grasped the back of her neck and picked up the rhythm. Ending each thrust way deep, and she got tighter and wetter...

"This is...this is just..."

"Good. Too good. So fucking good," she finished for me, and I laughed, and she laughed, and I came. And...there she was right behind me. Soni closed her eyes, and tears slipped from the corners. I kissed them away as the delicious grip of her pussy milked every drop from me.

I laughed, and she cried and fuck... I might be in love with this woman.

chapter eighteen

Sonja

The alarm on my cellphone blared to life. Six-fifteen had come far too early. I tried to shut it off as quickly as possible, but the sound still started Atlas out of his sleep.

"Oh, my god," he groaned, covering his head with a pillow. "What was that horrible sound?"

I chuckled. "Good morning," I whispered before kissing his shoulder.

Atlas rolled over, pulled me into his arms, and threw the blanket over both our heads. "What time is it?" he asked, his voice deep and gravel rough with sleep.

"A little after six."

"Why are we up at such an ungodly hour?"

"Well, my kids'll be up in a few. I usually make them breakfast before school."

"Hm," he grunted. "Do I need to leave?"

"Do you want to leave?"

"Fuck, no."

I laughed, and he pulled me in tighter, working his hips just the tiniest bit so that his morning wood rubbed against my bare ass.

"I was hoping to spend the day with you...unless you have something to do."

"Besides you? Nothing on the schedule."

He laughed. "That's what I like to hear." Atlas's hands began to wander. Cupping and gathering one breast and coaxing the nipple to a hard peak. "I like waking up next to you."

"Me, too." I sighed as his other hand smoothed over the rise of my hip and between my thighs. He flexed his hips, pressing his dick against me more firmly, and I felt my body readying itself for him. "Atlas…" I whispered.

"Yeah, Soni?" he answered, a smile in his voice. "Is there something you want?"

"No…there's something I *need*," I said, letting go of the playfulness and letting that need bleed into my words.

"Is it me? Am I what you need?" he asked, and I heard that same need in his voice.

"Yes," I said breathlessly. "Yes, I need you."

He sighed and grasped my chin, turned my head so he could reach my mouth. His soft, nibbling pecks quickly slid into a deep, searching kiss as we undulated against each other. His hand slid down the back of my thigh, cupped my knee, pulling it upward, opening my hips so he could slide that same hand between them. I gasped when his hand caressed my sensitive, swollen pussy.

"You're already so wet…" he whispered, slipping two fingers into me so sure and deep that a loud moan spilled out of me. How could I still be so ready after the thorough fucking he gave me last night? That was a question I would explore later, but right now, I reached back to take the hard length of him in my hand.

"Shit…" he cursed softly and thrust into my fist. Then he suddenly went still and alert.

"What?" I asked.

"I heard something," he whispered.

186

I held my breath and listened…and then I heard it, too. Nadia was up and moving around. Usually, I had to drag her out of bed by her ankles, but today of all days, she chose to wake up all on her own.

"Shit," I cursed, but for a completely different reason than he had a moment ago.

"So I guess that means we'll have to put a pin in this?" he asked his lips pressed against my shoulder.

"I'm sorry," I said with a grimace, hating that life had intruded on what had promised to be a perfect morning.

"Don't be. I'll still be hard when you get back."

That made me laugh but also made me want to stay in bed.

Atlas kissed me one last time and nudged me out of bed. "Hurry up and go so you can hurry up and come back."

After a quick pit stop in my ensuite—where a quick glance in the mirror confirmed that orgasms were, in fact, good for my skin—I went out to the kitchen.

Nadia bounded down fully dressed and decidedly perky for a kid that stayed up late watching TV. She sat right down at the breakfast bar, and I slid a plate of bacon and eggs in front of her.

"Did you sleep with me last night?" I asked as she shoveled a forkful of eggs in her mouth.

Nadia rolled her eyes. "Morning, mommy," she said around a mouthful of food.

"Is your brother up and moving around?"

"Yeah, but he's still not dressed yet."

I nodded, knowing that probably meant I would have to drive Nadia to school to make sure she made it to homeroom. "Lemme go put some clothes on case I have to drive you in."

I popped Winston's plate into the microwave and went to my bedroom to change into something suitable from the carpool lane. In my bedroom, I found Atlas sprawled across my bed in a deep sleep. I smiled and had to restrain myself from climbing into bed with him and covering his face with kisses.

I heard Winston talking to his sister out in the kitchen, and for a moment, I allowed myself to consider how it would be if me and Atlas were dating, and the kids knew about him.

How would that look?

Maybe he'd be at the breakfast bar drinking a cup of coffee, listening to Nadia talk about cheer squad drama. Maybe Winston would ask him about the film they had studied the night before.

I closed my eyes...

But no matter how hard I tried, I couldn't picture it. I didn't see him and my kids in the same space.

"Mom?" Winston called out from the other side of my bedroom door. "I got Naddy. Thanks for breakfast."

"Okay, thank you, son. I love you."

"Love you, too, mom,"

Atlas lifted his head, rolled over, blinked sleepily, and then smiled. "Does that mean you can come back to bed?" he asked.

"Yes."

"Good." He threw back the duvet, revealing his naked body and that he was still, indeed, very hard. "As promised..." he waggled his eyebrows.

I yanked my t-shirt over my head, stripped off my leggings, and dove into bed. Atlas caught me and wrestled me underneath him like he was wresting an overactive toddler. His mouth found my left nipple, and I moaned, opening my hips wider so that he could settle deeper. The edge of his teeth

188

scraped the peaked nub, and I let out a moan and wrapped my legs around his waist.

"Hmm...I think I might have found a cheat code..." he whispered, kissing a trail across my chest to my right nipple.

"A cheat code?"

"You know... like when you're playing a video game, and you're trying to unlock the next level, but it's too hard, so you look up a cheat code and—"

"Oh, it unlocks the next level," I said, finally getting it.

"Yup, and I think sucking on your nipples like this ..." he paused for a moment to cover my nipple with his warm mouth and sucked hard, sending a frisson of pleasure through my body. "And when I used my teeth..." He scraped my nipple with the edge of his teeth, and my hips bucked under him. Atlas laughed. "Yup... a cheat code. I wonder..."

Atlas swiped my nipple with the flat of his tongue and pulled it into his mouth. Sucked hard. Harder. So hard, it almost hurt, and I felt it in my clit.

"Oh..."I moaned, cupping the back of his head. I opened my eyes and looked down at him. He was looking up at me. While looking in my eyes, he did that thing with his teeth again. Longer and harder and my hips bucked and rolled under him. Pleasure sparking in my clit like he was sucking that, but he wasn't. But, oh, God...

"I'm coming," I whispered.

He nodded.

"I'm coming. Why am I coming?"

I closed my eyes, pleasure rolling through my body as I held his head against my breast. His self satisfied laughter met my ears as I came down.

"What the fuck was that, Atlas?" I asked.

189

He looked up at me and smiled. "I told you. I found the cheat code." He pushed up on his elbows, and I felt the blunt tip of his dick against me mere seconds before he thrust inside. Filling me, stretching me, claiming every inch of me as his.

* * * *

Apparently, when I tried to picture Atlas in my kitchen, I'd pictured him with too many clothes on. But leaning against the counter drinking a cup of coffee in his black boxer briefs with those thick thighs on display? This was far better than anything I could have imagined.

"What are you grinning at?" he asked.

"You."

"Me?"

"Yes, you. In my kitchen, drinking coffee in your man panties."

"Man panties?"

"Yes, man panties."

"Excuse me… these are dry-wicking boxer briefs. Athletes wear them."

I raised an eyebrow. "They do? In something besides fitness ads designed to make housewives buy these man panties for their husbands?"

"Hmmm…" He set his coffee cup on the counter and walked toward me. "See…I'm not a husband. So that can't be who those ads are for."

"So maybe designed to make girlfriends buy them for their boyfriends?"

"Close, but I bought them for myself."

"Ahh, I got it. Designed for men who want to seduce their way into the beds of middle-aged women to give them amazing head and bone-melting sex?"

"Ding! Ding! Ding!" he sing-songed then kissed me. Sweet kisses that you give someone when you've spent hours skin-to-skin, mouth-to-mouth, and inside of each other, but it's still not enough.

"So what do I need to do for some solid food? Eggs, bacon…"

"You're hungry? But you ate so much this morning," I joked, my voice pitched high in faux disbelief.

"I could always eat more of you, Soni."

It was already eleven in the morning. We'd spent most of it and all of the night fucking, but I still wanted him to eat *me*.

Atlas notched his hands under my arms and lifted me up onto the countertop. Those same hands found their way under my top to play with my nipples and… *fuck*.

I broke away from the kiss. "I'll make you food…" I panted. "I'll make us food. I can't come anymore because I'm sure there are no calories left in my body."

Atlas laughed. "I thought you would say that."

"I'll get the eggs. You look under that cabinet over there for the pots and pans."

I went to the fridge to gather eggs, cheese, butter, and bacon while Atlas pulled out a griddle pan and a saucepan.

"Oh, no. There's a good fry pan under there…"

"I don't make scrambled eggs in a frying pan. I make them in a saucepan," he said matter-of-factly.

I stalled for a minute and stared up at him in wonder. "So, you're making the eggs?" I asked.

"Yeah…is that a problem?" he asked.

"I mean, you asked me for solid food. I just assumed—"

"You assumed you would be making breakfast for me? Oh, no… I mean, you can make the bacon and coffee, but I'm very particular about my eggs."

"Oh, okay."

He smiled at me. "You're staring at me like I'm the first man who has ever stood at your stove."

"Well…" I smiled at him, but it was a stiff smile because he was the first man at my stove. My own son had never even boiled water on my stove.

Atlas kissed the tip of my nose. "You've been to my condo. I think our ranges are pretty comparable. I'm not gonna break it, Soni."

"I know."

I wanted to tell him my stunned reaction wasn't fear that he would break my stove, but at the idea that he wanted to use it at all. But instead, I handed over the eggs, cheese, and butter. "I'll make the bacon, but you need to explain why you're making the scrambled eggs in a saucepan."

Atlas smiled. Not the big smile — though I love that one for different reasons — but the lopsided half-smile that he had on right now as he unwrapped the unsalted butter. It's the same smile he smiled before he kissed me the first time.

"So… do you know who Sir Ian McKellan is?"

I stood alongside him while he explained how he was up late with insomnia when he stumbled upon a video of the thespian making eggs on YouTube.

"So you just put it all into a cold pan," he said.

"What?"

"Yeah…all of it. Eggs, butter, milk…where's the milk?"

I grabbed the milk from the fridge and handed it to him. "This is insanity."

"You better get started on the bacon," he said with that sly half-smile.

While the bacon sizzled on the griddle pan, Atlas scrambled the creamiest eggs I'd ever seen my life. Once the breakfast was prepared, we pushed aside my work on the table and sat down to eat.

As he pushed eggs onto his fork with a piece of toast. Atlas flipped through my coursework along with the notes I'd taken.

"We talked about you starting a blog weeks ago," he said as he observed my list of to-dos. "Why haven't you done that yet?"

"I started it, but I wanted to give some thought to the strategy you discussed in the last class."

"Smart. Do you have anything written yet?"

I nodded and nibbled on a piece of bacon. "Like ten?"

"Let me see them."

"You don't have to—"

"I want to. Let me see your work."

"Don't you want to finish eating your breakfast first?"

"Soni..., I'm gonna fuck you again after breakfast, so can you get your laptop so I can see your work?" he asked again.

I bit my lip and left the table to grab my laptop out of the living room.

"Hmm...eating breakfast in our underwear was a good idea," he called out to my back.

I returned from the living room with my laptop in hand and sat in front of him. Leaning over his should, I entered my password and pulled up my document files. "Here you go..."

"Okay," he said, then looped his arm my waist, pulling me into his lap as he read. "Hm...I like how you'll framing these."

193

"Thanks, I thought it would be cool to have an information series that could create a little interest for those mix-your-own-medicinal classes you suggested. Estelle agreed to let me host it at her studio."

Atlas looked at me and smiled. "This is pretty damn good, Soni." He kissed my shoulder. "I'm really fucking proud of you."

Something in me swelled, and I realized that the reason why I couldn't imagine him in my kitchen earlier wasn't because he didn't belong here. I just would have never been able to imagine anything as good as this.

A thoughtful frown creased Atlas's brow. "Good medicine."

"What?"

"*Good Medicine*. That's what you should name your business. *Good Medicine*."

"That's actually perfect," I said with a nod. "I like that. I think you're right." I cupped his cheek, in my hand, and gave him a sweet kiss. "The last time my mother saw me, she reminded me that love and sex are good medicine, too."

"Oh, really?" he asked with a raise of his brows. "Do you agree?"

"Hmm... maybe? I think I need another dose to be sure."

Without another word, Atlas stood up, tossed me over his shoulder like a woman-sized sack of potatoes, and stalked back to my bedroom.

chapter nineteen

Atlas

It was nearly four in the afternoon when I finally left Soni's bed, and that was only because it was almost time for her kids to come home. We both agreed that it wouldn't be a good look to have them stumble upon their mother in bed with her lover in the late afternoon. But tonight was the homecoming game for her kid's school — my old alma mater — so I could look forward to sitting next to her in the stands and maybe stealing a few kisses.

Kairo had already left me half a dozen messages, each one more agitated than the last. I knew I should have called her to let her know I wasn't going to be in, but I did manage to get some work done from Soni's bed. And really? I didn't need to be in the office every day. Neither did she. Besides, we had that standing appointment at *Cutz 'n Cocktails* and had planned on going to the homecoming game together anyway, so I would make my apologies when I saw her.

I was only about five minutes late for our appointment, but Kairo was already in the chair when I came in.

"Hey, Atlas!" Krissy chirped as I came in. "Give me a minute, and I'll get your drink ready."

"Thanks, Krissy," I said with a wink. "What's up, everybody? Hey, Kairo."

"What's up?" my friend said flatly but didn't bother to look me.

"Hey, sorry, I'm late."

"For work or for your haircut?" she asked.

"My bad. I should have called to let you know that I was working from home today. But I set up a time to do that interview with the chick over at *Village Journals* and finalized the slide deck for the webinar."

"Cool. Great," she said.

"Cool."

Kairo would probably have a bit of an attitude for the rest of the evening, and with good reason. But I wasn't going to worry about it too much. She was usually happy as long as I carried my end of the workload.

My phone vibrated in my pocket, and I couldn't suppress a smile because I knew that it was probably a message from Soni. I pulled out my phone and saw that I was right.

Soni: I'm sore in places I didn't know I could be sore.

The grin on my face stretched a mile wide.

Me: really? I thought all of that yoga would have made it a little easier for you.

Soni: I don't typically hold positions that long. And I definitely don't hold them while a two-hundred-pound man fucks me within an inch of my life.

Remembering how I'd had her in a standing split in her shower before I left this afternoon made me bite back groan. She really could hold those poses for a long time.

Me: hey, don't body shame me.

Soni: the only shame is that your body isn't next to my body right now.

That time I didn't bother trying to bite it back. And it must have been loud because it drew the attention of everyone in the shop.

"Who the hell has you grinning at your phone like that?" Jerricka asked as she flicked off her clippers.

"I'm guessing its the same person that has him distracted and absent from work these days," Kairo muttered.

"Hey... that's not fucking fair. I've been getting shit done. I just worked from home today."

"Home?" she questioned with a raise of her right brow. "More like you worked from Sonja's home today." She said Soni's name with such disdain that I couldn't help getting a little irritated.

"I'm confused... I thought one of the perks of working for yourself was the ability to make your own schedule. Granted, I should have called you to let you know, but I got my work done, and I'm here now, ain't I?"

"Barely..." Kairo spat back.

"Oh, no! Is the fearsome twosome about to break up?" Sheba asked, trying to lighten the mood.

"Don't be ridiculous," I said. "Kairo is just acting childish."

"I'm acting childish?" Kairo scoffed. "You're the one over there texting like a preteen girl."

I shook my head. "Jealousy is a motherfucker."

We've been going back and forth like this for days, and I was tired of it. I told her that things between Soni and I were developing into something more than a fling. She's my best friend and my business partner, so I felt like that was something she should know. But apparently, that was a mistake because she has done nothing but complain about how this thing with Soni was making me lose focus. For the life of me, I couldn't figure out why.

"What's the deal, Kairo? Why does this bother you so much?"

"This is not a conversation for the barbershop," she said as Jerricka brushed the loose hair off of her and unsnapped the cape. "I'm gonna get a couple more hours of work in," she said as she stood up to fish her wallet out of her pocket.

"Ohh... kay? I thought we were gonna hit happy hour before the game—"

"Nah, I have a few things I have to take care of. I'll meet you at the game. Save me a seat."

Kairo walked out before I could say another word. I stared after her for a moment then looked at Jerricka.

"Is something else going on with her?" I asked.

Jerricka shrugged. "I have no idea. She doesn't talk to me like that. Come on, I have another appointment in forty-five minutes, and ya ass was late."

I sighed and climbed into the barber chair so Jerricka could get started.

"So you and Kairo have been friends since you were kids, right?" she asked as she draped the cape over me.

"Yup. Since we were like seven or eight."

"I can tell. You two fight like siblings." She picked up the boar bristle brush and proceeded to beat me about the head under the pretense of brushing my hair.

I grimaced and ducked my head away. "Damn, do you have to be so rough?"

Jerricka sucked her teeth then forced me to turn my head forward again. "Maybe you should talk to your friend," she suggested.

"I've tried talking to her. You see how she is. She hates the idea of me and Sonja together because she thinks I'm gonna hurt her or something."

Jerricka let out a dry laugh. "Did you ever think that maybe this isn't about your relationship with Sonja? That maybe it's about your relationship with Kai?"

"My relationship with Kai? What about my relationship with Kai? Did she say something to you?" I asked, turning to look at her again.

Jerricka repositioned my head roughly. "I'm not as close to her as you are, but I do consider her a friend. Maybe consider the fact that this relationship with Sonja might be triggering something for her."

I frowned. What did one thing have to do with the other? For the life of me, I couldn't see how these two things related to each other, but instead of asking more questions that might insight more violence from Jerricka, I suffered quietly through my haircut.

An hour later, with a fresh cut and a possible concussion, I went back to *The Coworking Spot*. Kairo was at her desk, working on graphics for our next marketing campaign, and didn't look up when I came into the room.

"You wanna talk?" I asked. "Or are we gonna keep sniping at each other like this until one of us rage quits the business?"

"Only one of us in this room has ever abandoned the other," Kairo mumbled under her breath.

"Ah." I pulled out a chair and sat down. "This about me leaving. I thought we were past that."

"It's in the past, but that doesn't mean that we're past it."

I rolled my eyes. "Come on, Kairo. I've apologized for that a thousand times, and I've been home for three years now. Isn't that enough?"

"Not when I see you getting into this situation that is doomed to end, which will give you another excuse to leave."

I clenched my teeth. "Everything always comes back to this…" I scrubbed my hands over my face. "What more do you need from me, Kairo? I'm here. We're building this business together. Things are going well. What more do you want?"

"I want you to not fuck a client—"

"I'm not just fucking Sonja. And do you really think I would run out on you if things go to shit between her and me?"

"It wouldn't be the first time…" Kairo said mockingly.

I leaned forward, elbows to knees, and covered my face with my hands. "Can we just have it out already? Can we just have it out so we can get past this?"

"What's to have out? You stole my girl, you stole the project we worked on for a solid year, and the following we built, then took it around the country to make a million dollars in sponsorships and workshops led by *The Big Guy in the Tiny Home Truck* living his best, nomadic entrepreneur life."

"The truck and the social media following…yeah. I stole that. I would say borrowed because we're using that same following now, but whatever. The million dollars? That was money I earned, but I put that in the bank, and that's what we used to start *The Coworking Spot*. But your girl, Kairo? I did not steal your girl."

"Ruby. Her name was Ruby, and yeah, you did."

I sighed. "For the last time, Ruby decided to tag along at the last minute—"

"Yeah, after you fucked her."

"Okay, I broke bro-code or whatever, but I didn't do it to intentionally hurt you. And as far as the truck goes... the plan was always for the two of us to make that road trip together. You're the one who changed your mind and decided to go to straight to grad school—"

"Yeah, because unlike you, I had to make real money to pay off my student loans, and I wasn't going to get a job with that kind of salary on a bachelor's degree. I didn't have a bunch of disposable funds to play around with on the stock market. And more importantly, you agreed to wait. Then I woke up to find all of it gone."

"Yes, that was fucked up, but you said you understood. I couldn't be here anymore. I was suffocating. You knew that better than anyone else, but now you're throwing it back in my face. I'm so confused. What is this argument even about?"

"Let it go, Atlas," she said, waving me off dismissively.

"I have let it go, but apparently you haven't."

"Yeah, it's easy for you to get over. You're not the one who was left behind. You're not the one who only got updates on her so-called best friend from social media."

"Okay... I get that. And if I haven't apologized for that specifically, I'm doing it now. I'm sorry, Kairo. I'm sorry for leaving you behind."

Her mouth twisted. "Yeah, sure. Okay."

"No, seriously, Kairo. Look at me."

My friend let out a heavy sigh and swiveled toward me in her chair, but still didn't look at me. I waited patiently until she did.

"Clearly, you resent me for leaving."

"Yeah, I do. But more than that, I feel like you're always looking for another reason to leave."

I sat with that for a moment. Heard her feelings and let them sink in. From where she sat, what I'd done was a betrayal. She feels like I abandoned her, and I understood that. She wasn't the only person who felt that way. My mother had voiced the same sentiments when I finally came back home.

"Okay...I hear you. And I get that this thing with Soni may look like it's doomed to tank from your point of view. And... I'm not entirely sure why you're so pessimistic about that, but I need you to know that no matter what happens with her and me, I'm not going anywhere. I'm home now."

Kairo sighed and slouched in her chair. "How can you be so sure?"

"I know... my track record is shitty." I cracked my knuckles. "I'm impulsive and unreliable... but I'm working hard to be someone different. I spent so much time being responsible when I was a kid that I kinda rebelled against it in the worst ways for a few years. But I'm here now."

Kairo nodded. "And this thing with Sonja...if it doesn't work out, it's not gonna trigger some shame spiral that will make you buy a ticket out of town again?"

"Heh...the shame spiral," I said with a dry laugh. "I have done a lot of internal work since I've been back. Even you have to agree that I've experienced a lot of personal growth, right?"

"Yeah, I'll give you that. But you didn't answer my question."

"Right, Sonja..." I chewed my bottom lip and cracked my knuckles some more as I tried to picture how things would turn out between us. Part of me worried that it would be over between us once the course ended. She would be busy getting her business off the ground, and she was already a busy mom. Where would I fit in?

But then I remembered being in her bed, drinking coffee in her kitchen, and worshiping her pussy in her garden, and I know I would do almost anything to stay in that picture for as long as she wanted me.

"You're going to call me crazy, and maybe I am, but I don't think things are gonna go left with me and Soni. It feels different, you know? Like it might be something."

Kairo nodded. "Have you told her?"

"Told her what?"

"That you're falling in love with her."

I laughed nervously and shifted in my chair. "Is that something people do? I mean, aren't you supposed to wait until you know for sure that you're in love before you make those sorts of declarations?"

Kairo shrugged. "I can't even ask Jerricka out on a date, but every time I'm around her, I want to tell her that I'm falling for her, so maybe I'm the wrong person to ask. Is that how you feel around, Sonja?"

"Honestly? Whenever I think about her, I feel like there's no other person I want to be with. I want her so bad that it makes me sick just thinking she might not want the same. I mean, all she has to do is smile at me, Kairo, and I'm gone. It's just — what?"

"Whenever you talk about her, you lapse into this weird language and get a big dumb smile on your face. It's kinda disgusting."

I rolled my eyes. "Breh, you asked me about my feelings."

"I didn't ask for all that," she said with a laugh. "But if that's how she makes you feel, you should tell her that."

"You think I should? I mean, we're supposed to see each other at the homecoming game tonight."

"Well," she said, standing up. "There's no time like the present."

Was I ready for that? Kairo wasn't wrong when she said that Soni was a grown-ass woman, and being with her would mean that I would have to grow the fuck up, too. She already had two kids. She didn't need another one. And those kids... would they accept me or make it difficult for us to be together? They weren't toddlers in need of raising, but that almost made it seem harder and scarier.

But I wanted her. I wanted *us*. So there was no time like the present to make that known.

chapter twenty
Sonja

My knees bounced as I scanned the crowd pouring into the football stadium. The stands were vibrating with intense energy, that excitement around the Red Raider's homecoming game. The sun was low in the sky, painted bright orange, pink, and red across the horizon. It was just cold enough to make it feel like football season. The players weren't on the field yet, but there was still about five minutes until game time.

"Are you cold?" Birdie asked, chaffing my arms over my denim jacket.

"A little bit."

Agostina, who was sitting on my other side, cut her eyes at me.

Okay, so I lied. I wasn't cold. I was nervous. Atlas was supposed to come to the game tonight, and my whole family was here —well, my siblings, at least — and I was nervous because he was going to meet them. And that felt big. *It was big.* Hence the bouncy knees.

Birdie kept her arm around me. "So…remember when you said that I could ask you for help?"

"Yeah. Are you ready to take me up on it?"

"Yeah," she said, dropping her gaze. "It's been harder than I thought it would be to find another job. I'm worried that I might have burned my last bridge."

I sighed. Birdie was the type who liked the hard lesson. I hated that she seemed bound and determined to learn that way. She was a great chef— mostly self-taught, and she could be amazing if she got out of her own damn way.

"Well, now that your career is trashed, and your reputation is ruined, I guess it won't matter if you finally track down your baby daddy?" Aggie asked.

Birdie rolled her eyes. "Don't y'all ever get tired of that joke?"

"It's not a joke," Estelle interjected. "We really want to know. Come on, Bird. Who was it? One of your instructors? A visiting chef? Some TV star from the Food Network?"

"I'm never telling you," Birdie said flatly.

"What are you gonna do when Amarettos asks about him?" Estelle countered.

"Like I said before, I'll deal with that when or if it happens. But for now... that's not drama any of us need."

Estelle rolled her eyes and shook her head. Wordlessly, I begged her to let it go. Estelle and Birdie were friends, but sometimes they went after each other relentlessly. That's the last thing I needed tonight. My nerves were already shot.

"You can stay as long as you need," I said to Birdie. "Just let me know when you're ready to move in."

The marching band stood up and started playing the school song, and everyone got to their feet as the Red Raiders took the field. I spotted my son Winston wearing number twenty-five, the same as his favorite cornerback. His sister and the rest of the cheerleading squad weren't too far behind. She was still on the junior varsity squad, but the way she's been practicing, I was sure she'd make varsity during the basketball season.

Once all the players had been announced, and the opposing team was on the filed, we all settled in for the game.

And that's when I spotted him.

Atlas was standing at the bottom of the stands, searching the crowd. My belly did a lazy nervous flip when he spotted me and smiled.

"Hey! Look! It's Atlas and Kairo!" Estelle said, then stood up and waved them over.

Without being asked, Agostina switched seats with me, wedging herself between Birdie and me and leaving the seat at the end of the row empty. Atlas sat down. Shoulder-to-shoulder, engulfing me in his warmth and his scent.

"Hey, Sonni," he whispered, smiling that filthy smile that made me remember all the things we'd done last night, this morning, and this afternoon.

"What's up, Sonja?" Kairo said, drawing my attention away before I could engage in a level of affection that wasn't fit for public display.

"Hey, Kairo. Nice seeing you again."

Kairo grabbed an empty seat next to Estelle and Deacon.

"Strange seeing your instructor here," Birdie said sarcastically.

"Not really. I was a Red Raider once upon a time. We come to homecoming every year," he said.

"And yet we've never seen you in the crowd. Seems like a man of your size would be hard to miss, " Birdie said with a raise of her brow, turning on that sparkle again. It was slightly annoying that she kept trying to flirt with him.

Atlas squinted at Birdie and smirked. "Well, I wasn't here to see your sister all of those other times, was I?"

Deacon must have overheard that comment because his head whipped around, and a frown creased his brow.

"Leave the man alone," Agostina said, pinching Birdie so hard that she yelped. "It's good to see you, Atlas."

"Same, Aggie," he said with a wink.

"You still have that crystal I gave you?"

Surprising the shit out of me and my sisters, Atlas dug the pink palm stone out of his front pocket.

"You're carrying that around?" I asked in disbelief.

"Yup. Have been since Aggie gave it to me."

Birdie elbowed Aggie, and she elbowed me, both of them silently screaming about his perfection as if I didn't know already.

"What? Am I doing it wrong? I was supposed to carry it around, right?"

"Yeah, of course. I just didn't expect you to…" I shook my head and smiled. "Don't worry. You're doing it right."

A shy smile twitched at the corners of his mouth. "I wouldn't want any of those old, ego-driven patterns to resurface."

"Do you feel like it's working?" I asked, my voice low and soft and just for him.

Atlas closed his fist around the palm stone. "Hmmm…"

That hum…it was sound he made more than once when he was inside of me. Hearing it now, my skin flushes and tingles under my clothes. He smiled like he knew.

"I think it might be," he said finally. Atlas leaned in closer so that he could whisper in my ear. "I really want to kiss you right now."

"Me, too," I said. Hating the way my breath came too quick and the prickle of sweat on my top lip, but loving that my body reacted to him so acutely. Loving that he could make me feel this way.

"But I can't, huh?"

I shook my head.

"Okay." He pulled away, and I almost leaned into the space he left. "Game's starting."

"Greenville has won the toss and deferred. South Pointe will receive the kick." The booming voice of the announcer echoed around the stands.

Winston jammed his helmet down on his head and jogged off the sideline.

"Let's go, Winston!" I screamed, cupping my hands around my mouth so that my voice will carry.

"What's his number again?" Atlas asked.

"Twenty-five," I said point him out. "In the backfield."

Atlas nodded, then his face went serious as South Pointe lined up for the kickoff. Winston got into position, covering his receiver. His posture was relaxed but alert. The kicking team went into motion. The kicker punted the ball high and straight down the center—a pop-up. Winston took off, a quick cut put him right in front of the receiver, and as soon as the other boy caught the ball, my son drove him into the ground.

"Yes!" I whooped, punching my fist into the air. My family and everyone else that came to support mine and Estelle's kids were on their feet, too. But I was surprised to find Atlas on his feet, too. Clapping hard and using his index and middle fingers to emit a loud whistle.

"Godamn!" he said once we all sat down. "Your boy is fast. You didn't tell me he was that good."

I smirked. "My baby is a star. You ain't seen shit yet."

That was no humblebrag. Winston was talented, and I loved to watch him play.

The score was 14-0 by the end of the first quarter. Halfway through the second, when it was clear that South Pointe's offense never got off the bus, Atlas turned to me and gave me a pointed look.

"What?" I asked, hyped up from the game and being near him.

He leaned in to whispered in my ear, "I really want to kiss you. *Need to.* Do you wanna go under the bleachers and make-out?"

A giggle spilled out of me before I could rein it in. "Make-out under the bleachers? Are you serious?"

His gaze dropped to my lips before he answered, "Very."

Now I couldn't stop looking at his lips, and yes, I wanted to go under the bleachers and make-out. "Uh…we're gonna go get some cocoa before the concession stand gets crowded," I announced.

"Any of y'all want anything?" Atlas asked.

"No, thanks," Aggie piped up.

"Nah, I think we're good," Deacon said from the row in front of us. His tone sounded stank. I tapped Estelle on the shoulder, and when she looked at me, I gestured at her husband. She rolled her eyes and shrugged as if to say, who knows?

I answered her shrug with one of my own then stood up. Me and Deacon were friends, but I wasn't as close to him as I was to Estelle. And I couldn't imagine why he would be pissed off and throwing stank attitude at me or Atlas.

"We'll be right back," I announced and followed Atlas down the stadium stairs. At the bottom, he reached from my hand and practically dragged me into the darkness under the bleachers. Making sure that we were far enough from the light, Atlas backed me up against the wall. The cold brick penetrated my lightweight jacket, but it was soon forgotten when he covered his mouth with mine. He kissed me long and deep until, panting, I had to push him away to catch my breath.

"Something tells me you've had many make-up sessions under these bleachers," I whispered between the soft pecks he made on my lips.

"A few," he affirmed. "What about you, Sonni Watts?"

"Well, back then, I was Soni Malone, and no… you're my first."

He pulled away a little and looked into my eyes. His heavy brows dipped into a frown. Are you serious? No one asked you to come down here just so they could kiss you breathless and feel you up?"

"Nope. I was a good girl."

His brow smoothed, and a filthy smile stretched across his mouth. "Are you still a good girl?" he asked. His hand snuck under my coat, and I drew a sharp breath when his cold fingertips found my skin. "Or are you going to let me feel you up and kiss you breathless?"

I grabbed the collar of his jacket and pulled him to me. "I'm not a good girl."

If this was the kind of make-out session I missed out on in high school, part of me felt deeply sad for fifteen-year-old me. She should have experienced this. She should know this longing, this overwhelming desire to devour and be devoured by someone else. To be wanted this intensely. Because forty-year-old me was completely blissed out on the feel of his tongue and his hands on my body. Good god, I was dangerously close to yanking down my jeans and begging him to fuck me.

"Hm… as much as I want to, that's not gonna happen,' he moaned into my mouth.

"What's not gonna happen?"

"That thought that just went through your perverted little mind."

I looked up at him and laughed. "You were thinking it, too."

"I was," he said, grabbing a big handful of my ass. "But this isn't the time or place."

"Agreed. We're adults. We shouldn't be doing this." I cupped the back of his head and brought his mouth to mine again. He moaned, clutching me closer.

"Soni," he muttered, pulling away again. "You wanna come to my place after the game?" he asked, his voice soft and hopeful.

"I want to, but we usually meet up at *Kinfolks Diner* for pie and milkshakes after home games."

"Oh…" He bit his lip. "I know we just spent the night and whole day together, but I really, really, really want to spend the night with you. I…" He stalled mid-sentence, and a strange look came over his face.

"Hey." I cradled his face in both my hands. "What's wrong?"

"Nothing's wrong, Soni. This is perfect. You're perfect." He shook his head. "I had this weird argument with Kairo today. I mean, it was my fault. I didn't show up for work and didn't answer her phone calls, so she was pretty pissed. Rightfully so."

"Oh." I stuffed my hands into the pockets of my jacket. "The argument was about me?" I stepped back and looked up at him.

"No, the argument was about me. I mean, my track with Kai is shitty. She saw me falling into old patterns, and it pissed her off because she thought--"

"She thinks I'm distracting you from your work." I looked down at the toes of my boots. "I mean, I get it. I thought this would be—"

"Hold on, Sonni. Let me finish."

"Okay," I whispered. I blinked and swallowed around the tightness in my throat. The ground felt unsteady under my feet, so I leaned against the wall. Just a moment ago, he was kissing me and asking me to come back to his place now he was…

Breaking my heart?

"Remember that night we ran into each other in the Village, and we ate ice-cream, and you told me that it wasn't a good idea for us to get involved?"

I nodded.

"Earlier that same day, Mr. Kemp said something to me that I haven't been able to get out of my head—"

"Mr. Kemp?" I looked up at him and frowned. "If this is how you let me down easy, you can stop—"

"Let you down easy? Sonni, I'm trying to tell you that I'm falling for you."

"I… what?" My lungs refused to fill with air. I was trying to take a deep breath, but my lungs literally refused to expand.

Atlas smiled at me. "Pick up your jaw, Sonja."

"But you just said…"

He nodded. "I said that I'm falling for you, and I know I shouldn't put pressure on this thing. And maybe you want to end things when you finish the course, but—"

"I don't," I said, shaking my head.

"You don't?"

I shook my head no again. My vision was blurry. I blinked to clear ant tears ran down my cheeks. Atlas cradled my face in his hands, kissed away my tears, and then kissed my lips.

"We can take it as slow as you want. I know that you have to consider your kids and—"

"Why don't you come with us to *Kinfolks* for pie and milkshakes after the game?"

"Are you sure?"

"I'm sure."

"Okay." A big smile spread across his face, and when his lips pressed against mine again, a little tremor rushed through him. One that echoed through me. "Are you cold?" he asked softly.

"A little," I lied for the second time tonight.

Atlas nuzzled his nose against mine. "Maybe we should actually get some hot chocolate." He kissed the tip of my nose, then reached down and laced his fingers through mine.

chapter twenty-one

Atlas

"Are you sure you want to do this?" Kairo asked as I parked my car across the street from *Kinfolks Diner*. "I mean, don't you feel like meeting the fam is a lot at this stage?"

"Kairo...I swear..." I cursed, killing the engine. "Before we went to the game, you're all *'confess ya feelings, Atlas.'* And now you're telling me that we're moving too fast?"

"I said to tell the woman you love her, not sign up to be a stepdaddy to her kids."

"I can't fucking believe you." I opened my car door and stepped out onto the street.

"I'm just saying it's a lot. Don't you think it's a-fucking-lot?"

I rounded on her and dropped my voice. "Soni's kids and family are important to her. How do you think this works out if I said, 'yeah, nah. I don't want to meet your people, but can you come back to my place after you're done with them so we can fuck?'"

"Is that why you're doing it?"

"No! I'm doing it because I want to be with her for real. Not some fling. Not some guy she sneaks in her house after her kids go to bed."

Kairo nodded and stepped around me. "A'ight. I just wanted to make sure you were sure."

I sighed and followed her to the door of the diner. "Why are you like this?" I asked with a groan.

"If I don't call you on your bullshit, who will?" she asked.

"I think maybe you should focus on your own shit. That shit being the pretty barber you're already in love with," I said as we stepped inside.

Kinfolks was as small meat and three type restaurant in a wedge-shaped building in the only major intersection in The Village. It was one of the few places that still held on to the cultural integrity of the neighborhood. This neighborhood used to be a mill village. When the mills closed, the people who lived here hung on, poor whites and Blacks living shoulder-to-should in a community that had been all but abandoned. Gentrification, or — as the city officials like to call it — urban renewal brought new energy to this part of town. Artists set up shop here. Scrappy entrepreneurs like myself, Kairo, and the girls that own *Cutz 'n Cocktails*, Estelle with her yoga studio, and other Instagram worthy businesses. But truthfully? It's not the neighborhood I grew up in. Places like *Kinfolks* needed our support.

"Hey, Mr. Kemp!" I called out to the older man to where he stood behind the cash register. "Why are you in here so late? Ain't Mrs. Kemp waiting for you at home?"

"Don't you worry about Mrs. Kemp. Let me worry about her," he grumped, folding his arms over his chest. "You're the one who's out in these parts after hours. Don't you and your crew usually drink yourselves silly over at the bar across the street?"

"We do, but not tonight. I came here to see my lady and get one of those crown and coke floats."

"Your lady?" Mr. Kemp asked as he pushed his glasses up on his nose so that he could ring me up.

"Sonja Watts. Remember I talked about her in the barbershop that time?"

Realization dawned on Mr. Kemp right before my eyes. "Sonja Malone. Little Soni Malone was who you were talking about?"

"Yeah?"

Mr. Kemp grunted and continued to ring me up. When I handed him my credit card, he held onto it for a moment with his mouth pressed into a hard line. Finally, he glared at me and jabbed a finger in my direction. "Soni Malone is not a woman you mess around with. You hear me?"

Stunned, I let out a surprised laugh. "Mr. Kemp, I have no intention—"

"I know about your reputation. I heard all those stories you told in the barbershop, and Sonja Malone is not one of those women. She is not someone you mess around with," he repeated.

"Yessir," I said, swallowing hard around a rush of nervousness. Kairo gave me a knowing look, and I suddenly wondered what I was really getting myself into.

"They're in the other room at them tables in the back."

"Thank you."

There was a coat tree next to the doorway of the dining room. I took off my jacket and hung it there before I went to the rowdy group at the tables in the back of the dining room. Birdie spotted me first. She smiled and tapped Sonja, who was involved in an energetic debate with Estelle.

"Why are you poking me?" she snapped at her sister. Birdie pointed, and Sonja's eyes landed on me.

Oh, God. That smile. *I'm fucking in love with this woman.*

"Hey!" Soni jumped out of her seat, skipped over to me, grabbed my hand, and pulled me over to their table. "I'm so glad you're here."

I greeted everyone at the table — including Estelle's suddenly sour-faced husband. Not sure what that was about.

"So...okay. Please explain the second play of the third quarter — or just the whole third quarter to Estelle. She doesn't understand why our defense won the game."

"Sonja, you're just all about defense because Winston plays cornerback—"

"And you're the same way with Scottie because he plays quarterback. Scottie is great, but our offensive line sucks."

Estelle gave me a pointed look, and Sonja did too.

I shrugged. "Soni's right. The way I see it, Coach Pierce doesn't have an answer for the 4-4 defense. Which is mind-blowing because—"

"Because a majority of these high school football coaches use that play!"

I haven't played football in years, but I've never been more thankful than I did at this moment. The woman next to me, the woman who let me kiss her, and fuck her, and maybe even love her, also loved football and fuck... *I want this.*

Sonja grabbed her milkshake and gave me a sly look. "What?"

I reached for her, drew my hand down the middle of her back. "Nothing, I just..." I bit my lip, then shook my head.

"Hey, Kairo," Estelle said, tipping her chin in my friend's direction. "I'm surprised to see you hanging out with the old married folk."

Kairo rolled her eyes and sat at a chair near the head of the table. "I know," she groaned. "But honestly? I'm just here for the milkshakes," she said, handing me mine. "Once I reach the bottom of this cup, I'm gone."

"Thanks, friend. Super supportive."

"You felt like you needed a support system?" Soni asked.

I took a big sip of my milkshake. "Mm... these really are good."

"There they are!" Deacon said.

We all looked toward the gaggle of teens in Red Raider jersey's and cheerleading uniforms pouring into the dining room. The two that wore Sonja's face looked at her. She tittered nervously and shot out of her seat.

"Great game, y'all!" she chirped, and everyone applauded the kids who looked sheepish — especially her son Winston who'd been the star player who snatched down two interceptions tonight.

"Sit down! Sit down!" Estelle said.

"We're not staying long," the boy who must be her son Scottie said.

"Winston, Naddy, come here," Soni said, her voice nervous and pitched too high.

"How many of those have you had, mom?" her daughter asked under her breath as she pulled up a chair at the table behind us.

"Nadia Watts, I'm an adult, and it's Friday night. I can have more than one drink."

"Cut it out, Naddy," Winston said, squeezing into the chair between his Aunt Birdie and his mom. He kissed his mother on the cheek, and she hugged his neck. And when she did, he noticed me, and a frown creased his brow.

Shit. "Great game, man," I said, sounding like every old head at every high school homecoming game.

"Wait...ain't you, Atlas James?" he asked.

Soni frowned, then looked at me and back at her son again. "How do you know him?"

Winston gave his mother an incredulous look. "He played cornerback, mom. And he still holds the record for most interceptions in a single season."

I squinted at him, slightly skeptical. "Seriously? That record hasn't been broken yet?"

"Twenty-six interceptions in one season? Fuck, no!"

"Winston!"

"Mom! It's Atlas James. How do you know Atlas James?"

I sat back and my chair and looked at Sonni. This was her thing. She needed to decide how to tell them. She licked her lips nervously, and I instinctively rubbed her back to comfort her.

"Mom!" Nadia squeaked, her eyes wide. "Are you dating this guy!"

Soni cringed. "Uh...yeah," she said, then cleared her throat. "Yeah, I am. We are."

I glanced at Winston, who looked as if being stunned twice in one evening had wiped all words from his brain. Nadia, on the other hand, was laughing in a way that might be borderline hysterical.

"Wow," Soni's daughter said finally. "Good for you, mom."

Soni let out a breath and laughed, too. At that moment, I realized that all of the adults were holding their breath, waiting for Winston and Nadia's reactions.

"So... did you have any special drills you did the year you made all of those interceptions?" Winston asked, skipping right over his mother's announcement.

"Uh...yeah."

We talked football for an hour more until Mr. Kemp came in and announced that it was closing time. Everybody filed out onto the sidewalk. While the kids said goodbye to their parents, I turned to Kairo.

"That went surprisingly well."

Kairo made a sound of agreement. "If you don't count the death stares from Deacon, it was a home run."

"Yeah, what's that about?" I asked, looking over my shoulder to find the man glaring at my back.

"I don't know, but are we on for brunch on Sunday?"

"Oh, yeah. Definitely."

"Cool. I'm out."

I stood on the corner and watched Kairo cross the street to the little lot behind The Coworking Spot, where she left her car. Once I was sure she was safely in the car, I turned back to Soni and the rest of the group.

"Me and Amara are gonna stay at your place tonight. Do you mind?" Birdie asked.

"Of course, I don't."

"I don't think she's going home tonight, anyway," Agostina, who had been quiet most of the night, said. She turned to me and waggled her eyebrows.

"Are you riding back with us?" Deacon asked, louder than necessary.

Soni looked at me and smiled. "Yeah, thanks, but I think I'm gonna catch a ride back with Atlas," she said, walking toward me.

I shook my head at her. Nadia was right. My Soni-girl was a little drunk and a lot adorable.

She slid her arms around my waist and looked up at me. "Take me home," she whispered.

"Soni, I swear…"

She pushed up on her tip-toes and kissed me. A real kiss. Not a peck on the lips. Birdie and Aggie whooped and whistled, and I took that as a ringing endorsement. Despite Deacon's open disgust.

"Okay, baby…I'll take you home."

Soni was chatty and nervous on the drive to my place. Practically vibrating in her seat. She hadn't been this tense around me since the day in the greenhouse, and I wasn't sure what that meant.

"This is a nice car," she said, running her fingers over the woodgrain dash. "I didn't realize you even had one."

"Why? Because I ride my bike everywhere? It's a good way to keep in shape, and I don't have to worry about parking."

"That's a plus."

I slowed to a stop at the light a few blocks from my house. The orange light filtering in the windows from the streetlights illuminated her face. I reached over the console and squeezed her thigh. She covered her hand with mine then took it in both of hers.

"That went okay, right? The kids seemed okay with it, right?"

"They're your kids, Soni. You would know better than me." I kissed the back of her hand. "Are you okay with it?"

Soni nodded then looked at me. "Yeah, what about you? Are you okay with it?"

"Yes…more than okay."

A nervous smile twitched at her lips. "Good. Me too."

My apartment was clean, but not nearly as inviting as Soni's garden had been last night.

"Should I light some candles?" I asked as I dropped my keys on the end table.

Soni shrugged out of her denim jacket. I took it from her and hung it on the coat rack next to the door.

"If you want to," she murmured then looked up at me. Lips parted. Pulse thrumming at the hollow of her throat.

She didn't care about candles.

Soni slipped her hands under my shirt, pushed it up and over my head. Her touch was featherlight, almost ticklish. Goosebumps covered my skin. That soft touch made my nipples — and other things — hard. She peppered soft kisses across my chest, and her tongue lapped at my left nipple, while her thumb swept over the right. She looked up at me again, eyes wide and glistening with unshed tears.

"How am I here with you?" she whispered. "Why do you want me? I'm—"

I kissed her before she could utter another self-deprecating word. "Why do I want you?" I asked. "How can I not?"

I pulled her Red Raiders hoodie over her head. She toed off her scuffed up hiking boots and fumbled with my belt buckle while pulling me toward the coach. Her kisses were hard and hungry as she unbuttoned and unzipped my flies. My jeans fell down around my ankles. I stepped out of them, and she pushed me down on the couch.

Soni stepped in between my knees and looked down at me. She was so different tonight. Last night she was playful and shy. Tonight, she stripped out of her clothes while staring down at me with such naked desire that it made my need for her swell into a scary feeling. Bigger than falling.

"Oh, God, " I whispered, watching her slip out of her panties. I sat up and helped her take them off, dragging my open mouth across her belly. Sinking my teeth into the flesh if

223

her hip. I slipped my hand between her thighs. Soni moaned and draped herself over my shoulder, her hands caressed my back. I touched her everywhere. Her beautiful heart-shaped ass, her smooth, round thighs, the backs of her knees, her ankles.

"I want to kiss every inch of you. Taste and worship every part of your body, " I murmured, slipping my fingers between her drenched pussy lips.

She sighed...a sweet wanton sound. I tipped my head back, and she cupped my face in her hands, kissed me, stepped back, and pushed against my shoulders. I frowned.

"Lay back," she whispered, gently urging me backward again.

I rested my back against the couch and moaned softly. I hadn't bothered to turn the lights on, but the curtains were open wide, and the city lights illuminated the soft curves that I wanted in my hands. She was beautiful.

"Look at you...how could I not want you?" I asked softly, shaking my head.

She kissed me. Kissed my mouth made a trail of kisses down my neck. Caressed the expanse of my chest while her kisses got wetter until she was sucking and licking a path down to the waistband of my briefs. Her fingers plucked at the elastic, and I grabbed her wrists.

"Soni...the last time you did this, I only lasted three minutes."

She smiled at me as she sank down to her knees. "It's okay. I know how to get you ready to go again."

I cursed and then lifted my ass a little so she could pull them down and off. The hungry look she gave my dick nearly made me come.

"You're gonna ruin me, aren't you?"

A tiny crinkle formed between her brows and she ghosted her fingertips up the length of me. "I thought we were actively trying to ruin each other for other people."

Gripping me in her fist, she held my dick steady as she gave the tip a sucking kiss. I grabbed fistfuls of the couch cushions and whimpered. Soni smiled, wiggled on her knees, drew the flat of her tongue up my dick, and sucked the tip into her wet, hot mouth again. She did it all while looking right at me. Right into my eyes and that intensity….it was too much.

I closed my eyes and let my head fall back on the couch.

Soni's other hand slid up my inner thigh, fingertips sifting through the hair where it grew thicker in the crease of my thigh. She lapped at the tip, swiping away the precome, and splitting the opening with her tongue before swallowing me down.

"Oh, fuck, Soni," I whispered. My hips jerked and instantly I was so close—

She fisted a handful of hair and tugged.

"Ow!" I looked down at her. "What the fuck, Soni!"

That sly smile of hers reappeared right before she swallowed me down again. Looking me right in the eyes.

"You don't want me to look away?" I asked, running my hand through her short, disheveled curls.

She shook her head and laved my shaft with her tongue.

"You want to look me right in the eyes while you ruin me?"

"Yes," she whispered, taking me deep, straight to the back of her throat. I cupped her cheek, felt her jaw stretch. I thrust deeper into her wet mouth. Soni moaned, her eyes sinking closed for a brief moment, then she fell into a rhythm, gripping my dick in her fist so tightly, and god, I was lost. She looked up at me, tears streaming down her sweet face, and I knew she was, too. Her other hand cupped my balls then teased at the sensitive place right beneath. I spread my knees.

"Soni...that feels so good."

She pulled away, still stroking me. Just the right amount of pressure, but not enough to come. The fingertips of her other hand slipped further, teasing across my ass and precome spurted out of me. Was she going to...?

Oh, yes...

She circled that opening shyly, watching for my reaction. I scooted lower asking for more without really asking.

Her cheeks flushed, and she smiled.

"Wait," I grabbed her hand. She frowned—confused until I brought those fingers to my mouth, sucked them, making them wet. Then I trailed those same fingers from my mouth back to where she had them. I looped my hand around her neck and pulled her in close.

"I told you we had this in common, but my shy little pervert needed to see it for herself, huh?"

"I'm curious. I know how it feels to me, I want to see how it feels to you."

"That's fair. And you do like to be even-Steven, don't you?" *This woman...this fucking woman.* The kiss she gave me made me want to come out of my skin. Deep, wet, and my dick twitched in her loose fist. I closed my hand over hers, squeezing hard, and fucking into that tight fist as her fingers circled my ass.

"Don't be shy about it, Soni," I growled against her lips. Tension and need turned my voice into something like sharped rocks rolling around in my throat. "It's okay, Soni-girl. I want it. I want you to do it. Just—"

The tip of her finger found it's mark and she applied the tiniest bit of pressure. My back bowed, and my breath panted

226

out of me as her wet fingers slipped deeper while her other hand made delicious twisting motions up and down the length of my dick.

"Mmm... Soni. Fuck," I moaned through clenched teeth. I kissed her, trying to keep the sounds inside, but they came out anyway. At least I thought they were just sounds, but no... these were words. I was making—saying words. Laughter spilled out of me as I came, and those words came right behind them.

"Soni... I love you. I love you."

She looked up at me, eyes wide. "You love me?" she whispered.

I held her face in my hands, kissed her. Kissed her again. "Yeah," I said, then laughed. "Yeah, I think I do."

Her bottom lip trembled, and she climbed into my lap; wrapped her arms and legs around me. I hugged her to me. This felt good. So good.

"Atlas?"

"Yeah, Soni-girl?"

"I think I'm falling for you, too."

chapter twenty-two

Sonja

"Hi! I'm here to pay the fees to form an LLC?" I said as I stepped up to the counter at the *Revenue and Business License Division* on Main Street."

"Are you sure? That sounded like a question," the woman with the close-cropped natural hair and gorgeous complexion asked.

I smiled. "Yes, I'm sure. I'm here to pay the fees to register my business as an LLC," I repeated with more confidence.

"That's more like it! Love to see a woman starting her own business." She leaned across the counter and lowered her voice. "Especially when it's one of us."

"Thanks, sis," I said with a wink.

"You have all of the necessary paperwork?"

"Yes, I do." I presented the thick packet of paper and leaned my elbows on the counter while she processed them.

All of the planning and hard work I'd done her the last five weeks had finally culminated into an actual business registered in the state of South Carolina. A month ago, I didn't think I could do this, but now I was official. Of course, the hard part would come when I opened my cart and started to fulfill orders, but I was a goddamn business owner.

As I stepped outside of the *Revenue and Business* offices, I felt an overwhelming need to share this with someone who understood this feeling. Someone who guided me and helped me through the process. That person could only be Atlas.

He answered on the first ring with a smile in his voice.

"I just registered *Good Medicine* as an LLC. I'm officially a business," I blurted.

"How do you feel?"

I smiled as giddiness rushed through me. "Accomplished. Badass...kinda terrified."

"There's nothing to be afraid of, Soni. You have all the tools you need to be successful. You know what comes next—"

"And I have you in my back pocket in case I fuck things up."

"You do, but you're not going to fuck things up. You've got this."

"I do. You made sure of that."

He chuckled. "Hey, so you're downtown, right? Do you want to meet up for lunch or something?"

"Yeah, how about the little cafe in that courtyard near Richardson garage?"

"That's actually perfect. I'm half a block from there now."

"I'm up by the bookstore, but I'll see you in like fifteen."

The desire to pick up a light jog to get to him faster swept through me, but instead, I took my time. I looked up at the bright, October blue sky as I made my way to the cafe. It was the kind of day that was a crisp reminder that Autumn was descending on the south.

I saw Atlas from half a block away, sitting at an outdoor bistro table, bathed by golden midday light."

Goddamn, looking at him actually made me ache.

All of this was so unexpected. I didn't expect to start my own business doing something that was practically second nature to me. I didn't expect this big man who seeped into the little cracks and crevices. We'd been at this for a few weeks now. We spent almost every day together. He ate dinner at my house and slept over most nights— well, we stayed at his if we were going to get a little adventurous.

And that part…that was surprising.

I did things with him that I'd never dreamed of even mentioning to my ex. I mean, it definitely helped that he was down for anything with the added twist that he could also get as good as he gave. That led to many bouts of giggle-laden bedroom antics. I swear, being with him was changing me in all the best ways. It made me feel strong, confident, and liberated in a way that I've never felt before. With him, I felt more like myself than I've ever felt.

And yes… the whole *I love you* thing was a bit terrifying. But when he said that he loved me, I knew that he loved me and not some idea of who or what I once was or who everyone thought I should be. With him, I was Soni. No one else. I wasn't ready to say it back, but I felt it.

I definitely felt it.

Atlas looked up at me at just as that thought crossed my mind. It must have shown on my face because one corner of his mouth kicked up into the same wicked grin that had graced those lips last night before he slid inside of me.

That man…that gorgeous man was inside of me last night and this morning.

Tossing aside prudence and propriety, I trotted the rest of the way to him. He opened his arms, and I leaped into them, straddled his lap, and kissed him—too hard and too deeply for the sidewalk. But I didn't care. The only thing that mattered to me was the way his big hands gripped my waist, how he shifted his hips, settling me right up against his quickly hardening dick, and the soft moan I swallowed with his kisses.

"I think I forgot to tell you this…but you do laugh when you come," I whispered on his lips.

"I do? I'm glad to finally have that confirmed," he said, then traced my lips with the very tip of his tongue.

"It was a delightful discovery, and that sound is officially ranked among my favorite things."

"Well, that's good because the sound and look of you when you come is definitely mine." His hand slid up my back and pressed me closer, deepening the kiss from playful teasing to something that made me grind into the hard length pressed against the seam of my jeans.

"Do we need to take this to my car?" he asked. "I'm parked at the Richardson garage."

Images flooded my mind. Images of him in the backseat of his Lexus with the leather seats and woodgrain door panels. Me straddling him —just like I was now— sinking down on his dick. A shiver rushed through me.

Atlas's smile broadened into something sexy and predatory. "You are so turned on by going at it like a couple of teenagers in the back seat."

"I am. I really am. But I'm also starving so we should definitely eat. But maybe after…"

"Whatever you want, Soni."

Whatever you want…

Had I ever had someone give into my whims so readily? The fact that he both inspired those desires and would readily indulge them made me second-guess eating first. It might be good to really work up an appetite.

"Okay," Atlas said, giving me a soft slap on the ass that made me squeak before he pushed me off of his lap with gentle hands, and urged me inside so that we could order.

With sandwiches, salads, and a cookie as big as my head for us to split. We reclaimed our bistro table and settled in to eat. Just as Atlas took his first bite, his phone rang. Annoyed, he picked up his phone and immediately frowned.

"Sorry, babe. I have to take this.

"No worries. Go ahead."

He pushed away from the table and answered the call pacing a few steps away from the table for a bit of privacy. I caught scraps of the conversation, but mostly I just watched him move. Admired his erect but somehow casual posture as he handled his business. A knowing smile crinkled the corners of his eyes as he made his way back to our table after ending his call.

"Were you looking at my ass?"

"I mean, it's just so perfect and round and just sitting up there like a bitable snack."

He grunted softly as he sat down. "The thought of you using your teeth on me always gets me halfway hard."

"So file that away for later?"

"You mean later, like when you're fucking me in the backseat of my car?"

The way he phrased that... like I was going to be the one in total control, using his body for my pleasure...

It almost made me want to tip our half-eaten sandwiches into the trash and drag him to the parking garage.

"Yes," I said finally. "After we eat."

"Good...I'd like that." He picked up his sandwich and took a hearty bite as if he wanted to get lunch over with, too. "Oh," he said while still chewing. "That was a client call.

She's going to have her boss stop by while we're here. I did an online consultation a week or so ago. They've been having issues with their payroll system, and he's going to write me a paper check. I figured it was now or never. Normally I wouldn't interrupt lunch—"

"It's okay."

"Thanks…it's the part of the job that I hate, you know?"

"Pros and cons of being your own boss. I guess I'll know all about that soon enough."

"Unfortunately," he grumbled. "Speaking of which, how's your online store coming along? Do you have everything set up for presale?"

"Getting there. Aggie is helping me write some of the copy, and we'll do the product photos once we get the first batch made."

He popped a chip in his mouth and nodded. "When do you think you're going to cook up the first batch?"

"This weekend. It's a full moon, and Mama said we can cook it up at the Apothecary."

"What does the full moon have to do with it?"

"We do a full moon ritual every month, so we'll already be together. Also, it's the perfect time for me to birth this thing. I've been nurturing this business all this time, creating recipes, and solidifying the branding, and all of the other things that go into making a business. Tonight is when it all comes together."

He smiled. "I love that. I'm so glad your family is supporting you through all of this."

"Me too."

"But honestly? That's not the part that makes me nervous. I'm kind of worried about production once the orders start coming in. My sisters are going to help me, but it's going to be a lot of work.

"Well." He licked salt off of his fingers. "I'm available for boxing, post office runs, or whatever you need help with when the time comes."

"Really? Isn't that some kind of conflict of interest or something?"

"I mean…" He tipped his head and scrunched up his face thoughtfully. "Maybe there is a little grey area, but I'm the course creator, the business owner, and the instructor. It's not like I'm going to receive any sort of disciplinary action for helping my lady make her dreams come true."

Surprise straightened my spine. "Your lady?" I asked.

"I mean… that's what you are, right? Unless you prefer to be called my girlfriend—"

I leaned across the table and stopped his mouth with my kisses. "I'll be your lady," I murmured against his mouth.

"Hm…good." Atlas smiled and kissed me again, and the world didn't matter--

"Sonja?" a familiar voice barked. "What the fuck is going on here?"

Eric?

I looked over my shoulder to see my ex-husband standing over our table, a look of barely checked rage on his face.

Stunned. I was stunned. So stunned that it took me to a minute to make sense of this.

"Deacon told me you were dating some young guy, but I didn't want to believe it, " he said, shaking his head in disbelief.

Atlas glared at Eric then looked at me. "You know this guy, Soni?"

"I'm her husband, asshole—"

"Ex-husband," I corrected. "What are you doing here?"

"I'm meeting up with Atlas to settle up some business."

234

Realization dawned on Atlas's face as he realized the person who owed him money for a consult and my ex-husband were one and the same. "You're her husband and the guy who owes me fifteen thousand dollars."

"Ex-husband," I corrected again.

"That's how you know each other. Oh, fuck. This is fucked," Atlas muttered.

"We have two kids, thirteen years, and a mortgage between us, so yeah. I know her," Eric continued as if he didn't hear me correct him the first two times he called me his wife. "The question is, how do *you* know her?"

"Nah. A better question is, how do you know *him*, Atlas?" I asked.

"I told you. I did an online consult with someone from his company, but that was months ago. Long before you started the *Entrepreneur Academy*—"

"Ahhh, so you're the one who has been filling her head with this childish dream of making money from her handmade lotions and creams—"

"Childish?" I scoffed.

"You have been mixing up those bullshit remedies with your mom since we were kids. Everybody knows that it's bullshit and that your mother is a snake oil salesman."

"Oh. Wow." I thought I couldn't be more stunned than I was when Eric first walked up, but now he'd disrespected me and my mother in the span of three seconds. "You know what?" I pushed away from the table and stood. "I'm just gonna go."

Atlas grabbed my wrist. "Baby, don't—"

"Baby?" Eric repeated so loudly that his voice echoed. "Is that what's going on here? Atlas, are you fucking my wife?"

"Ex-wife! I'm your ex-wife. You divorced me. Remember?"And now my voice was the one ringing and echoing in the quiet corridor between the buildings. Frustration made tears spring to my eyes, and I tried again to back away. Atlas held onto my hand and stood up slowly.

"Eric…you should give me the money you owe me and walk away," he said. "Now." His voice was colder than I'd ever heard it.

"How did you know she was my wife? Did you look her up online or something?" My ex-husband sucked his teeth and pulled out his checkbook. "I knew I shouldn't have trusted you to look at my finances. You're probably telling her about all of my —"

"You fucking idiot," I growled. "I did your payroll. I probably know everything he found and what he told you to do to fix the mess you made over there since I quit. Lemme guess. You still haven't hired anyone to do the payroll, and that's why you have to write him a paper check, huh?"

He scoffed. "I can't believe you, Sonja. Running around with some guy half your age? What are you even thinking about? Has he met my kids? Been to my house?"

"It's *my* house."

Eric glared at the two of us in turn. "What kind of example is this to set for our children? *Our daughter.* I really expected better of you, Soni," he said, finally then turned and walked away.

I stared after him in wide-eyed disbelief, feeling humiliated in a way that I'd never been in my life.

"Soni--"

"I can't believe this," I snatched my hand out of his grasp. "He just disrespected and degraded me in public."

"I'm sorry—"

"That's how we look to everyone, isn't it? Some woman running around with a guy half her age?" I turned to him and looked him in the eye. "And Deacon... why would he do that? Why would he make me into some whore who brings strange men home? In my bed. Am I in the wrong here?"

His shoulders drooped. "Soni...why do you care what about everyone thinks? You and me are in this relationship. Not your ex-husband. Not Deacon. You and me." Hesitantly, he took a step toward me, but when he reached for me, I drew in a shaky breath. "Don't do that, baby. Let me hold you."

I crumbled into his embrace. Hating the fact that I still wanted his touch even though I didn't want to need it. "I'm humiliated."

"Don't be. He's the one who made an ass of himself. Not you."

Wasn't that the same thing?

I pushed away and looked up at him. "I don't think I can do this."

"Do what?"

"This." I gestured between us. "You and me. I should never have let it happen." I turned my back to him and grabbed my things.

Atlas wrapped his arms around me, pulling me back into his chest. "Sonja, don't," he said softly, his lips against the nape of my neck.

Gah... it felt so good to be held. So good to be held by him. It would be so easy...

I wrestled out of his embrace and walked a short distance away from him. "It's just too much to handle. My focus should have been on my business. Not on you and now..."

"Really, Sonja?" he asked softly, then he made a sound. A sound that made me stop what I was doing and turn to him.

"Not even two seconds before that asshole walked up, you told me you would be my lady, and now I'm nothing more than a distraction? Is that what you're saying right now?"

I shook my head. "I know what I said." I looked down at the pavers under my feet.

Atlas moved in close again. "Did you mean it? I meant it. I meant every word I said. Did you mean it?" His hand slid around my neck, thumb skimming my throat in that way that always made me feel claimed in a way that I knew I should resist.

"How far can this go, Atlas? I mean, I have kids. One headed to college and one in her sophomore year of high school. I don't have time to hang around with my boyfriend."

"So let me find the time. I'll find a way to fit in around all of the other things."

I looked up at him. "The evidence of my life with him will always be around. I know you're uncomfortable with that."

"Yeah, but that's my problem. I want to be with you, Soni. I'll get over it."

And his gaze was steady and sure right now. Much steadier than I felt. Did that mean that he was sure of what he wanted? Could I even trust that he understood exactly what that meant and what he was getting himself into? "And the kids... are you ready to play a role in their lives? Because that's non-negotiable. Do you want to be a part of my life in that way, Atlas? Because that's what it means for me to be your lady."

A furrow formed between his brows. "Of course, I'll have a relationship with them. Don't know how that will look, though. I honestly didn't think that far in the future, Sonja. I just know that I want to be with you."

And there it was.

I backed away from him with a sigh. "I think we should step back and think about where things between us are going, Atlas. I love spending time with you, but... I really can't afford to be distracted now."

He shook his head. "I can't believe this. You're breaking up with me, and I haven't even done anything wrong."

"We're not breaking up. I just want to take some time to figure out if this is what we really want."

"No," he said, his voice soft. "You need to decide if *I'm* who you really want." Atlas rocked back on his heels and looked up at the sky. "Kairo said this might happen. It still sucks."

"I'm sorry—"

Atlas shook his head again, leaned in, and kissed me on the forehead. "When you're ready. I'll be waiting for you."

chapter twenty-three
Sonja

It was the first full moon of Autumn. The blood moon. The Hunter's moon. The moon of dying grass. The leaves were starting to turn, the days were getting shorter, and the crisp bite in the air lingered long after the sun came up. During the full moon, my sisters and I gathered on the Malone land and did our "witchy thing" as Eric called it. It was also the night I wanted to start mixing up the samples for *Good Medicine*. Infusing the mixture with good intentions and divine feminine energy. And of course, good laughs and good booze with my sisters and my mom.

When we were younger, I wondered why my father didn't join us. He took in the moon from the back porch in his favorite rocking chair. He claimed that he had Cherokee blood, but we never really knew if that was true. He said his mother was forced to leave the reservation when he was too young to remember any of the rituals and ceremonies, but part of me wondered if he wished he'd tried harder to find his family. This land was his by birthright, but we knew next to nothing about the man who left it to him.

Either way, Eudora and Grover's land was the best place to be at moonrise.

She came up fat, red, and round on the horizon before the sun had fully set. Now she hung heavy in the sky, right over our bonfire. Bathing us in her cool light.

I closed my eyes and breathed deep. Taking in the fragrant scent of dry leaves and my mother's lavender fields. A deep calm descended on me, and I was glad I decided to come out here — even though I wanted to hide in my bedroom. Not that I didn't have a right to feel that way after what happened with Atlas and Eric.

My bedsheets still smelled like Atlas, but I was pretty sure it was already over between me and Atlas. I still couldn't wrap my head around that they knew each other. Even though I knew it was just business, it still felt like a betrayal of sorts. Well, better that it happened now rather than later when me and Atlas were months or years deep into a relationship. After that outburst from Eric, I knew it was too soon for me to date anyone. I didn't want to welcome that kind of drama into my already fractured home.

My sister Aggie threw another log onto the pit-fire and picked up the mangled rake that we used to stoke it. I pulled my blanket around my shoulders and folded my legs so that I could tuck my feet under it.

"Where's Mama and Birdie?" I asked.

Aggie sighed and took the Adirondack chair next to me. "She's trying to convince Naddy to join us."

"Hm. Good luck with that."

Aggie dug a pointy piece of clear quartz out of her hip pocket and sat it on the small round table between us. "What's going on with you?" she asked.

I debated lying, but instead, I shook my head and said, "I don't want to talk about it." My voice cracked with emotion, and my older sister frowned at me.

"Okay," she said, never one to push. But knowing her, she'd already read my energy and knew exactly what was going on.

"You don't have to stay out here the whole time, but at least come out and set some intentions," my mother said, her voice carrying on the night air.

"What's the point, GG? I don't believe in any of this stuff," Nadia grumbled. She was walking hand in hand with Amara, who took in the fire with big eyes and an excited grin.

Me, Agostina, and Birdie, who was walking toward the bonfire behind them, gasped audibly.

"Mama, I—"

My mother held up a hand to silence me, and I went quiet almost involuntarily. She grasped Nadia by the shoulders and turned her so that they faced each other. "Now what did you say, chile?" she asked in a voice so soft and low that I barely heard her over the roar and crackle of the fire.

Nadia cast a furtive glance at me, and Mama gave her chin two swift taps. "Don't look at her. She doesn't have the answer. I asked you what you said."

My daughter swallowed and then squared her shoulders. "I said I don't believe in this stuff."

"What *stuff*?"

"All this witchy stuff that you guys do out here on the full moon. Daddy says it's nonsense, and I don't know, I kinda agree with him."

I clenched my teeth.

"Daddy says, huh?" Mama echoed. "Your daddy is a smart man, and he knows a great many things, but he don't know nothing about this. This is woman business." She covered Nadia's heart with her hand. "Do you believe in yourself?"

She looked confused for a moment. "Yes?" she said finally.

"You believe in me? Your mama? Your aunties?"

"Yes, ma'am," Nadia answered a bit more confidently.

242

"Well..." Mama cupped Nadia's cheeks in her hands. "You believe in this. That's all this is, chile. Malone women, coming together to share they hopes and dreams and hurts. To find strength in each other. You understand?"

Nadia nodded. "Yes, ma'am."

Mama patted her cheek, then they both made their way to remaining chairs around the fire. When she was settled in, Mama's gaze finally met mine, and I thanked her wordlessly for steering my daughter straight. I knew Eric was nonreligious and often called my family's rituals and traditions silly and nonsensical, but I thought he only said those things to me. Not our daughter. The fact that he would try to taint her that way pissed me off.

Agostina reached across the space between our chairs, grabbed my hand, and squeezed it. I looked at her, and she gave me a slow blink.

Let it go.

I closed my eyes and exhaled, letting it go. I had a lot to let go of tonight. That was what the full moon was about.

It never used to be this hard for me to get grounded enough to commune with the moon. I didn't dare say that out loud, though. Mama would probably launch into a tirade about me living too far from the family land and not paying attention to the cyclic nature of life and seasons. She wouldn't be wrong. I used to feel the moon phases in my body— all of us were once hyper-aware of her waxing and waning. Now it seemed that Aggie was the only one among us who paid real attention to it anymore. She planned her business around it, and that really seemed to be working for her.

"Hey, Aggie... remember when you were going to write that book about planning your creative business around the moon?" I asked.

My sister's head was tipped back, eyes closed, her face bathed in cool moonlight. "I remember. How old was I then? Like twenty-five?"

"Twenty-seven," Mama corrected. "It was the year of your Saturn return."

The obvious was left unsaid. It was also the year that my sister lost her mind.

Agostina has and probably always would be sensitive, but it wasn't until her twenty-seventh birthday that we found out just what that meant.

She heard voices in empty rooms.

Felt the presence of entities in her bed, in the shower, sitting across from her at the kitchen table.

We joked that the Boo Hag was visiting her, but when she started talking to those spirits out loud, we all became a little concerned.

Aggie was the wild child among us. She loc'd her own hair at fourteen, covered herself in sigils and religious iconography the moment she was old enough to get inked without the consent of a parent. She was also the one who dabbled in drugs. Not just the lightweight shit like weed, but the scary addictive stuff. Me and Birdie thought that might be what was going on when she started rambling on about staying up all night to talk to the spirit of the man who lived in the little blue house up the street. During what we thought was an especially episode, we took her to the ER. The placed her on a seventy-two-hour hold that ended up lasting thirty days. After lots of testing, Aggie was diagnosed with Bipolar II and put on a treatment of medication and talk therapy. She hasn't had a manic depressive episode since.

Of course, Mama and Daddy didn't really believe Aggie was mentally ill. As far as they were concerned, it was just the ancestors speaking through her. When I asked Aggie, she didn't totally disagree. She said the anti-psychotics quieted the voices, but didn't silence them. However, when she did any sort of repetitive work, she often slipped into a meditative state that allowed them to come through. I'd seen it happen, and if I hadn't experienced it for myself, I wouldn't have believed it.

"Well, someone else already wrote one," Aggie said finally.

"Yeah, but is it rooted in our kinda magic?" Mama asked as she passed Aggie the jar of homemade hooch.

"Nah, it's European influenced."

"So no one has written your book. That's your book to write, so write it."

Aggie brought the jar to her lips and took a generous sip. The big sister in me nearly said something about her drinking on her medication but thought better of it. She was fine, and knowing her, she probably didn't take her meds today to make sure she was okay to drink.

I shut my mouth and took the jar of hooch when she passed it to me. When I brought the clear liquid to my lips, I smelled nutmeg and vanilla...maybe some allspice and honey for sweetness. The first swallow was hot and aromatic as it made it's way to my belly. When I opened my eyes, Nadia was looking at me expectantly. I was much younger than her when I participated in this sacred ritual for the first time. I stretched out my hand and passed her the jar.

Naddy pushed Amara off of her lap and took it from me. After one hesitant sip, she coughed and immediately tried to pass it on to Birdie.

"No, ma'am! You need to take a proper swallow of that before we can continue," Birdie said.

245

My daughter looked at me, and I shrugged. "Birdie's right."

Naddy frowned and looked down at the liquid in the jar before she brought it to her lips and took another swallow. She was still holding the liquid in her mouth when she tried to pass the jar to Birdie again. My sister simply stared at her until she managed to muscle down that mouthful of liquor.

"Good girl," Birdie said, and took the jar from her.

"Can I have some?" Amara asked, reaching for it.

"No, ma'am. You have to be at least seven years old. Ain't that right, mama?" Birdie said to her daughter.

"That's right, Bird. Your time will come soon enough," she said, patting a pouty Amara on her knee. "Do you know what a luck charm or a mojo bag is, Naddy?" my mother asked, turning her attention back to my daughter.

"You mean...like the cereal?" Nadia joked.

"Nadia Watts—"

"I'm sorry, GG," she interrupted before I could scold her any further. "I mean... yeah. I kinda know what it is."

My mother gave me a look that instantly made me feel ashamed. I wasn't doing right by my daughter.

"Everything in this world has its own power," Mama said as she pulled items out of her sweater pockets. "Every herb, every flower, every rock, and even the words that come out of our mouths have power. It's our job to know how to use it."

I leaned forward to see the items my mother had in her lap. A fingertip-sized bit of John the Conqueror root, peppermint leaves, dried basil and bay leaf, a cinnamon stick, an alligator tooth, and a small green flannel pouch. Mama was making me a mojo for success and abundance. My eyes teared, and I swallowed around the unspoken love I felt in her actions. Like I said, Mama Malone may not hug and kiss you, but as a conjure-woman, this was one of the many ways she showed her love. Making that mojo under the full moon infused it with all the power of those herbs and her good intentions.

Mama stood and walked over to me, the mojo bag fat with all of her good medicine. "Once I give this to ya mama, it's for her hands and eyes only," she said as she tied the bag closed. "I bind this bag to my daughter's purpose," she murmured then held it out to me.

"Thank you, mama."

She leaned in and gave me a kiss on the forehead, then went back to her chair. The bag had a long string. I hung it around my neck and tucked the actual bag itself into my bra. The magic felt warm and alive against my skin.

"When we were little, we would make trips to the coast to visit mama's family during the summer. You remember that, Aggie?" Birdie asked.

"It's one of my favorite memories…" she murmured. "Mama and her sisters would drink homemade hooch and dance."

Mama took a swallow of said hooch and grunted. "Me and my sisters didn't dance. We walked the damballah."

My mother stood slowly. Stood up erect and strong, and as I watched her, she seemed to grow taller than her five foot four inches in height. Bigger than her narrow frame. Her presence surrounded us like an embrace.

And then… she began to dance.

Feet slightly apart, knees bent, she pushed her chest forward, exhaled in a deep, sonorous breath that pushed at the flames of the fire. The sound like big and rich, resonated and then settled in my bones. Then her hips contracted forward, spine unfurling one vertebra at a time only to throw her head back and start the sequence over again. Her body a serpentine line. The moon on cradled on her shoulders.

Aggie threw off her blanket and stretched her arms over her head. Fingertips to the sky, and then like a whip, her spine arched, long locks flying, and then I was on my feet.

There were always drums when my mother and her sisters danced. But we needed nothing but the moon, our bodies, and our sacred fire tonight. The drumbeat was in our feet and our hearts.

I couldn't tell you how much time passed, but at one point, we were all on our feet — even Nadia. With tears in her eyes, I watched my daughter discover the thing that bound us together as family and as women. I took her in my arms. My mother and sisters enveloped us.

"This is what it means to be a Malone woman," Mama said in a breathless whisper. And at that moment, I knew that my daughter would never question if all of this was real again.

chapter twenty-four
Sonja

The bonfire had burned down to a few ruby embers when
Mama stood and made her way down the path to the
apothecary. Wordlessly, we all followed her. Nadia fell into
step with us. Eager to participate in cooking up the first batch
of *Good Medicine*. I was more than a little nervous. This was
going to be the first time I made such a large batch, and
consistency was key.

The air in the apothecary smelled strongly of basil and
allspice. Mama mopped the shop every Friday with a wash to
draw abundance and prosperity. The sweet, familiar smell
brought back pleasant memories of manning the cash register
with my mother while she smiled and helped customers. The
smell was particularly strong, which made me wonder if she'd
washed the floors again to prepare for me.

"In here, girls," Mama called when she heard us come
through the screen door.

I followed the sound of her voice back to the small kitchen
behind the cash wrap. It was galley style with all of the
appliances and cabinets against the back wall. This was where
she made all of the remedies she sold in her shop.

"Well, we have work to do, don't we?" Birdie said as she
stood up. There was a dark twinkle in her eye.

I looked at my other sister, my mother, Nadia.

"Show me them recipes," my mother drawled, holding out her hand for my beat-up composition notebook.

I clutched it to my chest, suddenly nervous about my mother reading its contents. She taught me everything I know, and I worried that she might find my recipes childish or simplistic—

My mother snatched the notebook out of my hands.

"Mama!"

"Quit stalling. This booze is starting to work on me." She pushed her reading glasses up on her nose and opened the book.

Agostina grabbed a big box that had been left by the front door and slid it onto the counter. "So, we can change them if you want," she said as she began to open the flaps on the box. "But, I thought they might be cool to sell along with your skincare herb garden seedlings?"

My breath caught in my lungs as she lifted one of the tiny pots out of the box and passed it to me. "Oh, my god, Aggie. What did you do?"

She smiled and ducked her head. "You know how I can get in that deep meditative state when I'm at the wheel. I started making these tiny little bowls and couldn't stop. They didn't sell all that well, so I figured they would be perfect for you. Threw one of those milky green glazes on there that you like and voila! *Good Medicine* medicine bowls!"

The bowls were palm-sized and delicate like all of her work. "This is perfect."

"Mom?"

"Yes, Naddy?"

"Is it okay if I take some pictures of this stuff? I think it would be awesome for your Instagram."

I turned to my daughter and smiled. "That's an excellent idea, Naddy."

"A'ight, y'all," Birdie said, clapping her hands together. "Let's get started."

It was a lot of work. I knew it would be before we even started. Excitement buoyed us for a few hours, but around one in the morning, our energy began to wane. I sent Nadia up to the house because she was practically sleeping on her feet. Birdie cut out not too long after. Mama fell asleep at the cash wrap with her head resting on her folded arms. That left me and Aggie filling tins and medicine bottles with salves, cremes, and oils, and sticking on labels. In the early morning light, we took product photos with her fancy camera and uploaded them to my online store.

"This looks so good, Aggie. Thank you."

She leaned into me and rubbed my upper back. "You're welcome. Now help me get Mama up to the house."

"Fine, but you wake her up. I'm not trying to get punched in the mouth. You know she wakes up like the house is burning down."

Aggie laughed. "I'll nudge her if you snatch me back the moment you see I'm in danger."

We walked Mama back up to the house without incident, and I crashed the moment I found something soft enough to fall asleep on and didn't wake up until a little afternoon. Nadia didn't go to school, but it was okay for her to miss a day or two. Especially for something like this. Arguably, she may have learned more by helping me last night than she would have learned in school anyway.

With the wagon loaded up, we drove home. I was still tired, but a lot less anxious now that I had enough product to launch the shop after my presentation next week. Damn…. I still needed to put the finishing touches on that, too.

"Atlas liked all of the photos from last night and left you a comment. You want me to read it?" Nadia asked.

My belly did a nervous flip. "Sure."

"He said, 'Wow! Y'all were really up all night working! Looks like it paid off. *Good Medicine* is off to a good start!' And then there's a bunch of emojis."

I could almost hear the excitement and encouragement, and that made me smile. "Like his comment and tell him thank you for me."

From the corner of my eye, I saw Nadia's fingers fly across the screen of her phone.

"Mom?"

"Yeah, Naddy?"

"What happened between you and Atlas?"

"Nothing. What makes you think something happened?"

"Well, he hasn't been around in a while."

"He's been busy," I said with a shrug. "I've been busy, too."

"It's not just that. Me and Winston went to see him last Friday, and he said that y'all were taking a break."

I frowned. "You and Winston went to see him?"

"He's our friend, too, Mom," she said with an exasperated sigh.

"I'm sorry. I didn't realize that y'all had grown so attached to him," I murmured guilt swamping me. Eric was halfway right about me, introducing Atlas to the kids. What was I thinking? "What Atlas said was true. We are taking a break, I guess."

"I don't get it. Why? Did he do something to hurt you?"

"No, he's been perfect. It's just… it's complicated, Naddy. It might be too soon for me to date anyone."

"Oh, come on, Mom. That's just crazy. You were literally the happiest I've ever seen you when he was around. And he *clearly* loves you. I don't get it. You should be together."

A surprised laugh and shook my head at her. My daughter wasn't wrong, but how was this supposed to work? When we were just fucking and having fun, I didn't have to think about how he would fit into my family. But these feelings gave the relationship between us a lot more weight. I mean, should I spend some time alone first? Take some time to figure out who I was without a man in my life? Either way, I was too tired to figure it out now.

I turned the corner a block up from my house. As I approached my driveway, I saw that Estelle was just pulling into her garage. I haven't talked to her since my confrontation with Eric. She was competing with Atlas when it came to delivering the most text messages a day, but until now, I wasn't ready to talk to her. As far as I knew, Estelle didn't realize why I was keeping her at a distance. She deserved to know why.

"Go on inside, I need to talk to Stelle," I told Nadia as we got out of the car. "And turn on the coffee pot when you get in there."

"Okay, Mom." Nadia waved to Estelle as she emerged from her garage. "He, Auntie Stelle!" she called.

"Hey, Naddy!" Estelle called back.

I shoved my hands into the pockets of my jacket and crossed the street. Estelle had stopped in the middle of the driveway, forcing me to come the last couple hundred feet. There was a silent challenge in that, and I didn't begrudge her.

"Hey, friend!" she said as I approached. "Wait. Are we still friends?"

"I don't know, Estelle. Are you and Deacon on the same page about me dating Atlas?"

Estelle frowned and moved in closer. "What are you talking about, Sonja?"

I told her about the confrontation with Eric. Recounted the way he had shamed me for dating a younger man and how he'd implied that he and Deacon discussed the matter at length. "He didn't make it a secret that he disapproved when we were all at Kinfolks that night," I reminded her.

Estelle sighed. "I'm so sorry, Sonja. We had a huge fight about how he behaved that night. I didn't realize that he'd talked to Eric, too."

"What was that about, Estelle? Doesn't he know that Eric was the one who asked for the divorce?"

"Yeah, he knows. But they're also friends, Sonja. Who knows what Eric has been telling him?"

I clenched my teeth against the things I wanted to say. Eric had no right to talk shit about me. Our marriage was over. That was what he wanted. I had every right to move on. To date someone else.

"So that's why you've been ignoring my text messages and my phone calls. I thought our friendship was stronger than that."

"I thought so, too, but you weren't there, Estelle. Eric did everything but pin a scarlet letter on my chest. He humiliated me." I shook my head. "And with all of this stuff I'm trying to do, I just didn't have the energy to deal with it or explain myself—"

"I'm so sorry," she said again, then stepped forward and pulled me into a hug. "I'm so sorry he did that to you."

I wrapped my arms around my friend and buried my face in her neck. I'd felt so alone in all of this and didn't realize it until this moment.

"Is that why you're not talking to Atlas, too?" she asked.

Words failed me, so I just hugged her tighter and willed myself not to cry. I missed him. No matter how complicated this thing was, no matter how good and right it seemed to let him go because he wasn't ready for this… I missed him.

"Oh, Soni… he's miserable, too."

I pulled away and looked at her. "Really?"

"Oh, honey. He's been pacing around the doors of my studio like a lost puppy and asking after you."

"Well, shit." The thought of him hurting…that did me in. "I didn't mean to hurt him, Estelle. But he shouldn't waste his time on me."

Estelle cradled my face in both her hands. "What makes you think he would ever think or feel like it was wasted time?"

"He's too young, and I come with too much baggage."

"Have you seen that man's shoulders? I think he's perfectly able to carry some of that baggage for you. And more importantly, he's willing. You should give him a call, Sonja."

"I'll think about it."

When I finally got myself together, I walked back across the street to my house and got in the shower. I smelled like woodsmoke, hooch, and every herb I'd touched last night. And god, I was so, so tired. The kind of tired that needed help to shut down. I would usually climb into the tub when I felt like this, but I was too tired to even do that, so a shower would have to do.

I thought about what Estelle said.

Was Atlas really ready to help me carry all of this baggage? That day at the cafe he told me that he'd never really considered how it would work, but he knew that he wanted to be with me. Was that enough?

There was also something else I didn't consider...

Maybe this wasn't meant to be long term.

Could I do that? Could I be with him, wholly and entirely in the moment without any expectation of forever? That was still worth it, right? I've only known the man for a couple of months, and already he has enriched my life. And as my clever, observant daughter said, he clearly loves me.

Clearly.

He loves me.

Me.

"Stupid woman," I murmured. I had everything I wanted right in front of me, but I was too stubborn to see it— to see him for what he was.

My man.

Dammit. It was time for me to stop being stupid and go get my man.

chapter twenty-five
Atlas

At the end of each cohort of *The Entrepreneur Academy*, we have a sort of graduation ceremony where each student gives a presentation. Over the last few years, it has become one of my favorite things about the course— not because it meant that the cohort was finally over, but because we all got to see how six weeks of intense focus could become a thriving business. It was really special because their family members got to see all of the incredible work they'd done, too. That's not to say that everyone who completed the course went on to become successful entrepreneurs. But at the very least, they had the tools they needed to get started. In this cohort, only two of my students registered for an LLC—Heather and Soni.

It had been thirteen days since I walked away from her on the patio of that cafe. My gut told me it was the right thing to do. She needed space and time to think about what she wanted from this—if she wanted us.

I didn't expect it to take this long, though.

Call me cocky, but I thought that she loved me. She may not have said those actual words, but I could tell that she felt it. I saw it in her eyes whenever I said it to her. But here we were. Thirteen days without talking or seeing each other, and I was trying not to lose my shit.

Watching the door, I paced the length of the room, straightening chairs. The space we rented for the graduation party was in *ArtCrush*, a place up the block that was primarily studio space for a group of eclectic, but well-known local artists. To keep the rent down, the hosted events in their common areas, and it's worked out well for us so far. The front half of the building was set up for a seated audience with a podium and a desk where I sat to make sure the slide decks my students had made were projected on the wall. I passed by that desk now and ducked into the hallway just to the left of it to check my phone for the hundredth time.

The thing hadn't bleeped, dinged, or vibrated in hours, but I thought…. Hell, I didn't know what I thought. I also didn't know why I was calling Soni for the second time today. She hadn't answered any of my previous calls, but I was too stubborn to believe that I should just give up.

The call went straight to voicemail. "Hey…I know I already called today. I don't know why I keep calling. I know we're taking a break or broken up or whatever, but I just wanted to say… I can't wait to see you tonight. I hope we can talk. If you don't want to, I guess I'll have to accept that this is it for us. But shit… I don't want it to be over, Soni. I don't want us to be over…"

I said goodbye and hung up the phone after that. What else was there to say? I'd left similar messages over the last few days, and she only responded once to let me know that she wasn't ready to talk yet. I knew I had to respect that.

But damn...

I missed her.

Kairo seemed to believe that all I missed was the sex. And yeah, that was partly true, but it was much deeper than that. I let myself feel things for Soni that never wanted to feel for anyone else and her pushing me away cut deeper than it

258

should. Especially since I hadn't done anything wrong. This was all a reaction to that confrontation with her ex-husband.

Fuck. If I knew it was going to turn out like this, I would've punched him the moment he raised his voice at her. What the fuck was wrong with that guy anyway? Humiliating the mother of your children like that in a public place? What kind of man could live with himself after treating my Soni that way?

My Soni.

Was she even mine? Had she ever been?

I scrubbed my hand over my face and stuffed my phone back into my pocket. This shit was driving me crazy. But what could I do about it? Run from it?

Honestly, that was exactly what I wanted to do. I wanted to pack up my shit and run away from this because if she didn't want to be with me, I wasn't sure why I needed to stay here.

Kairo made me promise I wouldn't, though. So I won't.

A comforting din of noise built as the space began to fill, and people said their hellos and found their seats. I leaned against the podium and watched the doors at the back of the room. I knew she was going to be here. She'd emailed the slide deck for her presentation two days ago. They looked good. Better than good. They were branded with her colors, and her brand identity was evident in each one. She'd also mixed her first batch and was prepared to open her cart before the end of class. That day at the cafe she was so nervous about it, but now it seemed as if she didn't need my help at all.

I just hoped that didn't mean that she no longer needed me.

"The caterer has everything all set up in the hall," Kairo said.

"Good. I'm looking forward to hitting that cheese and charcuterie board," I said, smoothing my hand down the buttons of my dress shirt.

"Have you talked to Sonja yet?"

"She'll be here tonight," I said after shaking my head. "Maybe she'll have something to say to me then. Either way, she sent over the slides for her presentation tonight. They look good. I can tell that she worked hard on them."

Kairo dropped a hand on my shoulder and squeezed comfortingly. "For what it's worth, I hope the two of you work things out. You were good together."

I rolled my eyes. "You're saying this now? After everything you predicted would happen has actually come to pass?"

"That doesn't mean I wanted it to happen," Kairo said, her brows knitting together. "You know that I want happiness for you as much as I want it for myself, right?"

In truth, I didn't. I'd never thought of it that way. Being back home sometimes felt like a long list of obligations I had to meet. Things I had to do for others. I couldn't be sure if I did those things, met those obligations because I wanted to make them happy or if I did it simply because it was what was expected of me. Except when it came to Soni. All I wanted to do was make her smile and cry happy tears.

"I know now," I said after clearing my throat. "I want the same for you, too."

Kairo squeezed my shoulder again then tipped her chin at the woman who just entered the auditorium. "Yeah, well. I guess it's time I quit being a punk and ask Jerricka out. Maybe it was won't end with me finding a new barber."

Jerricka waved and smiled as she found a seat. Kairo gave her a wink. I raised my brows and looked at my friend.

260

"Tonight?" I asked with a raise of my brow.

Kairo shrugged. "I've put it off long enough, I think."

"A'ight then," I said, giving her a playful shrug. "It's about damn time."

She practically skipped down the stairs to where Jerricka sat. A bright smile spread across the pretty barber's face, and Kairo sat next to her, turning on all the charisma that she'd held back all of this time.

Best friend is in love. You love to see it.

And then, flanked by her sisters and with Nadia and Winston in tow, Soni came through the door. She was wearing one of those dresses that I always associated with African women. It was green and covered with a big floral print and clung to her soft, generous curves, hugging her body the way I'd dreamed about for the last two weeks. I stepped around the podium and met them at the back of the room. "Hey, y'all."

"What's up, Atlas!" Winston grinned, and I dapped him up. "The flyer on Instagram said there would be food?"

"Down that back hall," I said with a laugh. "But make sure you leave some for the rest of us."

Nadia gave me a quick hug, then followed her brother. Little Amara waved shyly, and Birdie leaned in to give me a kiss on the cheek. Aggie grabbed my hand and pressed a seafoam green pebble into my palm.

"What's this?"

"Green aventurine," she said with a one-shouldered shrug. "Just in case you need a little boost of confidence." She raised a knowing brow at me then grabbed a seat next to Birdie and her niece.

"She gave me one, too," Sonja said with a laugh before opening her hand to show me her matching gemstone.

Her voice. God, I missed that raspy, bluesy voice of hers. "Soni... this dress. You look beautiful," I murmured.

"A little better than a raggedy band tee and ripped jeans, huh?"

"I love you in that raggedy tee and jeans. And in this dress. I love you any and every way you'll let me, Soni."

She looked up at me. Her mouth was painted red, her lashes were dark, framing her smiling brown eyes. Eyes already bright and twinkly with unshed tears. I wanted to hold her. My chest literally ached because I missed the feel of her against it.

"I got your message earlier. I'd like to talk after this. Maybe we can go out for a drink?"

"A drink. Okay." But it wasn't okay. A drink sounded formal and not at all promising, but I'd keep an open mind. Maybe drinking a little would lead to kissing and me spending the night in her arms. "Are you ready for your presentation?" I asked, changing the subject in an attempt to keep things light.

She gave me a shrug. The movement exposed the smooth round of her shoulder. I wanted to kiss it.

"I had an excellent instructor. I think I've got it in the bag."

"The instructor or the presentation?" I asked.

She tapped her chin in faux contemplation. "At this point, I'm pretty sure I could bag both." She gave me a wink and stepped around to me to go find a seat down front with the rest of her cohort.

Relief washed over me. Maybe I had nothing to worry about.

I spun on my heel and went straight to the podium. This was my favorite part of teaching this course, but I was suddenly anxious to get it done and over with.

"Good evening, everyone! And thank you all for attending the presentation and graduation party for the seventh cohort of *The Entrepreneur Academy!*"

The assembled audience clapped and cheered, then I launched into a little spiel I'd written to explain the course as well as promote *The Coworking Spot* and the other courses we offered. Then it was time for presentations.

The assignment was to use the work they'd done during the six-week course to create a simple business plan. In that plan, they would summarize the problem they planned to solve for their customers, identify their target market and how they would sell to them, and present a financial plan with their projected profits and losses. A lot of their presentations were short and sort of vague, but heavy on branding and marketing, which was to be expected. Only Heather and Soni had a meaty enough business plan to really demonstrate how much a person could get out of the course if they applied themselves. Which is why I saved the two of them for last. Soni second to last because I thought attention-starved Heather would like to be the last thought on everyone's mind before they went to mingle and drink free booze.

When Soni came to stand at the podium and introduce herself, I noticed something about her that I hadn't earlier. Well…two things. The first was that her ass looked amazing in that dress, and the second was that the shy, sweetness that I came to associate with her was all but gone. Correction: she was still sweet in more ways than one, but in her nude heels, and modestly sexy dress, Sonja Watts looked like a boss.

Not a lady boss, or a girl boss, or a mompreneur or any other hashtag she might use to describe herself, but a boss.

And, well… It kinda made my dick hard?

Soni cleared her throat. "Atlas?"

"Yes, Soni?" I answered, realizing once the words were out of my mouth that I'd answered her like we were alone and not in front of an audience.

She glanced over her shoulder at me, cheeks red, a smile on her sexy mouth. "Can you start the slide deck for me, please?"

"Oh! Yeah, sorry. My bad. I got a little distracted."

"Clearly!" Birdie piped up from the back of the room.

Soft laughter rippled through the crowd.

"Thank you, Atlas," Soni said, and I was thankful that I was sitting behind this desk, and no one would see how hard hearing my name on her lips had made me.

"Hi, I'm Sonja Watts, and my business is a *Good Medicine*, a herbal health and beauty brand created with centuries-old recipes rooted in Gullah culture."

Sonja's presentation was tight, well-researched, and entertaining. The slides weren't all text and graphs but were interspersed with pictures and videos, one of which I recognized from our day trip to Brevard. She had notecards, but she barely glanced at them because she knew her shit.

Yes… my lady was a boss, and it made me so fucking proud that I had to remind myself not to jump out of my seat and clap like a fan. Thankfully her family didn't have to adhere to such propriety and let their pride in her show.

"Thank you, Sonja," I said after the applause had died down. "And for our final presentation, we have Heather Mills." I looked at Heather and was met with a searing glare. Maybe having her present last wasn't the best idea.

Oops.

Twenty minutes later, after we took a group photo and handed out the certificates, I looked around for Soni. I spotted her on the other side of the room in what looked like a painfully serious conversation with one of the realtors that sold commercial property in the Village. She looked like she needed rescuing, and I was happy to do it.

I wove my way through the friendly crowd as casually as I could, trying to catch her eye and signal that we could leave whenever she was ready. But when I was just a couple of feet away, Heather stepped into my path.

"Atlas, hey! Can we chat?"

"Sure, Heather." I stuffed my hands in my pocket and put an extra foot of space between us.

"I just wanted to say that it was really cute of you to make me present after your girlfriend. Like anyone was going to be able to follow her up after she put in so much extra *work*." She sneered when she said work as if to imply that Soni used sex to get extra help.

I rolled my eyes. I was sick of this chick. Her and her annoying ass friend Ashley. Sick of their snide remarks, bullying behavior, and know-it-all attitudes. Thankfully, this was the last day of class. I could finally stop biting my tongue.

"Tell me something, Heather?"

"Hmm?" she leaned in.

"Are you more upset about Soni supposedly putting in extra work or the fact that I never considered you for the job?"

Heather's face fell. "This is very unprofessional. I could report you for sexual harassment—"

"How? On what grounds? I never went out for drinks with you, no matter how loudly and often you and your little friend begged. I treated you with professional courtesy the entirety of this course. Even when you conducted yourself like a mean girl in a high school lunchroom. What would you have to report, Heather?"

Heather's mouth opened and then closed again, clearly unnerved by the fact that I wasn't intimidated by her threat. This wasn't the first time I had to deal with someone like this. Unfortunately, it wouldn't be the last either.

I glanced over Heather's shoulder and saw that our conversation had drawn Soni's attention. "Well, if that's all, Soni needs my attention. Good luck with your business." I stepped around her and closed the short distance between me and Soni.

"...I have quite a few smaller spaces that might work for you. We should get together soon to look at a few," the realtor said as he pulled a business card out his pocket and handed it to her.

"Oh, I wouldn't want to waste your time. Brick and mortar isn't something I'm considering right now."

He shrugged. "Well, that's okay. You could just call me if you'd like to have lunch or a drink."

Soni glanced at me, a stunned expression on her face. "Oh, Travis...I don't think..."

And that was when he noticed me. I wasn't sure how he could have missed me since I was standing just to the right of him. "Hey, Travis. You mind if I borrow, Sonja for a minute?"

Travis looked up at me and then frowned. "Sure. Nice chatting with you, Sonja."

"You, too, Travis," she said, smiling stiffly.

When the realtor had finally maneuvered a reasonable distance away, Soni turned and looked up at me. "I suppose you want to talk now?"

"Please," was all I could manage.

She looked around, spotted one of her sisters, and signaled that we were leaving, but instead of heading toward the door, she took my hand and lead me deeper into the building.

We wove through the crowded hallways until we came to an exit door. She pushed it open, and we were standing in a garden behind the building. It was beautiful back here. Japanese myrtles in full autumn colors of orange, yellow, and red hung over red brick walkways that lead to little alcoves with benches.

"How'd you know about this?"

"Aggie's ceramics studio is right through there," she said, pointing down a walkway that led to a series of low buildings on the edge of the property.

"Huh. I wish I would have known she was this close. I could have come over to visit."

"Nah…Aggie's kind of protective of her creative space. If you want to visit her there, you have to make an appointment."

"Of course," I said with a nod and a laugh.

"She's quirky but lovable," Soni said, slightly defensive.

"I know. Her little weirdo tendencies are endearing."

Soni nodded and wrapped her arms around herself. "And she's a big fan of you."

"I noticed." I reached in my pocket and pulled out the bit of aventurine she gave me when she came in. "But what about you? Are you a fan of me?" I asked softly.

"Big fan. Huge!" she said and smiled just as big.

"Soni, you're cold. I want to hold you. Can I hold you?" I stepped forward with my arms outstretched.

"Not yet," she said, placing a hand in the middle of my chest in an attempt to push me away. "I'm not done apologizing yet—"

"I accept your apology," I said, then wrapped my arms around her and lifted her off of her feet.

"Atlas!" she protested feebly, her arms circling my neck. "You need to let me say this."

"Okay, but... you feel really good in my arms right now so don't say anything like you don't want to see me anymore—"

"That wouldn't be an apology," she said with a husky chuckle. She cupped my face with both her hands, closed her eyes, and touched her forehead to mine. "I'm sorry I pushed you away. I never expected Eric to act like that, and some of the things he said put real doubts in my mind."

"Doubts about me?"

"Doubts about us." She took a deep breath. The tension it her body made me want to hold her tighter. "I just want to make sure you know what you're getting into."

"Your house? Your bed? The clan of witchy Malone women? Your daughter and big-head son that came by here and bugged me every day instead of heading straight home from practice?"

Sonja gasped and pulled away to look me in the eyes. "They did?"

"Yes, they did. Hell, Winston showed up here ready to fight me on that first night because he thought I hurt you."

Her eyes went wide. "Oh, my god. I'm so sorry."

"Don't be. I know how it feels to worry about your mom's heart." I laughed, remembering how he had arrived at *The Coworking Spot*, puffed up and angry. "It was good for us. We bonded over it. But anyway, I know what I'm getting into, Soni. I want all of it. I'm ready for all of it."

"And what if we're together for a long time, and you want kids of your own?"

I shrugged. "What about it?"

"I'm a forty-year-old woman. I'm too old to give you babies."

"Well, I've never really considered having kids anyway."

"You say that now, but you might change your mind later."

"Jesus, Soni. Stop thinking about all the ways this could go wrong and consider all of the ways this is so right. You need to change your mindset."

She laughed. "Is that all I need? A mindset shift?"

"Positive thinking leads to positive outcomes."

"That simple, huh?"

"Yup, that simple."

"Are you going to put me down anytime soon?"

"After I kiss you, but I need to know something first."

"What?"

"Is that lipstick kiss-proof? You look so pretty . I don't want to ruin your—"

I didn't get my answer because Soni's lips met mine, and then I didn't care. I moaned, and when my lips parted, she slipped her tongue into my mouth. Just the taste of her tongue made me wish I had somewhere to lay her down so that I could taste all of her. I slid one hand down her back and palmed her ass. Squeezed one cheek until she squeaked my name.

"Come home with me tonight," I demanded.

"Okay," she whispered and then sucked and nibbled on my lips until I was moaning again. My dick was so hard that I swear the thing was trying to weasel out my waistband to get inside of her.

"Ahem!" a loud voice interrupted. "Excuse me!"

"Oh, shit," Soni whispered. "Is that Nadia?"

Hesitantly, I opened my eyes and was embarrassed to find not only Nadia but her brother and her aunts standing just outside the exit door. "Yup…" I lowered Soni to the ground slowly. "It's Nadia and all the rest of them."

"Oh, shit," Soni said again with a laugh. She went to step away and turn around, but I held her against me. She gave me a confused look. "What?"

Without saying another word, I glanced down between us, and when she saw the state I was in, she began to laugh.

"Not...the response I need right now."

"What do you want me to do?"

I leaned in close and whispered. "You know what I want you to do, but obviously you can't do it right now."

That only made her laugh harder.

"Soni," I whimpered helplessly.

"Okay, okay," she whispered, kissing me sweetly.

"Yo, seriously? If y'all are done eating each other's faces, the rest of us would like to go get some dinner, please," Birdie complained.

"Give us a minute," Soni said.

"Alright, but just a minute," Aggie said with a wink. Then they all went back inside.

"Hey," Soni whispered the moment looking up at me.

"What, Soni-Girl?"

"I love you," she whispered even more softly. A tear escaped the corner of her eye, and I wiped it away with my thumb. "And yes, the lipstick is kiss-proof. The mascara is waterproof, too."

chapter twenty-six
Sonja

It was First Friday, and I was back at *Artisan Depot*, but this time, I was setting up my own shop next to my sister Aggie. It took a bit of creative negotiation to get the fiber artist that had bought the booth next to Aggies to swap with me, but as far as I was concerned, the extra money I paid to make that happen was worth it. Our concepts blended together seamlessly but were still two distinct businesses. The waist-high shelf that served as a partition between the two spaces was home to the skincare herb garden kits that we'd planted for display. The bright green shoots of basil, rosemary, and lemon balm filled the space with an herbaceous scent that made the pop-up shop feel and smell like home.

I stepped back and crossed my arms, taking in both spaces critically. Aggie came to stand next to me.

"What do you think, sis?" I asked.

She draped an arm over my shoulder, tipped her head, squinted, and then smiled. "I think I was right about you not needing me to help you do this."

"I rolled my eyes. "Do you want me to say you were right?" I asked.

Aggie smiled and shrugged. "I'm just saying. I would be nice to hear."

I turned toward my sister and grasped her by the shoulders so that we were looking at each other square on. "Agostina

Malone, my widdle sister, you were right. I didn't need your help. You knew that I could do this on my own, and I did. Thank you for believing in me."

She smiled and wrapped her arms around me. "I'm so proud of you, sis. You're gonna have all of the success you want and more."

I squeezed her tighter, knowing that she was right because Aggie didn't say things that weren't true.

"Oh, look," she said, stepping back to hold me at arm's length. "Here comes another thing I was right about."

Before I even turned around, I knew she was talking about Atlas. I felt his presence the moment he came through the door and not just because he was a big guy. He just brought so much good energy into the room with him that it was impossible to ignore.

Atlas was carrying two big monstera plants that I'd brought from home to fill the empty corners of our booths but forgot to get out of the car. Paired with that big bright smile that I could wait to kiss, he looked like a housewife's fantasy.

"Yes," I agreed. "You were right about him, too."

Atlas bit his lip as he drew closer, and that inspired all sorts of dirty thoughts. The heat arching between us made my cheeks burn.

"Hey! I know exactly where those need to go," Agostina giggled nervously, then stepped forward and grabbed the two big plants from his arms.

"Aggie, that plant is as big as you—" he tried to protest, but she'd already snatched them both from his grasp and moved onto her side of the partition between our booths. "What's with her?"

"I don't know. Maybe all of this sexual energy passing between us made her uncomfortable," I said, looking up at him.

"Sexual energy? I was just delivering the plants you asked me to get out of your car." A grin spread across his face as he wrapped his arms around me.

"Right... it had nothing to do with all that lip biting, winking, and big dick energy you just brought into the room."

"I did not wink!" he said, but didn't disagree with anything else I said. "I don't know, Soni. I feel a way about you objectifying me like this."

"What kinda way?"

He leaned in close. "The kinda way that makes me want to drag you across the courtyard and see if you can keep quiet while I make you come in that lobby bathroom with Chloe sitting at her desk typing away?"

My mouth opened on a little gasp, and he kissed me as I thought about him locking us in that bathroom, yanking off my jeans, and lifting me onto the countertop. "That...I'm pretty sure that's sexual harassment," I stammered.

"It's a fantasy, pervert. I never said I was going to do it!" he said, clutching his imaginary pearls.

"I hate you," I said, trying to push him away.

"No, you don't. You love me," he teased in a sing-song voice.

"Gah! Still so damn smug."

"Like I told you before, I have a good reason to be." Atlas brushed his lips against mine, delivering a soft, sweet kiss before he let me go. "So are you guys all set up? Do you need me to grab any boxes of merchandise or moving anything heavy?"

"I'm good," Aggie chirped from her side of the partition.

I looked around. "I think I'm good, too."

"Okay, cool. I'm gonna head back to my place and grab some clothes for the weekend then meet up with Naddy and Winston for dinner. We'll head back down here to check on you after that."

"Okay," I said, rolling my eyes. "See you later."

Atlas only mentioned that he was grabbing clothes from his place because he seemed to think that it was time to cohabitate. I disagreed. Adamantly. We'd only been seeing each other for two months, and besides, I didn't get divorced just so I could move another man into my house. So what if he slept in my bed most nights? Sometimes a girl liked to get away and stay at her boyfriend's place where she could scream as loud as she wanted and walk from the bedroom to the kitchen naked it.

None of those arguments seemed to matter to Atlas, though. He wanted to move in because "It just makes sense, Soni." He'd even got the kids and Birdie, who was living me now, to side with him. I just wasn't ready. Or maybe it was like my decision to date him. I wanted it to be on my terms, damn it.

A chuckle and the flick of a lighter came from the other side of the partition. Aggie stepped into the little opening we'd left between our two booths blowing on the sage smudge sticks I'd made for us.

"You know what I'm about to say, right?"

I rolled my eyes again and took the lit smudge stick she offered me. "Fine, but don't push, Aggie. I mean it."

She shrugged her shoulder and smiled at me. "I wouldn't dream of it."

The social media campaign Nadia and Atlas helped me organize for the week leading up to this First Friday really paid off. There was a swarm of people waiting to get in when the doors opened, and it looked like we would sell out before people stopped coming. Which was great but also a little terrifying. This kind of popularity meant that I might be considering a commercial space sooner rather than later.

Things were just starting to calm down, and Atlas had sent me a text to say that him and the kids were on their way when an unlikely customer stepped into my booth.

Eric had always been a good looking man. Even when we were gangly teenagers working my mother's farm in the summer. He was the kind of guy that all the girls were pining after when we were kids in the nineties. Light skin, light eyes, and so-called good hair. Funny how those good looks didn't hit me the same way now that he was standing in the middle of my booth post-divorce.

"If you're here to humiliate and berate me again—"

Eric held up his hands, palms open and exposed. "That's not what I'm here to do, Sonja. I promise. I should've never reacted the way I did that day."

I folded my arms across my chest, and in my peripheral vision, I saw Aggie take the same sort of defensive stance.

"That almost sounded like an apology," I said.

"It is. I'm sorry, Sonja." Eric stepped a little closer, and now that we were mere feet apart, I could see that he was falling apart around the seams.

"You look tired."

His shoulders drooped. "I am tired," he said.

"Come here." I directed him to the table where I had my point of sale machine set up and pulled out the chair for him. "Have a seat."

"I don't want to take away from your customers."

"Aggie can handle my customers while we chat," I said, grabbing a bottle of calming, lavender and lemon balm from the shelf. I pulled up a wood crate and sat next to him as I opened the bottle. "Remember this?" I asked wafting it under his nose.

Eric smiled. "Hell, yes. This stuff was the only way I made it through that first year of being in business for myself."

I held out my hand. He took off his class ring and his watch before resting his hands, palm upward, in mine.

Eric had always handled stress poorly. This was nothing new. When we were married, I would run him a hot shower and massage him with this oil so that he could fall asleep.

"I'm sorry for calling your mother a snake oil salesman and belittling your business. I don't know what came over me that day," he murmured.

I poured a bit of the oil in my hand, warmed it between my palms, and proceeded to massage Eric's left hand. "You were stressed out. You always lash out when you're stressed. It's nothing new."

"Nah… it was more than that," he said, shaking his head.

I didn't really want to hear this. Things between us were broken beyond the point where they could be fixed. It was too late for this kind of conversation.

Using my thumb, I pressed into the heel of his hand. People who typed and texted a lot always held a lot of tension there. I massaged it until the knot loosened and then disappeared before I moved onto his right hand.

"Being divorced…it's not what I thought it would be," he said. "It's really kinda lonely."

"I'm sorry to hear that."

"I guess I just miss my family," he added softly.

I wasn't sure what effect Eric thought those words would have on me, but it inspired one that even I didn't expect. "You know, divorce is a lot different than I thought it would be,

276

too," I said. The knot in Eric's right hand was hard and more pronounced. I focused on softening it. Just as that area under his thumb began to feel pliant, I felt the energy in the room shift around me. I couldn't hear him or see him, but I knew Atlas was in the room.

"How is it different for you?" Eric asked, finally, when he couldn't wait another second for my response.

I stood up slowly, still holding both of his hands in mine. "It's not lonely at all."

Atlas rounded the corner with Nadia and Winston. Winston had that big grin on his face that he so rarely ever word, but Atlas always seems to coax out of him.

"Daddy?" Nadia said, a question in her voice. "What are you doing here?"

I turned away from Eric and looked up at Atlas. The look in his eyes asked a lot of questions that I hope I answered by stepping into his arms and kissing him.

"You okay?" he asked softly, his big hand gripping my side, clutching me to him possessively.

"I'm fine," I said, following my answer with another soft, reassuring kiss.

Eric stood and hugged our kids. "I just came by to see your mom's shop. Everywhere I went today, people were talking about it."

"Yeah, mommy's kind of a big deal," Nadia said with a smug smile. "Did you know that she sold out of her first batch of products in like forty-eight hours. We spent the whole weekend cooking up more."

"And had the achy backs and necks to prove it," I added with a laugh.

"Good. I'm glad you're doing so well, Sonja," Eric said with a tight smile. He glanced up at Atlas then glanced away just as quickly. "Well, I don't want to interrupt y'all's plans. I'll leave you to it!" Then he tried to make a quick escape.

"Hey, Eric," I called after him.

I slipped out of Atlas's arms and covered the short distance that he'd put between us. "That thing you said about missing your family? You don't have to miss us. We're still your family." I felt Atlas come up behind me. Silently supporting me.

"She's right," Atlas said. "You should come over for Thanksgiving dinner. We'd be happy to have you."

He should have stayed silent.

Eric's eyes widened, and that tight smile came to his lips again. "I'll give it some thought. You two have a good night. See you later, kids," he called over his should on his way out.

I turned to Atlas and looked up at him.

"What?" he asked with a sly grin.

"*We* would be happy to have you?" I repeated, putting my hands on my hips.

Atlas shrugged. "We would."

"Sir! It's my house! Who do you think you are inviting people over for dinner? On Thanksgiving of all days!"

"Oh... so does that mean I should tell my ma she can't come over either?"

"Atlas!"

Behind him, my sister and kids giggled and whispered conspiratorially.

"And you! You little traitors!"I growled, pointing at Winston and Nadia.

"Oh, come on, mom. He's over all the time anyway," Winston said with a shrug that looked dangerously like the one Atlas had just given me.

His hands circled my waist, and my body softened into his instinctively. "Seems like you're the only one who has a problem with this," he said.

I let out a frustrated sigh and glared at my sister.

"I didn't push!" she said, throwing up her hands like I'd aimed a gun at her. But then she dropped them just as quickly and laughed. "I didn't push *you*, anyway."

Preorder the next book in the series:

the bad in each other

a small town romance

Out of work Sous Chef, Birdie Malone is willing to do anything to get back in the kitchen.

Even if it means she has to start a YouTube channel and start building a career as a home cook to get noticed. Competing in her hometown's yearly low country foodie competition is start. And if she wins, she will finally get the position and recognition she's been desperate to receive. No one ever needs to speak about what happened between them. She can keep her secrets.

Self-taught chef Saxon Turner has is in danger of having his foodie travel show after he gets caught in a dark room with the Governor's daughter. Luckily, it's just in time to help to be a judge at for a foodie competition in his home state of South Carolina. Maybe this will be able to shed the bad boy image he's carried with him through most of his life.

Or at least he thought it would be until he saw that one of the contestants was Birdie Malone.

It's been six years since he's seen Birdie and he more than surprised to see the petite, brown skinned, talented chef competing in a small town food competition when she should be commanding a kitchen of her own. They'd clashed over his rigid adherence to tradition and her tendency toward reckless creativity and their passion was hotter than fire. The way he left things between them when she got kicked out of culinary school is chief among his regrets. He can only hope that she will trust and respect him again.

Birdie has made some mistakes on her life, but none greater than getting involved with Saxon Turner— a mistake that has left her with consequences she will have to deal with for the rest of her life. She just wants to win the money to start her own food truck business and ignore the fact that Saxon has unexpectedly become an unwanted distraction. But the passion, intensity, and creativity he inspires in her can't be denied. Will she be able to keep him out of her bed and her head in the game?

Flip through to read Chapter One!

chapter one

Saxon

Holding up her skirts and her thick thighs while trying to balance her on the stack of Carolina Gold Rice was a feat, but as far as I was concerned, it was well worth it. All of the satin and itchy tulle bunched around her waist were a secondary thought as I thrust into her slick depths. Her pussy clung to my dick every time I pulled out, and I couldn't get enough of the feel of her or the sounds she made as I fucked her in her fancy ball gown.

If only I could remember her name...

Yeah, I should be ashamed of being this specific kind of monster at this stage in my life, but what was I supposed to do when she stormed into my kitchen with her cute button nose turned up demanding to know why the servers were so slow with the champagne and why there were so few canapes. She was clearly someone of import, storming into my kitchen that way, but I couldn't place her face. Either way, I knew it was just an excuse to get me alone. The canapés were good, but nothing special; smoked salmon and pea vol au vents, Pea and prawn crostinis, beetroot blinis with garlicky mushrooms. If she was really looking to complain about the food, she would have said something about the deviled eggs. Still drunk from last night, I'd slept in and left the sous-chef with my recipe -- one that had received high praise when I made them for a

White House function eight years ago. But he'd left out a key ingredient and I could taste the hole in the flavors. Hell, anyone with a tongue could taste the damn hole in the flavors. But she wasn't concerned with the canapés or the deviled eggs. And I wasn't either.

Not now anyway.

"Oh, god," she moaned loudly, her southern drawl bleeding into those two words to draw them out long and twangy like the low country accents I grew up with.

"Shh…" I said, covering her mouth. "You don't want someone to overhear us, do you?"

With her free hand, she snatched mine away from her mouth. "I don't fucking care! Your dick is as good as everyone said it was. Jesus-fucking-christ!"

I leaned back and looked her in the eye. Took in her flushed cheeks and big brown eyes. She was classically beautiful. The sort of southern girl who would age into a well-heeled southern woman who took no shit. But that didn't explain away her comment about my dick. As good as everyone said it was? Had I seen this woman before? Fucked one of her friends? And how was I supposed to feel about that comment? Was it a compliment or…

"Oh, fuck. I'm gonna come," she moaned loudly.

Okay, …it was a compliment. I grinned and grasped both of her hips to hold her steady. If I couldn't shut her up, I might as well get in a good nut before we were discovered.

The buffered quiet of the dry goods room was filled with the obscene, wet sound of our bodies slapping against each other as I grunted and groaned my way toward a climax that felt like a moving target. It was my own damn fault. All the drinking I've been doing the last few days has resulted in a case of whiskey dick— hard as a rock all the damn time but can't come for shit.

"Oh, shit….oh, shit…" she chanted, and I felt her come around me, and thank god, my own body followed suit like a pavlovian response so that I came right behind her.

"Ahh…fuck!" I cursed, realizing that I sounded like some amateur porn star. Still, I let those satisfied, bullish groans spill out of me as I chased every bit of that pleasure, thrusting my quickly softening dick into her. This shit wasn't sexy, but I didn't really give a fuck because I finally had it. The relief valve on the tension I'd been feeling for the last week while taping my show in my hometown, I surrounded by all the things I'd gone to Culinary Institute of America to escape had finally released.

"Miranda?" a very surprised, very male voice said from behind me.

I cursed under my breath and bent to pull up my pants. If that was her man at the door, I at least wanted to put my dick away before it was time to throw hands.

"Charlie!" the woman I'd just fucked said, a wide-eyed look of surprise on her face. A face that now seemed vaguely familiar.

Oh no…

I turned to the door, and my suspicions were confirmed when I met the furious gaze of Charlie Benjamin Cartwright, the newlywed husband of Miranda Dunlevy, daughter of Governor Dunlevy of the great state of South Carolina.

Fuck.

"Listen, man. I didn't know—" I began my hands up in a defenseless posture.

"You didn't know?" Charlie interrupted. "Are you about to say that you didn't know that this was my wife of six fucking days? You were the chef at our wedding reception!"

I frowned. Oh, yeah. I had catered their wedding. The Governor had flown me in for that exact purpose. Slowly but surely, the drunken haze in my brain was penetrated by the fact that my reckless dick may have finally cost me my career.

"Charlie," I said, panting on my most benign smile. Or at least I hope it looked benign. "I'm really drunk and so is Miranda here. I'm sure that if either of us had been sober, I never would have fucked your wife—"

Oops. Those were the wrong words to say. Charlie's face went two shades redder if that was even possible.

"Well, I hope it was good for you because your career is over, you piece of shit."

I glance at the now sobbing Miranda. She was yanking down her skirts to cover the pussy that would possibly ruin my life. And I swear to god… "It wasn't even that good, to be honest," I slurred.

"You son of a bitch!"

Did I say that out loud?

Charlie's fist met my face, and the rest of me met the cement floor of the dry goods room.

* * * *

"I can't fucking believe you," Paula said as she smashed a bag of ice into my swollen face.

Either the Governor's son-in-law had a mean right hook, or I was so drunk that I didn't even get a lick in because I was waking up in the production van outside of the mansion.

285

"Of all the people in this entire ball, you decide to fuck Miranda—fucking—Dunlevy. Were there no other prospects, or are you just that fucking fatalistic?"

"To be honest…I didn't even see who else was in the room. I was too drunk for that. How bad is the black eye? I think I can still land a decent lay before we go. Put me back in the game coach."

"This isn't a fucking joke," Paula hissed. "Marty is trying to sweet-talk the Governor, but he wants your head, and he's making all sorts of threats." She tipped her chin in their direction, and I picked them out of the crowd easily.

Marty's body language told me that he was trying his damndest to get the situation under control, but the Governor was just glaring at me. Silent and stone-faced like he wouldn't be deterred. It hit me at that moment that my wayward dick hadn't just ruined my life, but it could possibly ruin the lives of seven people who made my pretentious travel and food show happen.

Á La Minute was born from a letter I wrote to the editor of a popular magazine that lauded French cuisine. It wasn't meant to be anything serious. Just my opinions without much deep consideration. It was also a dressing down of the elite in my industry and an accurate portrayal of my life as a line cook. That letter to the editor became a monthly thing, and then a column, and then Paula talked me into pitching a show. We were dating at the time and traveling all over Europe and the Far East. I wrote about our adventures and sold those flowery missives to other magazines and blogs. Gradually, I grew a reputation that supported her idea. I still believe she got that yes out of me in bed, but here we were. Us and six other crew members that had traveled from the US all the way to the

tiniest island in Indonesia—not Bali. Goddamn, laptop
entrepreneurs were destroying Bali. I refused to add my trash
ass narrative to that. But we traveled all over the eastern
continents, eating our way through native villages and
sprawling metropolis we could in the last six years.
Somewhere along the way, someone suggested that it was time
to head home, to do the same thing in the US, Canada, Central,
and South America. I thought it was a good idea.

Then they suggested Charleston. If I had any good sense
about me, I would've said no, but heh. No one has ever
accused me of having good sense.

I pushed up on my chair to try and get a good look at the
Governor and Marty, but my head swam, and all the bad
decisions I made earlier threatened to empty my stomach all
over my chef's coat. I lay back down.

"What did Marty say when he found out?" I asked, putting
the bag of ice over my eye again.

"He could make words for a solid minute, and then he told
me to get you out of here. He's really pissed, Sax."

"What are you waiting for?" I asked. "Get me out of here."

* * * *

Production rented a house on Folly Beach, so that's where
Paula took me. Back to the place where I could smell the salt
air and hear the waves and maybe figure out a way to spin this
into something debauched yet charming.

Paula went straight to the liquor cabinet when we came in.
Her phone would be glued to her hand for hours after all this.
Cleaning up my mess. Again. I would have to figure out a way
to make it up to her. Again.

I went upstairs and into the master bedroom, closing the double doors behind me. Stripped down to my underwear, grabbed a bag of weed, some rolling papers, and went out onto the balcony. Sea air greeted me the moment I opened the door, and I closed my eyes to take it in.

Of all places to show my ass…Charleston, my hometown. The place where my father would catch wind of my fuck-ups and add them to the long list of "Things Saxon Has Done to Disappointment Me." I wasn't sure what volume he was on, but it had to be a library's worth of ways he could condemn me.

To be honest, my bad boy persona was wearing a thin. That was part of the reason why we came here. Everyone thought that starting the new season with some good wholesome content featuring Saxon Turner, the down-home southern boy, would sell well to network bosses. I tried to tell them it was a horrible idea. I had too many secrets here. Too many ghosts were waiting to rise up and consume me that I was probably headed for that mediocre fuck with Miranda Dunlevy the moment that my plane touched down at Charleston International. There was no avoiding it.

This is the first time I've been home in six years, and this is the reason why. I couldn't be in this city without getting drunk. Too many memories get in. Hell, the last time I was in Chucktown, I'd basically linked arms with the devil and partnered up with him to ruin my own life. At the time, I had everything I wanted, everything I'd ever strived for. I managed to fuck it all away, much like I did tonight. I guess this was just a case of history repeating.

I flopped onto a lounge chair and plucked two papers out of the box to roll a nice fat joint. If I'd really and truly blown up my life, I didn't want to be sober for the aftermath. Paula must have moved to the patio because broken strands of her conversation wafted up to me.

"...Yes, he was drunk. He's been drunk since we got here..."

"...we were supposed to go up to N. Charleston to get some shots of him in his old neighborhood...I'm not sure. Maybe? If we had a few days, we could...yeah, I understand."

It sounded like Paula was trying to negotiate a few days off so that I could hide away and let the rumors die down. Part of me hoped that our network bosses didn't agree to it. I wanted to get the fuck out of here. Never mind the fact that I didn't have a home because I'd been traveling for the better part of six years, living out of hotels and a rucksack packed so tight that it was a wonder I managed to shoulder it half the time. I'd sleep in a Mumbai airport if it meant I was getting the fuck out of here.

I heard Paula's flip-flopped feet as she walked across my bedroom to the open patio door.

"Hey," she said softly. "Can I join you, or do you want to be alone?"

I gestured to the lounge chair next to mine. She handed me a bottle of water and sat down next to me. I opened it and passed her the joint, and she pulled smoke into her lungs without her usual prissy posturing. Yeah, I really fucked this one up.

"What set you off this time, huh?" Paula asked. "You were doing so good went we left Costa Rica. You were tanned and relaxed. You'd spent enough time there to sweat out all the liquor and traded whiskey for weed. Then we land here and—"

289

"It all goes to shit," I finished for her. I took a big pull on the joint and held the smoke in my lungs until it burned. "I told you that I didn't want to come back here."

"Yeah, you did. But you didn't say why."

"And you never bothered to ask," I countered.

"That's fair." Paula reached for the joint, and I passed it back to her. She took a long pull.

"So what's the verdict? Have I finally fucked it up beyond repair?"

She sighed, a plume of smoke seeping from her nostrils and between her lips. "The team is working on it. Scouring social media and all of the gossip sites to make sure nothing is leaked and planning what to do when and if that happens. Steve is willing to give you a few days. Let the Governor cool down before he approaches him to do damage control."

"So, I still have a job?"

"For now."

"For now," I huffed then brought the joint to my lips again.

"We're going to out to North Charleston to film the segment with Myles Lawson tomorrow. After that…take a few days, Saxon. Get your head together so we can finish recording and get the fuck out of this town."

The weed was doing its job now. Loosening my limbs, quieting my stomach, and letting the fucked up events of the day seep from my brain like the smoke leaving my lungs. North Charleston… that was the last place I needed to go, but my friend would know that I needed somewhere to hide. Myles was probably the only person in my life who wouldn't judge me too hard for the mistakes I made in the last six years. I was just worried that I might tarnish his reputation by mere association.

Coming March 2020!

About the Author

Often accused of navigating life without a filter, Tasha L. Harrison has managed to brand herself as the author who crafts characters and stories that make you feel all of the feels. She writes African American, interracial and intercultural erotica and erotic romance with heroines just as brazen, emotionally messy, and dramatic as herself and heroes that love them anyway.

She lives in Upstate South Carolina with her handsome hubbie, two not-so-smallish men, and one super needy boxer dog. When she's not writing filth, she's riding around with the top down on her Jeep Wrangler, Amber, blasting Southern Rock and pretending she's in love with the mountains when she really misses the ocean.

She also edits romance and erotica because love stories are her business.

Tasha's work and information on her editing rates and services can be found at tashalharrison.com

Acknowledgments

This is usually the point where I shout out all the many things that went wrong in the process and how self-doubt and anxiety tried to trip me up… AGAIN. But here's some news…it didn't happen! Get thee behind me neurosis!

Or, I mean, just leave quietly. It doesn't have to be a big "thing."

Anyway, for those of you who don't know, I started this book as a writing challenge back in September (of 2019 if you're reading this some time in the future). I named the challenge #20kin5Days, during which I would attempt to do exactly that! I didn't actually succeed in writing 20k but the challenge unlocked a skill that had been elusive to me up until this point: fast drafting. And from that challenge Sonja and Atlas were born. Brand new characters falling in love in a small town. Now her two sisters have a story to tell and I can't wait to get to those!

I would be remise if I didn't acknowledge the authors that rode with me during this challenge and afterward. Lucy Eden, Ash Dylan, L. Penelope, CM Lyon, and Jasmine Silva to name a few. I also want to shout out my Thursday write in crew: Katrina Jackson, Zaida Polanco, and Lucy Eden (again). Y'all are the real MVPs! We're about to make 2020 our bitch!

As soon as we can all make sure we take our ADD meds, decide what the fuck we're doing, and actually write during the write-in.

BUT ONCE WE DO THAT IT'S OVER FOR Y'ALL!

Once again, thanks for reading my words and supporting my little writing career. I can't wait to bring y'all more stories next year!

Tasha

CPSIA information can be obtained
at www.ICGtesting.com
Printed in the USA
LVHW010315100720
660306LV00018B/1393